William Tucker Washburn

Spring and Summer

Blushing Hours

William Tucker Washburn

Spring and Summer
Blushing Hours

ISBN/EAN: 9783337366124

Printed in Europe, USA, Canada, Australia, Japan

Cover: Foto ©Andreas Hilbeck / pixelio.de

More available books at **www.hansebooks.com**

SPRING AND SUMMER

OR

BLUSHING HOURS

BY

WILLIAM T. WASHBURN

———

NEW YORK AND LONDON

G. P. PUTNAM'S SONS

The Knickerbocker Press

1890

CONTENTS.

iii

Contents.

Contents.   ix

PAGE

The Great World (*Continued*).

Ꞁꓯ꓿RIAMBICS.

SPRING AND SUMMER

Ὀλίγοις καὶ πολλοῖς.

Brave little book, go forth,
  And wander with the wind,
East, west, and south and north,
  Thy kindred soul to find.
Let wealth nor fame thy step delay,
But with the humblest watch and pray.

If doughty stranger smite,
  Bid him lay bravely on,
Though through thine armor bite
  His weapon to the bone ;
And thank him for the joy to find
'T is not another friend unkind.

Brave little book, go forth,
  Thou man-child of my heart,
Among the least in worth,
  Yet bravely play thy part,
And prophesy the golden day,
When love and truth the world shall sway.

3

THE RUBY.

A starving child a ruby found,
    And thought the gem on fire,
With rags its wounded finger bound,
    The gem tossed in the mire.

MY MOTHER.

One name alone has power to move
   My soul, than every other,
Far dearer is that name I love,
   Thy sacred name, my mother !

All other ties at fortune's breath
   Are swift to fade away ;
Thy love alone through life and death
   Is stranger to decay.

Thy whispered prayers in childhood's ear,
   Thy foolish faith and blind,
All seasons of life's changing year
   With chord of music bind.

I 've heard the song the seraphs sing,
   That melts all creeds in one,
And makes the Virgin's glory ring
   From viewless sun to sun.

But dearer is that name I love,
   Outlasting every other,
Alone, of power my soul to move,
   Thy sacred name, my mother.

5

SPRING AND SUMMER

OR

BLUSHING HOURS

A FAMILIAR SPIRIT.

Thou wilt not sleep, when I am dead,
Thou wilt not press the wormy bed,
My Song, for mother's drowning prayer
Woke never heaven her child to spare,
As mine, that thou may'st never know
The long, forgetful, silent woe.
I sent thee from thy gentle home
In beauty's war to win the plume ;
Thy laden step comes back again,
With penury, care, and chill disdain ;
Yet wiser thou, who wouldst reprove
Who thee for lesser objects love,
And teach me, glory's smile unwon,
Thy dearer soul to prize alone.
Thy voice all ills by mortals mourned
To discord's charm divinely turned,
And through my softest feelings wrought
The sinews strong of strenuous thought.
And as in life thy spell has laid
The death-mists, that my path invade,

No less in death thy tender strain
Of life will charm away the pain :
For doubt not thou my trembling ea.,
Where'er I lie, thy voice will hear ;
Or mingled with the pulsing wind,
Or leaves, that wave their whispers kind,
Or borne on pinions white, that beat
The sullen earth in cadence sweet,
Thy comrade waves, that round thee played,
When first my step thy whisper stayed ;
And, so may fate forget my death,
My hope is I may rest beneath
The deep blue sky with stars embossed,
The winds, that drive with compass lost,
The crystal air, the brooding mist,
That paves the world with amethyst,
The changing splendor eve and morn
Of that wild shore, that knew me born
And happy, ere came down on me
Dark years and strange perplexity.
Where'er I lie, thy tongue will tell
My ear the tales, it loves so well,
Of eager boy, who sails amain,
Nor doubts the blessed isles to gain ;
Of shipwrecked Hope, that pricks alone
O'er quicksand, marsh and flinty stone ;
Of youth, who quickly catches fire,
If Beauty's finger wake the lyre ;
So must thou sing of Her, who knew
All stops of nature's music true,
Who all the songs from mountain spring
To crested wave had gift to sing,

Yet owned her love with simpler art,
Than those young rhymes that stirred her heart.
And thou wilt mourn the hapless Nun,
Coy, snowbound daughter of the sun,
Whose prayers too near my heart-purse stole,
And perilled fortune, fame, and soul.
And thou wilt paint the Maiden proud,
Tall, Arab-ankled, Clite-browed,
Who heard and sighed, who sighed and fled,
And left my heart uncomforted ;
Whose eyes still seem with love to beam
On mine, like stars in misty dream.
And must thou tell of Beauty's wiles,
The feigning sighs, the perjured smiles,
The song more melting than the moan,
From whitening wave and pine-leaf blown,
That, as with listless sail I lay,
And thought of one gone far astray,
Allured my simple shallop on,
Across the waste of waters wan,
To distant isle and grotto bright
With sunset's purpling amber light,
Where, thick with rose and ruby spread,
And lilies bending overhead,
Reclined, a Lady sang and pressed
A golden harp to snowy breast ?
Forgetful hours, how quickly flown !
Awake, death eyes me left alone,
Forsaken, faint, on desert isle,
With upas tree and crocodile
To lend me shelter and a tear,
And wolves to laugh away my fear.

Forsaken, but with mind untamed,
With secret wound and name defamed,
Again, to busy human kind
By fortune's aid my path I find.
Then wilt thou picture Pity's face
In love with sorrow and disgrace,
And tell of timid charms unknown,
Of all her house, to one alone ;
Light foot, on deeds of mercy swift,
Brave hand, the fallen to uplift,
Forgiving eyes, and smile as sweet,
As ever angel stooped to greet,
Now fondly turned, where wrath and hate
Alone with death my life debate ;
Not ill canst thou her merits tell,
Whose every motion pleased thee well,
Whose limbs by music's touch were formed,
Whose heart by music's whisper warmed,
Whose love was one enchanting song,
That stayed the eyeless hand of wrong,
Compassionate, devout, and pure,
That knew to pardon and endure,
Content to share, with bankrupt heart,
A wealth unknown to fortune's mart.
And thou wilt call up many a face,
That won thy fancy's modest praise,
On mountain side, in vale or town,
Where'er thy wayward wing has flown,
And echo Her electric voice,
That made thy chosen rhymes rejoice.
And thou wilt sing of Brother true,
Whose love in soil unfertile grew ;

And grieve o'er kinsmen long estranged,
And hymn a Mother's love unchanged,
And those blessed moments, trebly sweet,
When mother's kiss and children's meet.
And thou wilt sing of spirits knit
To mine by touch of kindly wit ;
Of Him, whose life-blood freely flowed
To help the slave on freedom's road,
Who, as th' impatient grave he neared,
With sacred song his mother cheered.
And thou wilt voice the Scholar's aim,
Th' insatiate eye, his heart of flame,
Who ragged, starving, racked with pain,
Holds kings and Gods in high disdain,
Believing truth alone is great,
All else beneath or love or hate ;
Whose footsteps never resting run
From age to age, from sun to sun ;
Whose touch unbolts the iron gate,
That closes fast on life's debate,
Who, pressing on, with torch alight
Invades the very soul of night ;
Nor backward turns, though on him glare
The sightless sockets of Despair,
But on, to realms, no comet's eye
Or new-born world's reproachful cry
Draws near ; whence, like a slender thread
By nature's deepest fountain fed,
The tangled stream of heat and time
Steals dimly forth with muffled rhyme.
And thou wilt sing His soul of pride,
And fate, to mine too closely tied,

Who, outcast of a sordid race,
His country's altar strove to grace
With laurel leaf, not lightly won,
Where greed and envy reign alone.
And thou wilt sing of holy creeds,
The consecrated spirit's needs,
Of martyr crowned with aureole,
And selfless love's immortal soul.
Of many a comrade wilt thou sing,
Who cheered thee in thy wandering,
And bring me many a message kind,
From hearts that kindred feelings bind.
Be this in life and death thy task,
No dearer boon from Heaven I ask.

MABEL.

I.

NEMASKET.

Broad, grassy fields, low hills, an azure sky,
   The pastures dotted with the grazing cows ;
   The stream that through the trailing bushes flows,
The elm's lithe beauty, pastime of the eye,

Old apple trees, the robin's melody,
   The constant whippoorwill, the whistling quail,
   The prophet spider's dewy rafters frail,
The gardener's care, the well-stored granary ;

How all thy charms, Nemasket, dearer grow
   Than when in thoughtless boyhood's opening
      bloom,
In haste each wood or river nook to know,
   Along thy wandering paths I joyed to roam,
The grape to gather or the line to throw,
   And happiest feigned when farthest from my home.

II.

HAYTIME.

Sweeter than the merry May-time
Is the happy toiling haytime,
When the harvest tall is curving
'Neath the engine's edge unswerving ;

When the blithesome, lightfoot lasses
Bind their hair with crested grasses ;
Seize their forks and follow after,
Mingling work with careless laughter ;
And, their generous labor over,
Homeward trip through fields of clover.
Such a day I homeward speeding,
Naught of country lasses heeding,
Dreaming, chance is, of fair Phryne,
Lydia, Pyrrha, or Barine,
Close behind me heard a shy, light
Step ; and, turning in the twilight,
Saw a dainty rustic maiden,
Swift of foot, though beauty-laden,
Pass me, and on my approaching,
Run as from rude hand encroaching ;
Till within a thorny thicket,
Like a nun behind her wicket,
From bright eyes, her bonnet twitching,
Soft she sang, with smile bewitching.
" Gentle youth, too much I fear thee ;
Come, I pray thee, come not near me."
Who can tell if friend or stranger,
Grew to me that rustic ranger ?

III.

IN ACCORD.

Than Mabel never fairer maid
  In fair Nemasket grew,
Her smile a sunshine in the shade,
  Her breath like honey dew—

What heart, a thousand times betrayed,
  Could doubt her accents true?

Our feet the daisies' tossing foam
  Across the meadow bore,
Where briery rose and piny plume,
  Above the trembling floor,
Repeated, "Love, let others roam,
  Before us lies the shore."

IV.

A MASK.

I hastened from my garden gate,
  The girls, a crimson cloud,
Were sailing to and fro in state:
  I shunned the garish crowd,
And sought a maid, whose loveliness
O'erflows her unpretending dress.

With lace and plume and sweeping trail
  The glittering throng draw nigh,
All arts they urge, but none avail
  To catch a constant eye,
That seeks a face, whose beauties are
A mask for every other fair.

V.

FORESTERS.

Love-faring through the forest shade,
  My darling's steps I drew ;
The frolic sunbeams round us played ;
  From leaf to leaf they flew.

They pierced the bramble's tangled gloom,
  They danced along the brook,
They woke the timid flowers that bloom
  By many a cloistered nook.

Ah, foolish is the world and blind,
  And blind I pray will be,
That envy's eye may never find
  The spot so dear to me.

VI.

SOMETHING AFTER.

HE.

The half-made kiss that mocks the sight
  Upon thy pouting lips
Be mine, and thine, these jewels bright
  No lips but thine eclipse.

And airy lace Love's hand shall place
  Around thy neck of snow ;
Each filmy thread would win to grace
  An angel from below.

And pearls would make a queen forsake
Her country, crown, and all,
From Beauty's trembling ear shall shake
Their colors magical.

And seasoned wine with spell benign
Shall teach thee to forget
An error, by love's word divine,
In sacred music set.

SHE.

The glass you fill fear not to spill ;
Alas ! your seasoned wine
Is growing green on field and hill
Beside the rolling Rhine.

Your pearls await some diver bold
On Coromandel's coast,
And fairies mold, in cave and wold,
The rubies poets boast.

And lace to try a spider's eye,
Or sift a sunbeam's rays,
Provokes a visionary sigh
That well the gift repays.

With all your wit, ill have you hit
A loyal lover's part,
Nor learnt love knows no praise so sweet
As proffered hand and heart.

VII.

FOILS.

They lie who say that gall is bitter,
They lie who say a bat will flitter,
The one is sweet, the other still
To my cruel lot, to her weak will ;
That wayward minx, who fairer grows
By telling blacker lies than crows ;
Alas ! that words that most forswear her,
But serve as foils to frame her fairer ;
And tricks that should unchain the mind
More closely love to beauty bind.

VIII.

INCOMPLETE.

" Hear the oriole's fuller throat
Pour the passion of his note,
See the golden buttercup
Drink the healing sunshine up ;
See the zephyr's pleading sighs,
The blushing rose's lips surprise ;
See the bees with murmuring wing
Soothe the flowers they rob and sting ;
See the waves love's lesson teach
To warming rock and trembling beach.
Strange that nature finds a bliss
In that quaint union styled a kiss."

Winning words from lovely maid
As through the treacherous mead we strayed,
But her laugh and flying feet
Left my answer incomplete.

IX.

WAITING.

The moon has risen, where art thou, my Love?
Dost thou not see the shadows beckoning?
Dost thou not hear the love-star carolling? '
Dost thou not heed what pleading zephyrs move

The trembling whispers of the vacant grove?
Nor listen to the low prayers of the spring,
Nor answer wooing nature murmuring
With voices that thy lingering step reprove?

Alas! what profit in the silvery ray,
That frets the eyelid of love's passion-flower,
That, changing night to a diviner day,
Imprisons all our life in one fond hour,
If treacherous beauty with deaf feet delay,
And torturing fears the gentle heart devour!

X.

THE LADY OF LIGHT.

Gentle lover urge no more
Willow tree and twilight hour,
Meet me, when with showers of gold
Morning floods the mountain old,

Where rock-rooted cloud-capped pine
Voices freedom's heart divine :
There beneath the eye of light
Proudly we our troth will plight :
If my lover faithless prove,
Then shall willows hear my love,
And with twilight's shadows gray
Mourning I will pass away.

XI.

SECURE.

Were you my lover at the spot,
And fancied that I had forgot ?
Forgot, how could I well forget ?
But mountain paths are often wet,
And, since one foolish word, with doubt
My wits have been so turned about,
I fear the treacherous eye of morn,
The dew-drop's guile, the robin's horn,
The butterfly's envenomed sting,
And danger's dart on beauty's wing,
And deem, sad source of woman's woes,
The best of friends the worst of foes,
And maiden's home no less secure
Than mountain glen with youth to woo her.

XII.

THE MESSAGE.

Wanton Sparrow, Venus' joy,
Let my prayers thine aid employ,
Fly to where in beauty deep
Gentle Mabel sinks asleep.

There, with fond encroaching wing,
In thick tresses cloistering,
Breathe in her unshielded breast
All her lover's cruel unrest.

Fever-seed and ice-king's breath,
Fear that hope encumbereth,
Timid pride, and anger meek,
Firm resolve as water weak.

At the sound of coming feet,
Let her heart refuse to beat,
And her voice forgetfully
Die in its own melody.

Let the sun rise and go down,
At a smile or at a frown ;
Let her, tossed through nights of pain,
With torturing day wish night again.

That if love thou canst not move,
She may pity those who love
And not unreluctant find
Pity treacherously kind.

XIII.

NO LICENSE.

My lover, pray do not come leaping
Across the wall, when folks are sleeping ;
You break my lilac branches down :
For them I care not, but the crown
My father's heavy hand will break,
If once his jealous ear awake.

Night-lurking lover in a garden
Is something neighbors will not pardon ;
I care not for them, but the smart
That follows busy rumor's dart,—
Bold rumor, that a license uses,
The prudish world to love refuses.

XIV.

THE DREAMER.

My soul soft slumber sealed,
  Soft slumber sealed my sorrow,
Beside me Beauty kneeled
  And bade my soul good-morrow.
Enchanting little maid,
  Debating sorrow's prayer
With veiling eyes afraid
  And cheek of roses bare ;
Why, Truant, art thou only kind,
  When slumber's cords thy lover bind !

XV.

BATHERS.

Her feet make white the golden sand,
  Bright shine her glances brave ;
In mine she locks her eager hand,
  We leap into the wave.

The happy waters round her press,
  Ah ! bitter sight and sweet—
They fold her in a wild caress ;
  They kiss, they part, they meet.

Was never naiad's face so fair,
  Amid the circling foam,
To whisper hope to fond despair,
  And lure the fancy home.

XVI.

THE HARBOR.

Fair maiden, winsome, proud, and coy,
  Ah ! wherefore dost thou shun me ?
Enchantress, raining life and joy,
  Turn, turn, and look upon me !

Ah ! let my hand thy soft touch wear,
  Why tremble, gentle maid ?
What should the water-lily fear
  Upon the dark stream laid ?

Ah ! closer bend thine ear's sweet charm,
  Till my heart in music break ;
What knows a pearly shell of harm,
  Though the wild waves' whispers wake ?

Ah ! blame me not if on my breast
  Thy sacred head I lay,
Like freighted vessel brought to rest
  In some deserted bay.

Forever there thou 'lt cherished be,
  By sheltering arms and brave,
That careless mock the fickle sea,
  The swift, relentless wave.

XVII.

THE PINES.

Beneath the pines no roses blow,
Beneath the pines no violets grow,
But underneath their fragrant shade
One summer day there sat a maid.
Her breath more sweet than violets are,
Her lips than roses lovelier far ;
And at her feet her lover sighed,
But long his suit the maid denied.
Fear not, fair maid, no eye shall know
Beneath the pines what kisses grow.

XVIII.

HASTE AWAY.

Haste away, thou idle Sun,
Now thy prying work is done.
Let thine ill-got secrets have
Burial in the western wave.
Think you all love's wiles to spy
With uncompromising eye ?
When the veil of darkness covers
From thy shafts two happy lovers,

Treasures thou hast never known
Mock thy garish splendor gone,
Beaming when the cloak of day,
The stars' night, is plucked away.

Then fond lips breathe words as sweet
As violets pressed by Venus' feet ;
And when words forget to flow,
Sweeter favors from them grow,
Making day's cold pleasures seem
Faded shadows of a dream.
Haste away, then, idle Sun,
That night's golden stores be won,
Lest love's angry arrows fly,
Blinding thy Cyclopic eye.

XIX.

THE FOOTFALL.

When tell-tale stars are laid asleep,
And muffling clouds love's secrets keep ;
How sweet the footfall light to hear,
That drives away our lingering fear.

Flow softly, fair Nemasket, flow,
Through banks that trailing vines o'ergrow ;
And safely to her lover's side,
With silvery voice my darling guide.

Between the pathway and the stream,
What wistful eyes in beauty gleam?
What careful hand, with coy delight,
Divides the forest of the night?

Oh! rapture mortal never felt!
Like spirits that in spirits melt,
Creep, creep, beloved, to my heart,
That sees thee lovely as thou art.

Oh! might I drink thy beauty dry;
Thou bliss that feeds my inward eye;
Close, closer, Love, thine arms intwine,
And clothe my soul with light divine.

XX.

FOND FORGETFULNESS.

I wrote me late a peerless song,
Painting absence' bitter wrong,
Homeless rhymes in music's chain,
Echoing their master's pain;
But when lengthening care has wrought
A miracle of unsunned thought,
And with fearful step I bring
To beauty's queen my offering,
In vain in their own loveliness
Rosy lips I strive to dress.
As each gentle word I frame.
Back the rebel starts in shame,
Till my soul a rhythmic breath
With honeyed charm encumbereth,

And nearer Heavens fold me round,
Speechless in cruel blisses drowned.
Ah ! roguish Love, that wove my lay,
Why should you snatch your gift away ?

XXI.

THE MISER.

Why so chary of a kiss ?
Think you, pretty maid, to miss
From a rose-encircled door
One sweet truant less or more ?
Foolish miser, not to know
Where one is plucked two others grow !
Riches come not but by spending ;
Profit waits upon wise lending.
How canst thou a miser be,
When nature wastes its wealth on thee ?
How can lips with honey stored
Thievish almoners, grudge their hoard ?
Love 's no painted butterfly
Wandering forgetfully,
Nor misty humming-bird to kill
Flowers that load its wanton bill,
But secret thrifty bee that knows
To bless the source whence bounty flows.
Frolic maiden, fair and young,
Wilt thou youth and beauty wrong ?
Time soon teaches youth to fly,
Youth too apt its wings to try.
Think you, when fond youth is gone,
Beauty lingers long alone ?

Prudent maiden, ah, remember,
Kisses grow not in December.
Grant me, Beauty, then just one,
Ere yon cloud unchains the sun,
Look, who knows if it were done !

XXII.

E PLURIBUS.

Learn, fair Cloisterer, in a trice,
How few kisses would suffice
To set the snow-king's daughter free
From love's importunity !
Quick a golden hundred coin,
And to them a thousand join ;
Then, on lips that die of thirst,
Let your hoarded treasures burst,
Till the stinging drops of hail,
Or wheat seeds springing from the flail,
Or silent stars that pave the sky,
Or sands on Jersey's beach that lie—
But stop ! look down ! I 'm half undone ;
I almost missed this tiny one.

XXIII.

. *THE GUIDE.*

Oh, where will you seek your truant May ?
But seek her wherever you will,
The birds will never the spot betray,
The sunken height with myrtles dight,

That mocks the mountain woodman's skill ;
A covert Love alone can find,
Nor Love, unless he spell aright
The notes, that point his footsteps blind ;
No starbeam, then, he asks for guide,
Nor firefly's small revolving light,
But presses up the mountain side,
Through interwoven branch and vine,
That rib the changeless leafy night,
Nor pauses, till above him shine
Two misty stars with promise clear,
Of guileless love's requital near.

XXIV.

BLUSH NOT.

Blush not, Lady, to have lain
Beneath my kisses' burning rain,
Beneath my kisses raining down
On thy crystal forehead's frown,
Staining with love's softer dyes,
Vermeil lips and veiling eyes,
Blush not, for if love can save
Beauty from the greedy grave,
Trust me, Heartpearl, thou shalt be
The gem of immortality,
Still, when Time's swift footsteps tire
Breathing forth contagious fire.
See how round this golden hair
Sunbeams break in colors rare,

This tell-tale hair shall serpent turn
And teach the gentle heart to burn,
Long after Romish prelates paint
Eve's tutor as a Christian saint.

xxv.

LOVE AND REASON.

Love, thine idle hour is past !
Think not such delights could last,—
Wisdom long delayed has come
To our violet-circled home.
Little hope of sunny weather,
When love and wisdom dwell together.
Seek some pretty youth to please,
Fretting for a new disease :
He with trembling hands will press thee,
He will cherish and caress thee,
Bind thy tangled locks with posies,
Stain thy feet with envious roses,
Call thee many a daintier name,
Than ungentle lips can frame :
Truth, that moulds my rugged lays,
Lacks the courtier's skill to praise.
Yet shall not thy little hour
Wholly fade, fond folly's flower :
Many sights will call thy face
From the past with tender grace,
Rainbows that round fountains play,
Blossoms drunk with purple May,
Dancing waves in sunshine dressed,
Moonbeams pale in cloisters blessed ;

All things poets feign divine,
Shall bid the golden moments shine,
When a frolic image gay
Held me captive to its sway.
But, fare thee well ! love cannot rule
Long the child of reason's school ;
Fare thee well ! when thou art gone
Proudly will I walk alone.
Fare thee well ! Nay, linger not,
Has thy wing its flight forgot ?
Stay, what languor numbs my veins !
Dizzy trances, icy pains !
Mute my tongue with sudden fears,
Mute my tongue, yet plead my tears,
Love ! ah, leave me not forlorn,
A pensioner of wisdom's scorn.

XXVI.

THE SURPRISE.

" Oh, sacred as the troubled tear,
   That tells of love too kind ;
Oh, sweet as kisses creeping near,
   Again fond love to blind.
Come tell me why, my Pretty one,
With downcast eyes you sit alone ? "

She turned, my pretty Mabel turned,
   Her cheeks with scarlet stain :
" My Sweetheart, how my heart has yearned—
   And have you come again ;
Have you come back again to me,
O prayed for long and fervently ? "

All ivory-gold her bosom shows
   Beneath her tangled hair,
That, rippling to her waist, o'erflows
   And showers upon the air
Bright sunbeams, that, with moonlight's ray,
In woven lustre round her play.

" But, Mabel, why this window wide ?
   Thyself unguarded here ?
Tell me what lover is to hide ;
   Confess to friendly ear."
Around my neck her arms she threw :
" My Sweetheart, say you love me true.

" My sweetheart, say you love me true,
   And will forever love ;
Though I forget myself in you,
   Oh, say you 'll not reprove.
Oh, say you 'll never love me less
Though I your heart too fondly press.

" They tell me lovers careless grow,
   When maidens prove too fond.
Alas, alas, how should I know ?
   I cannot think beyond
The moment, when my pulses feel
Like flame your whispers o'er them steal.

" Do you prefer me coy and nice,
   To lure you on and on,
My hands and lips all freezing ice,
   My heart to marble grown ?
O loved with longing infinite,
My hope, my tears, my heart's delight ! "

" But tell me why my Mabel wept ;
　'T was but a week unblessed."
"Alas," she sighed, "the minutes crept,
　It seemed a year at least.
I wept, because, I cannot tell,
I thought, perhaps, you were not well.

" I wept the wrong, my foolish haste,
　My parents' trust betrayed ;
I wept so much dear pleasure past,
　And then I grew afraid,
And wept I never might, O pain,
Have cause so sweet to weep again."

" My gold-hair maid, the harvest moon
　Lights many maidens fair,
And of the fairest is there none
　With Mabel may compare.
But fairer will my Darling shine,
If she forgets to weep and pine."

XXVII.

FORGET ME NOT.

Forget me not, when on the dreaming deep,
　Where all things are forgot, the heedless wave
Breathes its sweet burden of eternal sleep,
　An echo many-voiced from one still grave ;
Forget not him, who sang thy praise and thee,
May-Mabel, envy of the jewelled sea.

2

XXVIII.

THE HERMIT-THRUSH.

Unkind misfortune's only son,
　　Through forest drear I strayed,
The sunbeams withered one by one
　　Beneath the tremulous shade.
" What profits it to night's dull reign
　　Unheard to sing and hear
Fond echo's melancholy strain
　　Return love's accents dear."

I sighed, when from a lofty pine
　　A hidden hermit-thrush,
With sweet exultant joy divine
　　Clothed listening cloud and bush ;
The whispering leaves stood still, the stream
　　Delayed its petulant fear,
Fond Nature, wrapped in music's dream,
　　Bent nearer eye and ear.

Ungenerous who deny their best
　　And holiest soul to give,
Careless if in another's breast
　　A quickening answer live ;
Yet, Beauty, could I wish thou wert
　　Thus wandering lone, that I,
Unseen, might soothe thy bosom's hurt
　　With so sweet melody.

XXIX.

THE PAINTER.

What limner paints as love paints,
   What love paints like despair,
That traces beauty's lineaments
   Behind fate's prison-bar ?
Enchantress, whose companionship
   Once framed my hours in gold,
Whose whispers parting lip from lip
   Of love eternal told,
No rival needst thou ever fear,
Who art so pitilessly dear.

REVISITED.

Gray-hooded, o'er the trembling sea
A spirit walks in mystery,
  And summons love to hear
The sacred songs of long ago,
The tangled thoughts of joy and woe
  That sleep in sorrow's ear.

On plain and mountain far away
How often, wizard ocean gray,
  Thy well-remembered note,
Sad undersong of jocund morn,
Or on the twilight's pinion borne,
  Around me seemed to float !

Thy voice is still the same ; the gleam
Of morning's hope and sunset's dream
  Is on thee still ; but one,
Whose smile, like thine, in music woke,
How altered now her loving look !
  Her words how distant grown !

URSULA.

I.

FORBIDDEN.

One sacred name forbidden
  Within this volume lies,
A lurking lily hidden
  From all but loving eyes.

To-day and sweet to-morrow,
  And nevermore will bloom
The mystic flower of sorrow
  On love's deserted tomb.

II.

A VISION.

She stands upon a grassy height
  That guards our mighty river,
Fair, fair is she as the budding light,
  That makes the pine tops quiver.

The lily on her whiter breast
  Reflects a purer calm,
The violet to her warm heart prest
  Exhales a sweeter balm.

37

As graceful as the waving wheat
  Beneath the zephyr's breath,
She bends my gentle word to greet,
  Then swiftly vanisheth.

The purple flowers spring up to hear
  Her fairy footsteps glide,
And Hudson's freighted whispers bear
  Her name to ocean wide.

III.

THE FORTUNATE.

Brave Mountain Maiden, elfin child,
Whose haunting songs my step beguiled,
To pause within a mossy nook
That could no thought ungentle brook,
Thy charms let murmuring pine-leaf tell
To rocks and streams that own their spell ;
For how shall meaner minstrel sing
Such loveliness bewildering !
An eye, whose crystal arrows true
The lark through Heaven's gate pursue ;
A voice, that sweeter notes commands
Than laughing waves on summer sands ;
A darker tress than winter night,
When moon and star deny their light :
Coy hands, the children of the snow,
Where lurking dimples love to grow ;
The marvel of thy finger tips,
With tell-tale stain of roses' lips ;

A breast, where restless fancy feeds
On kisses as he counts his beads.
But ah, what profit to recall
Delights, that wound beneath their pall ?
The blind are fortunate alone,
The few unmocked, who have not known
Thy beauty, for who looks on thee
Is stranger to tranquillity.

IV.

EST LAUDANDA VOLUNTAS.

Kind Heaven has shed its utmost grace
Of beauty round thy lovely face.
Whate'er thy proud eye shines upon
Is fed with glory, like the sun.
Whene'er thy gentle voice is heard,
Deep in their grave our souls are stirred.
All gifts thou hast to true hearts near ;
All treasures unto angels dear.
Naked am I ; no less I strive
No vulgar gift my queen to give.
A few wild-flowers that dare not meet
Thine eye, are strewn before thy feet,
Poor nurslings of the desert drear,
Not for their hardy beauty dear,
But from a bounty all thine own,
To fortune's children never shown ;
That clothes with joy the darkest hour,
And arms a gentle wish with power.

V.

WINTER-BOUND.

No longer, Lady, winter-bound,
    The season disobey ;
See how through trembling bark and ground,
    The buds their sunward way
Are pricking fast ; with robin's song
    The hills and vales resound ;
Around us shifting shadows play,
    Bright-colored insects throng,
And founts, with nodding rushes crowned,
    And brooks that voice the May,
Forget the frost-king's fetters strong,
    And laugh with morning's ray,
Thy frowns alone in beauty's wrong
    Th' approach of spring delay.

VI.

TWILIGHT.

Lady, whose peerless loveliness
Consenting day and night confess,
In the gentle wedded hour,
When twilight breathes its magic power,
And stealthy from their noontide sleep,
Beauty's hidden spirits creep,
No lofty rhyme of beaten gold
The blossom of thy name shall hold :

But the pine-leaf answering
The robin's note shall sweetly sing
Thee, as dreaming sunbeam fair,
And holy as pale evening's prayer.

VII.

VESPERS.

Marvel of the flattered Heaven,
  Maiden, kneeling at thy shrine,
Like the spirit pure of even,
  Breathing morning's hope divine.

Holier than the candle's dream,
  On the conscious altar lying,
Shines with consecrated beam
  Beauty's vestal faith undying.

Clothed with lustre, like a star,
  Maiden, thou wilt never know,
What unceasing fires of war
  From thy gentle glances grow.

The clashing atoms' restless strife
  Wakes the sacred candle's flame.
Ah ! may the words that rob my life
  Weave a glory round thy name !

VIII.

THE VESTAL.

Crystal maiden calm and proud,
　Beauty's passionless despair,
Cold as the transparent shroud
　Consecrate immortals wear.

Ivory hands a bosom press,
　That the dreaming snowflakes cover,
O'er whose stainless loveliness
　Vainly wingéd blushes hover.

As vain the muse divides the light,
　That from duty's path secure
Fancy's wayward pinion bright
　May thy vestal steps allure.

Round a lily filled with dew,
　A thriftless murmuring bee delays,
That bidding oft its love adieu
　Still returns to sing its praise.

IX.

IN THRALL.

In vain the poet's eye has sought,
　Through Nature's cheating form,
The cradle of the breathing thought,
　That keeps earth's pulses warm.

The hidden home of sovereign love,
　Whose consecrated dream
Floats over meadow, shore, and grove
　O'er mountain well and stream.

Cease, toilers, on an idle quest,
　Unseen of mortal eyes,
Upon a vestal's marble breast,
　The god imprisoned lies.

The glances of his fading eye
　Have changed to music's grief,
Whose words the sunbeams' fingers tie
　To murmuring wave and leaf.

But fair and ever fairer grows,
　Fairer than tongue can tell,
The maid, whose saintly beauty throws
　O'er wingéd love its spell.

X.

A TEAR.

Belovéd, grant me but thy tear,
　I ask no other guerdon ;
Thy smiles the hoarding world may wear,
　I crave but beauty's burden.

Who deepliest loves the brooding night,
　Its longing and its sorrow,
Is first to catch the trembling light,
　And bid the dawn good morrow.

XI.

THE DEAF EYE.

Boast not that thine unaided eye
  Can spell the captive moons that ride,
With music's changing harmony,
   To deck the royal planet's pride.

When thy carved ear of marble cold
  Is deaf to prayers whose wandering sigh
Would wake a statue's sleeping mould,
  To breathe unbidden sympathy ;

Yet still, though faint with sad despair,
  My fancy aids thy glory's store
With no less self-forgetful care
  Than in love's first enchanted hour ;

When like a humble chimney-sweep,
  Imprisoned in his telescope,
I saw a star's large beauty creep,
  To paint day's nearer sky with hope.

XII.

IN FATE'S DESPITE.

In my deafness still to hear thee,
Like a spirit, singing near me ;
In my blindness to behold thee
Fairer through the clouds that fold me.

Still in fate's despite to love thee,
Cannot this, proud beauty, move thee
Something to forgive my boldness,
Something to forget thy coldness.

Pride has whispered, cease thy wooing,
Hopeless love is life's undoing ;
Shame has whispered, cease thy sighing,
Scorn best answers love's denying.

But my warm tears unforgetting
Still the frozen ground are fretting,
And upon thy window gleaming
Lie the cold, cold moonbeams dreaming.

XIII.

BEAUTY'S MALISON.

Oh, wayward child of music, why
    Shouldst thou his praises shun,
Whose heart, though hurt, could ne'er deny
    Of all thy wishes one ?
Oh, sweetest spirit of my song,
Why wilt thou so thy beauty wrong ?

Thy gentle glances from me turned,
    Thy pity changed to pride,
My wild entreaties cruelly spurned,
    Thy hand to mine denied.
Alas, I 've felt cold hunger's fang,
But love, how sharper is thy pang ?

Wilt thou of music moulded crush
   A leaf that murmured thee,
When all the forest lay at hush,
   To glean the melody ;
Before thy feet, though stained it lie,
   By whom it worshipped shall it die ?

Wilt thou destroy a sacred shell,
   That owns thy name alone,
And joys that sweeter song to spell
   Than listening waves have known ;
The voice that sullen surges love,
   Can it no more thy bosom move ?

Yet dearer loved than fairest thou
   Of lovely ladies all,
Within my soul thy name shall grow
   To passion mystical.
And often shall the tale be told
Of her to love so tender cold.

And when within the greedy grave
   Thy lover's woes are hidden,
One bliss his dying lips will have
   To breathe thy name forbidden ;
And o'er him many a bird will sing
Thy sweeter name than song of Spring.

XIV.

A DOUBLE CRIME.

Gentle maiden merciful,
  Wherefore scorn his servitude,
  Who, with faithful heart though rude,
Toils a garland fair to cull
For thee, whose name is Merciful?

Did thy lips my praise forswear?
  An evil oath and keeping it,
  A double crime wilt thou commit?
And heaven's hand, that writes thee fair,
And love that reads, alike forswear?

Remember, Sweet, no stranger's child,
  But of thy beauty's purity,
  An echo that forgets to die,
Love, banished, sings from winter wild—
Mother, listen to thy child.

XV.

LOVE'S GOALS.

Thou rudder of my thought and song,
  Oh, whither wilt thou guide me?
The sullen billows round me throng,
  The tempests ride beside me.

Will Beauty's pride my pathway urge,
Where icy chains on ocean's surge
Are laid, and cold and luminous,
   Heroic faces gleam,
And shadowy fingers beckon us
   To fame's unfading dream ?

Oh, rather may thy feelings warm
   Forswear thy breast of snow,
And learn the dearer, truer charm
   Thy lips of roses know :
And bend my course in rapid flight
From frozen sun and hopeless night
To smiling coast and land-locked bay,
   Where purple flowers encroach,
And with no crime but love's delay
   The trembling ear reproach.

XVI.

THE IMPEACHMENT.

Why are thy lovely eyelids drooping,
   Thy glances hidden in their sheath,
Like eagles from the mountain stooping,
   That tremble on the dewy heath ?

Why are thy charméd words delaying
   With faltering wing by music's nest,
Like bees that o'er the roses straying
   With balmy fragrance sink opprest ?

Why is thy neck with blushes staining,
  Like lily from the tempest's wound,
That bending pours its sweet complaining
  To crimson flowers that paint the ground?

Ah, Love, why art thou idly pleading,
  At beauty's cell disconsolate,
Like minstrel that with footsteps bleeding,
  In vain entreats the convent gate?

XVII.

LA BELLE DE NUIT.

I, the opal flower of night,
Stirred by languid melancholy,
In the moon's unreal light
Waken to the dirges holy,
Unforgetful zephyrs sing,
Round the sun's bier lingering;
While the bat from fearful wings
Quivering dreams around her flings,
And with exiled cry the owl
Answers earth's unquiet soul.
As the firefly's measured beam
Marks the music of night's dream,
Haunting visions timorous creep
From hoary mountain chambers deep;
Masking shapes that darkling fly,
Beautiful in mystery;
Airy visitants that give
Aspirations fugitive;

Pilgrim voices careless day
With clanging pinion sweeps away ;
Dear as echo from the grave,
Or fettered sigh in sea-locked cave,
Or hidden rivulet whispering
Promise to the ice-bound spring,
Or beauty's pale transparent face
Through the cruel wave breathing grace.

On my lips the moonbeam's kiss
Paints the shadow. of love's bliss ;
Cold as snowflakes light that rest
On the bird's deserted nest ;
Cold as vestal's wounded pride ;
Cold as hope of widowed bride ;
Cold as pity's touch that vain
From lovelorn hearts would steal the pain,
Hearts on bloodless kisses fed,
Happier with the unmocked dead.

For in my cloistered thought I keep
One passionate image mirrored deep,
Though ever doomed, imperial Sun !
With maiden eye the wish to shun,
Ah ! would my heedless charmer knew
Me not less fair, me far more true
Than the favorites golden crowned,
That drink the perfume of his wound ;
Generous love's unanswered prayer
Breathes a soul from its despair,
Immortal hope unknown to light,
Won from sorrow infinite.

XVIII.

THE STORM IN THE HARBOR.

Your eyes with golden light no more,
Fair Ursula, are brimming o'er ;
No more the music of your voice
Repeats the song " Rejoice, rejoice."

" Upon me rests like frozen pall
The shadow of the convent wall :
If Heaven the gift of love denies
Its barren bounties I despise."

Contented rest, fair maid, alone,
Love is but lovely when unknown ;
A moment's joy, and ever after,
Derision's cold, unfeeling laughter.

Her glance rebuked the words malign,
She flushed in loveliness divine ;
Coy rosebud wrapt in sable leaf,
What wins the heart like beauty's grief ?

I looked upon the mighty river,
" Must love and beauty part forever ?
Beneath the bank lies hid my sail
The faithful Hudson tells no tale."

XIX.

WARNING.

Where the pine and river meet,
Maiden, guard thy silvery feet;
Little for thy beauty's good
Works the Spirit of the Wood.

Underneath the forest's lid,
He in ambush lying hid,
Lures with evil's mystery
Thy white soul's security.

Seest thou not an ebon ray
Mid the waving grasses play?
Seest thou not the raven's wing
O'er thy path its shadow fling?

Love, no idle painted boy,
Tempts with hope of promised joy,
But the offspring of despair
Wooes thee to a demon's lair.

XX.

PHANTOM FEARS.

Confined in the grasses sear
On the meadow lies a deer;
Black against the cloudy sky
Ravens flock with boding cry.

Sadder sight, a lady fair
Gems with beauty sorrow's lair,
Lingering, where the brambles twine
Thick around the stunted pine.

Lady, linger not, nor heed
Words that will betray thy need;
Nature's warning voices hear:
Fly the shadows creeping near.
Better lurking adder smite,
Better wolf thy love invite,
Than on desolation's throne
Thou, forsaken, weep alone.

XXI.

FUGITIVES.

Haste, Lady, lay thy hand in mine,
  The moon is wrapt in mist;
The tell-tale stars forget to shine,
  By love to slumber kissed.

But, Beauty, be thine eyes my path,
  Hark how the wild wave calls;
Soon shall our sail defy the wrath
  Of churlish convent walls.

Haste, Lady, haste, look never back;
  There is no home but love,
And heaven lights fond lovers' track,
  Though far from heaven they rove.

XXII.

ADRIFT.

Fast, fast a-down the rushing river,
　To the pathless ocean wide,
The swift wind bears us onward ever,
　The wind and swifter tide.

And dark and ever darker grow
　The night and tempest-wing;
And high the waves their white hands throw,
　Like spectres beckoning.

But while in love's embrace I lie,
　What evil is to fear?
'T is bliss to live, 't were bliss to die,
　And Thou, belovéd, near!

And as deep in thy rippling hair,
　My trembling touch sinks down,
A music echoes through the air,
　That mocks the heavens' frown.

XXIII.

MEROPE.

Hide not thy laughter-loving face,
　Like weeping shame-veiled Merope,
Who deeming mortal love disgrace
　From alien sisters turned to die.

Ill-judged her grief, whose influence sweet,
  No wanton lure for treacherous Jove,
Gave wings of light to rooted feet
  And lent divinity to love.

With kindlier beam, Enchantress, shine,
  My stricken soul bid live again,
That having known thy face divine,
  Denies a mortal beauty's reign.

XXIV.

A CONVERT.

Beneath the light of hazel eyes
  I sank on beauty's breast,
As sinks a child in Paradise,
  To soft, reluctant rest.

" Oh, sing ! " I cried, " of beauty's flower,
  And breath like honey-dew,
Of love that knows the twilight hour,
  To changing pleasure true."

She sang : but, hark ! the woven strain,
  Of joy it tells, and sorrow ;
To-day the cheating golden grain,
  The iron tares to-morrow.

Of sinners' wail and wasting woe,
  And oh, the words—how sweet !—
Of hopes, from mercy's tears, that grow
  Beside the judgment-seat !

She sang till love, to worship won,
    Forgot its wanton sigh,
And, soul in soul, we floated on
    Through still eternity.

XXV.

THE WEAVER.

I have woven a net for thy feet,
Lest the slow leaden wind may entreat
        The swift airy flight
        Of their pinion light,
My rooted love's whispers to cheat.

I have woven a net for thy hair,
Lest the sheltering night should despair
        If the wild loveliness
        Of thy wandering tress
Spread its sabler wing on the air.

I have woven a net for thine hand,
Let its whiter charm serve as a wand,
        That shall tempt the cruel snow,
        Like step-mother, to throw
Its treacherous cloak o'er the land.

I have woven a net for thine eye,
That no glittering arrow may fly,
        To awaken the Sun,
        Ere his slumber is done,
That thy beauty's retreat he may spy.

I have woven a net for thy heart,
That no word from love's goal may depart,
  But like rose leaf embayed,
  Where the wave is ne'er laid,
Still whisper how lovely thou art.

XXVI.

LOVE-LONGING.

  Among the lilies lying,
  Pale Love, why art thou sighing?
The moonbeam cold and river fleet
Mingle their white gleaming feet,
And a star-born murmur thrills
The silence of pine-crested hills,
Unheeded, thee a rhythmic breath
With swift charm so o'ermastereth,
  Pale Love no longer sighing,
  Among the lilies lying.

  Upon the cold hillside,
  Shone Beauty golden-eyed,
With parted lips all passion pale,
Beneath the moonlight's crystal veil,
Lying clothed in garment rare,
In tangles dark of silken hair,
Lying clothed in kisses sweet,
That from her eyelids to her feet
Burned, like roses peeping through
The stainless drifted mountain snow,
Till love's deeper kisses sheathe
The chiding fears her whispers breathe,

Luring joys the immortals crave
From her heart's fast beating wave,
Swiftly gathering into one,
All raptures of the star and sun.

So on the cold hillside,
A homeless poet's bride,
My lovely lady, crimson white,
Shone apparelled in delight,
Like a truant sunbeam hid
Beneath the still night's closing lid,
From the fountain of the morn,
A gem by music's pinion borne,
On barren love's forgetful shore,
To blossom once and nevermore.

XXVII.

OUT OF THE DEPTHS.

No longer o'er a smiling sea
With swelling sail my bark I guide,
And, singing beauty's praise and thee,
Measure thy name with ocean wide.

For now, like dragon from its cave
In eastern mists that brooding lies,
The storm-rack o'er the shuddering wave
With evil-boding pinion flies.

Now, now the tempest's fury wakes,
From pole to pole the lightnings blaze,
The sea in living mountains breaks,
The salt waves flood the starry ways.

Yet none the less my heedless care,
   While instant death its dart delays,
Bids wave and wind their tribute bear
   To deck my lovely Lady's praise.

Sweet love, that sucks the violet's breath,
   Is fed no less with danger's flower,
Life's cradle and the realms of death
   Alike confess his sov'reign power.

With feather from the tempest's wing,
   Thy name traced on the fatal rock
Shall breathe delight, while perishing
   Thy lover sinks beneath the shock.

XXVIII.

ALONE.

Leave, Lady, leave your garden gay,
   The stately lily leave,
And steal with secret step away,
   Where none may see you grieve.

No daisies star your tangled curls,
   Your breast no roses deck,
And scattered lie the threaded pearls,
   That gemmed your snowy neck.

Alas! that modest glance and prayer,
   That censure love's caress,
Make lovely maid more fatal fair
   And love more merciless.

XXIX.

ADIEU.

The sliding bank a mossy oak
　Upholds with wrinkled, knotted claws,
Its heart, that turned the ligh'ning-stroke,
　With secret tooth the blind worm gnaws.
　　　　Ever the stream flows silently !

Amid the brambles winter bare,
　What glimmers in the moonlight cold?
Is it a beamy jewel rare,
　Or white lamb strayed from its master's fold?
　　　　Ever the stream flows silently !

Rained never jewel so crystal light,
　Nor pet lamb nursed on the mountain side ;
A kneeling lady gems the night,
　The queen of beauty, of sorrow the bride !
　　　　Ever the stream flows silently !

Upon her blue-veined feet her hair
　Unbound its fitful shadow flings,
Her belt, that knows her heart's despair,
　Around her waist too closely clings.
　　　　Ever the stream flows silently !

A ring her trembling kisses press ;
　Though fate be false, love is more true ;
" May God thy soul in mercy bless !
　Adieu !" she sighs, "my Love, adieu !"
　　　　Ever the stream flows silently !

From parted wave what bitter cry
The mountain's brooding echoes wakes !
On fitful wing the ravens fly,
The mouldering boughs the shrill wind shakes.
Ever the stream flows silently !

XXX.

NOVENA.

I.

Oh, Hope where other hope is none,
Oh, tender as the mercy shown,
Saint Magdalen, thy errors known.

Oh, lovely as thy name is bright,
Make intercession day and night,
For whom too late has loved the light.

Too late, oh, heart with sorrow riven,
For other pardon than of Heaven,
For other hope than sins forgiven.

II.

My bed the thistle is and thorn,
My hunger craves the tainted corn,
That starving beggars pass in scorn,

And putrid oil, that serves as lamp,
To cheer the ague-fit and cramp,
That dwell with me in cellar damp.

Dear Patroness, veil justice's eye,
From whom in last extremity
Of ill worse penances would try.

III.

Its sword will sorrow never sheathe ?
" Despair, be thou my hope, O Death,
To thee my spirit I bequeath."

I cried, but thought of one who grew
From vicious soil divinely true,
And blossomed in brave beauty new.

Thou holier name than Eucharist,
Oh, midnight's plume to splendor kissed
Of morning by the love of Christ.

IV.

Saint Magdalen, what need confess
How utter his unworthiness,
Whose prayers around thy altar press.

What sins of deed, of word, of thought,
The good undone, the evil wrought,
The simple to confusion brought.

Oh, widest circle of love's creed,
Incarnate mercy intercede
For him, whose sorrows weep and plead.

V.

Upon my lips a bleeding sigh,
Within my heart a bitter cry,
Dear Patroness, art thou not nigh ?

All words of joy are turned to pain,
The names I love curse back again,
Art thou not near, Saint Magdalen?

Saint Magdalen, dear Patroness,
Art thou not near, his grief to bless,
Whose prayers one only hope confess?

VI.

Oh, more than drink to lips athirst,
Or food to hearts by hunger nursed,
Or peace to sinful souls accursed.

Oh, more than mantle to the cold,
Oh, gathering name in Jesus' fold
Of outcasts from religions old.

Saint Magdalen, Saint Magdalen,
Again thy light and mercy rain
On whom the night consumes and pain.

VII.

Oh, love, that turnest law to shame,
Saint Magdalen, immortal name,
That shieldest heaven itself from blame.

Co-mate with that just hearted thief,
Who brave in agony of grief,
Accused the wise world's unbelief.

Twin souls of Christianity,
That sorrow will not suffer die,
Though Heaven's throne in ashes lie.

VIII.

Oh, praise Saint Magdalen, each leaf,
That chid'st forgetful nature's grief
With happy promise of relief.

Oh, praise Saint Magdalen, each wave,
That from the sullen ocean's grave
Upbraid'st the shore with whisper brave.

Oh, praise Saint Magdalen each bright,
Prophetic star, whose changeless light
Rebukes the sorrow of the night.

IX.

O name of love unmixed with awe,
O name above the curse of law,
O name that healest heaven's flaw.

Oh, loftier, than to know disdain,
Oh, brighter than to brook a stain,
Dear Patroness, Saint Magdalen.

Thou star of crystal ocean,
Where turgid streams unstaining run,
Shine gently on my labor done.

XXXI.

THE TAJ.

Not easily shall I forget
The Taj, 'mid cypress shadows set,
With column, dome, and minaret,
    Where sacred Jumna flows,

Rising in beauty picturesque,
With flowers adorned in arabesque,
   The lotus and the rose.

A Titan's chiselled passion cold,
With white magnificence untold
Apparelling the dusky wold,
   And drawing with delight
The worship of the bending skies
Around the tomb, where regnant lies
   An empress jewel dight.

But more immortal shines the glory
Of Jehanera transitory,
The emperor's child, whose simple story
   The waving grasses tell.
" Uncanopied, here sinks to rest
A pupil of the men of Cheest—
   Long loved and cherished well."

The perfume India's flowers of pride,
The song her birds in crimson dyed,
Have lost, around thy couch abide,
   True, unassuming maid ;
Yet sadder make another sleep,
A grave unsung, unblessed, that deep
   Within my heart is laid.

3
.

IN VAIN.

A voice from ocean's secret spring
  Repeats the burden sweet,
Pale sorrow, lay thy bleeding wing
  On the painless infinite :
Sweet song, by seraphs unforgot,
  My soul thy chiding heedeth not.

The crescent from the troubled sky
  Looks over the tossing waves,
Its tender, unobtrusive eye
  In light my spirit laves :
Alas ! fair empress of the sea,
  Thy promise may not comfort me.

The vision bright of lost delight
  My wandering path waylays,
With evil slight by day and night
  My very soul it flays :
And evermore in sad refrain
  I hear the words, " in vain, in vain."

TERA.

THE MAID OF ELBERON.

Who wanders o'er the barren sand,
  What winsome maiden fair?
Was never lady in the land
  Might match her graces rare.

Faint glances with fond fears dispute,
  As in the twilight's doubt
From trembling lid irresolute
  The love star peepeth out.

But never balm shall minister,
  So knoweth many a one,
To him, whose eyes once look on her,
  The Maid of Elberon.

REACTION.

" She is so beautiful," I heard
  A gentle maiden say,
Her lips with kindly feeling stirred,
  Like rose by morning's ray.

" Is she so beautiful ? " I said,
  And silent sat and thought
Not of another lovely maid,
  But one to music wrought,

Whose generous praise a rival's charm
  Had conquered for her own,
And careless clothed with strange alarm
  A heart to wounds unknown.

Not fashioned ill to tell or hear
  Of beauty's power she seemed,
Who like a distant vision near
  With soft enchantment gleamed.

A sunny glance of timid joy,
  A voice, the rivulet's note,
A golden tress, whose tangles coy
  Shadowed a pearly throat.

Time's touch may fret her vermeil cheek
  And whiter hand than snow,
But her brave spirit's beauty meek
  Shall ever fairer show.

III.

A NON-COMBATANT.

Winsome maiden, beauty's ward,
Needless care is it to guard
Thee from one, whose sober mind
Earthly hopes no longer bind.

What to me bright eyes aglow,
Underpeeping crystal brow ;
Or whiter hands that softer rest
Than foam-flowers on the billow's crest ?

What to me a languid neck,
Lilies nothing spare to deck ;
Or the tangled lingering light
Playing through thy tresses bright ?

Whisper not of dimples, where
Pinks and roses fade in air,
Nor of Arab ankle fine,
Lending speed to foot divine.

Whisper not of crimsons given
By the soft compliant even,
To stain a lip where haply lies
Bliss, a harsher heaven denies.

Dearer far to me than charms,
With which sense the will disarms,
Is that soul of tenderness,
, Thy coy glances half repress.

Dearer still, the record kind,
Left by grateful sick and blind,
Proving thee that miracle,
A woman good as beautiful.

Misery's homestead turned to joy,
Tasks that idleness employ,

Truth and comfort to despair,
Tera, these thy praises are.

And, alas, not such as these
Are the pleasing images
By which lovely maiden may
Find her fancy lured away.

IV.

BEAUTY'S FROWN.

A touch that sways the electric fire
　　May wrap the world in flame ;
A voice, that rules our heart's desire,
　　May kill with word of blame.

Enchantress, whose ungentle frown
　　My faltering tongue reproved,
To thy glad heart be never known
　　The thought thine anger moved.

" If she had cared to hear me speak,
　　She had not found so dull
The silence, whose fond eloquence meek
　　Proclaimed her beautiful."

But fare thee well, what thou hast given,
　　Thou canst not take away,
A face, whose beauty whispers Heaven
　　To one, who dares not pray.

When folly's favorites boldly press
Around thy silvery feet,
To wound thy modest loveliness
With feigning accents sweet,

Perchance thy sated ear may turn
From phrase of polished art,
And wish itself not deaf to learn
The music of the heart.

v.

TERA.

Frolic Tera, strive to find
For earnest question answer kind :
Who has the sunbeams robbed to dress
The beauty of thy silken tress ?
Or from crest of morning's wave
Fed thy crystal glances brave ?
Or placed for music's holiest cell
'Mid golden shade a pearly shell ?
Or bade swift-winged roses break
From snowy dimples in thy cheek ?
Or marble made thy shoulder rare
Than Pelops' daughters whiter far ?
Or from fleecy billows dyed
With richest coral's crimson pride,
Clothed a breast, where fancy's wing
Folded sits, while angels sing ?
What thorn has stung a dainty finger,
Whose frown forbids fond truth to linger ?

What hand with belladonna tips
The pouting charm of rebel lips ?
Or ties the wind's swift sandal on
A foot ill-framed from praise to run ?

VI.

THE PUPIL.

Like eagle on his lonely throne,
His wing's wide circle done, ·
But drinking with unsated sight
The large imperial light,
I stood in pride of strength, to beat
Despair beneath my feet,
Till seemed me but as idle breath
Wealth, glory, life, and death,
Nor love more that the light smoke curled
Fair from the valley world ;
So wrapt I stood in the high thought
By nature's passion wrought,
Nor, save the God-voice of my soul,
Knew other power's control.
But ah, what humble change is this ?
Why creeps my wing to kiss
The daisy sweet and violet
With crystal dew-drop wet !
Ah, why fair maid of hearth and home
Should thy far footstep roam,
Or by what sorrow spurred or hope
To seek the mountain's scope ;
And, with thy brave enchantment coy,

Like child that begs a toy,
Win from me secrets by me won
From th' unseen sun of sun,
Until the practice of thy voice
Such music weird employs,
Such mingled notes of sweet and high
In tangled harmony,
That I, forsworn, turn wisdom's rays
To deck a lovely face,
Ingolded by a wandering tress,
That prisoned sunbeams dress ;
Till, faint as April flowers that lean
The morning's blush to glean,
I bow before thy silvery feet
In servitude complete.
But thou, fair pupil, taught too well
The heart's deep master-spell,
Remember that thy teacher sues,
And spare the rod to use,
Nor press on him the tyranny
Of new authority,
Whose hand, though empty, owns to give
Treasures less fugitive,
Than those proud peaks, star-tenanted,
Rooted 'neath ocean's bed,
That sway the broad Pacific's pride,
And earth and sea divide :
For, if thou wilt the burdening tax
Of beauty's frown relax,
Doubt not my palsied hand shall set
High arch and minaret,
A splendor of immortal stone,

With jewels thick o'ergrown,
To temple thee, when greedy death
Thy bloom encompasseth,
And all of thee that is not mine
The gods to dust resign.

VII.

TERA IPSA.

Why to music's sleepless shell
Fancy will thy folly spell
A name, whose charmed melody
Summons beauty's image nigh ?
Art thou Tera's milliner
Thou must need apparel her
In texture of thy cunning loom,
The lily's snow, the rose's bloom,
Orient pearl and ore divine.
From the sun's most hidden mine ?
Why delight her languid neck
With golden serpent's coil to deck ?
Or on ivory shoulder set
Finer lace than spider's net ?
Why delight to make her sit
Demure, the while swift fingers knit
A task, whose airy meshes well
To prudent mind of fetters tell ?
Why delight from dimpled cheek
To lure her wingéd blush to speak ?
Or wake what fatal danger lies
Slumbering in ambush eyes ?

Foolish Fancy ! know'st thou not
Long ere this she has forgot
Thee, my master, and each word,
Beauty's faithful echo stirred ?
Deem, I pray, her picture is
One of wealth's poor forgeries,
And thyself a lacquey born,
Not to hold its charms in scorn.
Let her spurred by hunger roam,
Banished from her dainty home ;
Let her bleeding, ice-clad feet
From stolen sunbeams gather heat ;
Let her fair hand's timid prayer
Glean what envy loves to spare ;
Let her grope, all anguish blind,
O'er frozen stream, in hope to find
Aid gentler than her sisters win
From man's heart compact of sin,
Think you, to your altered eye,
This rose will peep so wooingly ?
Yet, alas ! in her must lurk
A touch of nature's handiwork,
That churlish thought would vainly try
With cheating comfort to belie ;
For yestermorn a beggar maid
Met me, wrapped in tattered plaid,
Whose reluctant, pleading face
Recalled the well-remembered grace
Of that cold blossom of the Sun
I had unwisely looked upon,
Till the treacherous masker bore
From avarice all its hoarded store,

And left me this dull opiate song
To solace hunger's torture long.
Spendthrift Fancy, cease thy dreaming,
Beauty's best 's but beauty's seeming.

VIII.

THE INTERPRETER.

Oh, lovely as thy gentle name,
Enchantress, what forgotten flame
    Awakes at thought of thee ;
Till eager grown, as thou art fair,
My soul forgets all other care
    Than thy dear face to see !

'T was not thy glances bending low,
Or rosebeam on thy lips aglow,
    Or sweeter voice than thrush.
'T was not my hand by thine impearled,
Thy tangled tresses o'er them curled,
    Thy swiftly mantling blush.

But that, like sunshine of the May,
Thy happy fancy loved to play
    Around each common sight ;
Till of what homely showed or mean,
The sacred ray that lurks unseen,
    Revealed its beauty bright.

Unskilled am I, with polished phrase,
Or music's sad persuasive lays,
    To touch a maiden's heart,

But oh, that thy kind eyes again
Might chase away the bitter pain,
That tells how fair thou art.

IX.

EMBARRASSMENT.

Beauty, could I but love thee less,
Not difficult it were to dress
In royal phrase thy loveliness.

But when I gaze upon thy face,
So blinding splendor round it plays,
Each word shrinks back in cruel disgrace.

As when a daisy rears its head
In hope to light the flowery mead,
And sees the dawn its radiance shed.

Yet, in thine absence overbold,
A basket have I made to hold
Thy gentle name's untarnished gold,

Of osiers lined with pencilled fern,
Where peeping rose-buds trembling burn,
And violets their eyes upturn.

X.

THE FINAL CAUSE.

The sunbeams sow the earth with power,
  And gem the trembling sea,
As I from night's unquiet hour
  Wake still to dream of thee.

Had Heaven meant me to be mute,
  Why should it mould so fair
A face, whose glance irresolute
  Allured to chide my prayer?

Had Heaven meant thee to be deaf,
  Why hid in golden net
Should peeping pearl for thievish grief
  A fatal ambush set?

Has beauty but created been
  To undo or be undone?
And has my madness shieldless seen
  The snow-child of the Sun?

Let not thine eye behold me, Sweet,
  But let thy mercy see
A captive bent before thy feet,
  To worship Heaven in thee.

XI.

THE PLATER.

The amber gods with unseen sway,
Dull lead in dazzling gold array ;
But subtler secret have I found,
One whispered word, and quickly round
My leaden soul bright fancies coy,
Of earth and Heaven the woven joy,
With cheating splendor gathering shine,
That half like thee I seem divine ;
The gilded dross all mortals laud,
Nor hoodwinked gods detect the fraud.

XII.

POSSIBLY.

" My little Maid with pouting lips,
   Once promise to be mine,
Your name, the Morning Star's eclipse,
   For ever more shall shine.
What hidden wealth in heaven remains,
Or locked in earth's unyielding veins,
Is yours———" From rosy lips astir
   Her doubtful accents break :
" Good lovers, but poor husbands, sir,
   I fear all poets make."

XIII.

LOVE'S AMBITION.

Could I entwine thy name through magic rhyme
　　With flowers Elysian that immortal bloom,
And fretted not by moth nor envious time,
　　Through distant ages breathe their sweet perfume,

Then should I envy not the lord, who binds
　　With iron chains the toiling earth his slave ;
Or, impious, with his cunning engines finds
　　The sacred gold hid in its rocky grave.

Nor him, his country's immortality,
　　Who plucks the guerdon of victorious war ;
But happy, Tera, in thy name would die,
　　The scorn of time, even from thee afar,
Unseen of any ray from fame's clear eye,
　　Like him who loved and named the morning star.

XIV.

THE DAY-STAR.

　　Beneath my feet the miners work,
　　Around my pathway poignards lurk,
　　The wolf's voice answers hunger's prayer,
　　Their warmth the winter breezes spare ;
　　A little while and misery
　　Its careless favorite dooms to die ;

And am I blamed that I beguile
Th' assassin hours with beauty's smile?
And lingering gaze upon a face
Where truant sunbeams gather grace?
Or is she blameless that would wound
A hand, whose careful joy has bound
Her brow with peerless diadem
To music fashioned gem by gem?
Has it, since when, become a crime
To frame in unforgetful rhyme
The Mystic Rose, and awestruck sit
Silent awhile and worship it?
Or must I, hopeless of the morn,
By night's last beacon left forlorn,
Unfriended watch all loveless-cold
The day-star's fading eye of gold,
Alien to her whose holy charm
Allures the soul with promise warm?

xv.

FAR AWAY.

Enchanting shape of moulded flame,
  No more my pride may praise
The magic marvel of a name,
  That still my spirit sways.

No more I watch thy blushes break,
  No more thy glance of fire
And wayward touch to passion wake
  Thy lover's lowly lyre.

From sorrow far, and far from one,
　Who worshipped beauty's face,
Beneath a cloudless summer sun
　The joyous hours you chase.

The locks my fancy loved to dress,
　With tangled sunbeams glow ;
The roses' perfumed kisses press
　Thy whiter neck than snow.

Fulfilled of beauty, thou, fair maid,
　Fulfilled of grief am I ;
Ah, would I in my grave were laid
　With one fond memory.

XVI.

THE LAMP OF LOVE.

Maiden shining from afar,
Like sunbeam changed to mocking star,
That to uncounted worshippers
With chainless bounty ministers,
How easily thou canst forget
His grief, who wove a fruitless net
To catch thy coy, reluctant feet,
Lingering o'er meadows sweet.
But, distant charmer, have a care,
Lest Love goaded by despair,
Far from daisy-crested field,
Or joys the piny mountains yield,

Seek the freighted secrets vast,
By ether's surging billow cast
On the rocky, treacherous shore,
Where poet-wreckers gather lore ;
Spells by sullen madness won,
Of sway to dim the noontide sun,
Or tear the unseen arm in twain,
That holds the double stars in chain,
Or checking earth's strong onward force,
To vapor turn the mighty corse,
Or the nameless comet call,
To pierce fate's adamantine wall,
From th' infinite sole visitant,
With message strange our law to daunt,
And prying back to regions blind
Chariot the freer mind ;
Spells of power to clip thee round
With icy words that other sound
Forbidding shall in fetters fine
Forever house thy soul divine ;
Or skilled to sheathe thy glance's ray,
Kindling on its tremulous way,
And bear each wayward prisoner bright
To soothe my sorrow's shrouded night.
Then rather let thy beauty brook
Kindly on his face to look,
Whose pride in scorn of sordid gain
Holds meaner lessons in disdain
Than th' immortal truths that guide
The universal ocean's tide,
From whose wave are idly tossed
Worlds, like shells with songs embossed

Of ages on their wrinkled rind,
Whose music lures thy lover's mind,
Though fed with bitter memory
Of golden blisses not to be,
Long to toil with art divine
In desert melancholy mine
Beneath one heedless star half-seen,
Thro' frowning rocks that press between,
To teach Earth's voices to forget
All songs save one to Tera set.

XVII.

A VOICE.

A voice from out the sea,
  Where all things are forgot,
Murmurs unceasingly,
  Forget, forget me not.

And thou, O fair of face,
  Flame-blossom of the wave,
Lacks beauty's Darling grace
  The meed of love to crave?

XVIII.

REMEMBER NOT.

Remember not, May-maiden bright,
  Whose sweet, unconscious loveliness
Rained joyance on my winter night,
  And breathed a healing balm to bless

A heart, that far too deeply wrung,
To wish another's bosom stung,
For thee can pray ; be all forgot,
Save two brave words, remember not.

Remember not ; through trembling leaf
  Thy peerless, budding charms appear,
Unfretted by a glance of grief,
  The honor of the purple year.
My inmost soul that drank their beam,
To feed its last and holiest dream,
For thee can wish, all were forgot,
Save two brave words, remember not.

Remember not ; base envy's tongue
  Would work thy tender breast annoy,
If memory's whispers fondly hung
  Upon thine ear's consenting joy.
The gentlest hope my heart can frame
Is that the sorrow of his name,
Who lives in thee, be all forgot,
Save two brave words, remember not.

Remember not ; thy beauty's crown,
  The crest of morning's brightest wave,
Have I not seen ? Nor less have known,
  Thy voice that lured me from the grave.
What recompense have I to give
To her, who taught my soul to live ?
Alas ! the wish, be all forgot,
Save two brave words, remember not.

Remember not ; the thought of thee
   At morning wins me from despair ;
And with its sacred melody
   At evening wooes me to the prayer.
Kind Heaven ! send me her sum of pain,
And all my joy bear back again,
And this sad wish, be all forgot,
Save two brave words, remember not.

Remember not ; if my dull thought
   Has gathered music from thy face,
As smoke, that curls from peasant's cot,
   Turns crystal fair in morning's rays.
My truest song, my deepest sigh,
That bears away my heart to die,
Is this sad wish, be all forgot,
Save two brave words, remember not.

XIX.

BROKEN.

With many a wistful madrigal,
That would from heaven an angel call,
   I have wooed thee, and have won
   Smile and glance that mock and shun.
And now that broken lies my lute,
And all its *misereres* mute,
   Many maids, with tear and sigh,
   Seek what Beauty passes by.

XX.

SELFLESS LOVE.

Thine eye, that robs the night
Of beauty, pours its light
On others ; not for me
Thy voice's melody.

The music of thy feet
Steals not my ear to greet,
Others thy winsome ways
Enjoy like morning rays.

Thy lips that roses stain
Will never ease my pain,
Thy beauteous breast of snow
For other's love will glow.

Yet will I never fret
My soul with vain regret,
When the prize is worth the pain
Our loss is greater gain.

THE SPIRIT OF LIGHT.

Goddess of Light, upon the mountains cold
   Thy throne is set. Thine eye, that knows no tear,
   Whose glances make the hungry eagles fear,
Breathes forth immortal fire and love untold,

That draw the chosen toward thine Alpine hold,
   Unrecompensed, save that around their bier
   Fame idly chants their name, warrior and seer,
And him the sov'reign, from whose hallowed mould

Laurel and myrtle spring. Thy cruel feet press
   Not mortal loves alone, but great gods slain,
Thy spoil, by braver hearts, that dreamed no less,
   So jealous madness wrought upon their pain,
Than thus to win thy perfect loveliness,
   A bliss too deep for men or gods to gain.

ESTELLA.

I.

SYRENS.

Fair is the garden of roses
In the twilight of purple and gold,
That for men's longing encloses
The bewitching light beauties of old.

Still are they sitting enmisted
In a splendor of wind-furrowed hair,
Still with a charm unresisted,
Are they luring us on to despair.

Wary the mazes they weave for us
In their grotto with mosses o'ergrown,
Softer the whispers they breathe for us,
Than the music from myrtle leaf blown.

Laïs or Phryne, the lawyer,
Fond Calypso or Circe divine,
Lamia, each bright decoyer,
Overpowers the hurt senses like wine.

Would, O my heart, thou wert done with them,
Will they nevermore suffer to sleep

One, whom swift beauty makes one with them,
　　Though a stranger from over the deep?

Still far from home, unreturning,
　　Must I follow the treacherous, bright
Eyes unextinguished of yearning
　　That bewilder, enchain, and delight?

Still in dark tresses entangled,
　　Must I hear the low, murmurous, warm
Music by sweet kisses jangled,
　　Like a harp where the honey bees swarm?

Nor for such light of love ladies,
　　Was I born where the spring frost is hoar,
Where every man at his trade is
　　At the plough, at the loom, and the oar.

Strangers to music and laughter,
　　Were my Puritan ancestors stern,
Harsher their now and hereafter,
　　Than the gardens, where ripe roses burn.

Not of such light of love ladies,
　　But a cloistering lily apart,
That of its beauty afraid is,
　　Was the maiden that fashioned my heart.

Gone long ago is the vision
　　Of the simple, the holy, the pure,
Left to me now but derision,
　　And the glances that deathward allure.

II.

A ROVER.

I owned no sober store
Of manners, names, or lore
    To plume my pride,
Nor science' mystic rod
To gold-bespangled lode
    My way to guide.

Unclad as winter's bough,
The wind went whistling thro'
    My body lean ;
And hunger-winged I sought,
Thro' ways with danger fraught,
    My food to glean.

I cursed the dullards, who
By thievish contract grew
    To misers hoary ;
For seemed to youth and me
Belonged the world in fee,
    And all its glory.

From hearth and home exiled,
The restless ocean's child,
    I shunned nor sought,
Nor cared to watch the plough
Across the meadows go,
    Nor planned for aught ;

Save, when my hour should chance,
To lie where foam-flowers dance
    Around my corse,
And careless back to give
Its bounty fugitive
    To nature's force.

But how shall I forget,
For oh, the joy of it—
    That hour of grace ;
When staying idle feet,
Where sea and river meet,
    I saw her face.

Together round her boat
The waves' swift pinions smote,
    A single oar
She held across the tide
Through blinding spray to guide
    Her keel ashore.

A cry of happy fear,
When first she saw me near ;
    And then she smiled.
She smiled in such a way,
Has from that fatal day
    My soul beguiled.

As back the waters flow,
I seize the veering prow
    And point it true.
Out leaps my lovely prize,

And shakes from laughing eyes
The briny dew.

Then in the breakers' dash
I catch an oar-blade's flash,
And soon the boat,
Forth from the shingly sand,
With fond reluctant hand,
I push afloat.

Her eyes one arrow send,
One touch her fingers lend ;
Then swift she flies,
With speed of feathered oar
Along the barren shore
In lovely wise.

Swift touch, but lasting chain !
Swift joy, but endless pain !
O heart, love-laden !
In hope again her cry
To hear, I hover nigh
The dark-eyed maiden.

A glance, a word, a touch,
Are these joys overmuch
For life to give !
Yet seemed my years had flown
On fruitless wing, nor known
Till now to live.

And as the evening grew,
I bent my footsteps true

To watch the light,
With holy cloistering charm,
From her proud window warm
    The chilly night.

Then, with diviner eyes,
The starry heavens surprise
    My wondering gaze,
That sees another ocean
Sweep on with measured motion
    Thro' timeless space.

And wizard fancies strange
With reason interchange,
    And fire my brain,
To seize Orion's sword,
And make my love adored
    Through Heaven's reign.

" O heart-beloved !" I cried ;
" Beyond the starry tide
    Or eyeless night,
On music's wing thy name
With breath of sacred flame
    Shall scatter light."

Then grew her chamber dark ;
But at her window—hark !
    What sound is there ?
Wide is her window flung,
And as with jewel hung,
    Enchants the air.

Beneath her white arm's yoke
The earth new beauty took,
   And bending skies
Fairer returned the bright
Pervasive liquid light
   Of languid eyes.

I hear the ocean's moan ;
My pretty bird has flown
   Back to her nest ;
And as the winter wave,
Where beauty finds its grave,
   Cold grows my breast.

Sad parting when by one
Is all the parting done ;
   O winsome maid,
Could I but softly creep
And watch thy face asleep,
   My grief were stayed.

True hand, dost thou not hear,
Sure foot, wilt thou not bear
   To beauty's side
One, whose immortal love
Nor earth holds bribe to move,
   Nor heaven wide !

I thought, and in an hour
Within the maiden's bower—
   Oh, who has seen
A flower so lovely laid

Beneath night's sober shade
As thou, my queen !

Enmisted in her hair,
One gleaming arm lies bare
Her face to shield,
That, like coy beauty chidden
With peeping charms forbidden,
Shows half concealed.

O maiden, wilt thou miss,
I thought, one guileless kiss ?
Not thine the blame.
And as who worships death,
Upon her perfumed breath
I press my shame.

III.

THE MAID OF THE DELAWARE.

Oh ! came you by the Delaware
When apple trees are white ;
Saw you a lovely maiden there,
Breathing beauty infinite ?

Beside the flowery bank she sits,
A child of sweet twilight,
And with forgetful fingers knits
A work of magic sleight.

The shadows on the mountains lie,
  With sliding foot the river,
A merry note, a plaintive sigh,
  Its heart unburdens ever.

But sweeter than the melody
  Of wave, of leaf, or bird,
The song that lures the passer-by,
  Once heard, too often heard.

Ill-fated thou, if once shall hold
  Thy name that fairy loom ;
The sunbeams, turned to ashes cold,
  Shall shroud thy path in gloom.

IV.

PRUDENCE.

Gaze not on her glowing eyes,
If your soul's content you prize,
Nor the tangles of her hair,
Deeming love is fettered there.

Think not from her ruby lip
Safely poisoned drops to sip,
Once but feel her fond caress,
Thickest dangers round thee press.

Vain thy warnings ever prove,
Prudence chiding sacred love ;
Swift I fly, but swifter far
The wind-shod feet of Venus are.

4

v.

THE MYSTIC.

What lovely vision hovers
  Beneath the starless night ?
What hand the veil uncovers
  That sunders night from light ?

That weaving marvellous
  The weaver hours have wrought,
To shroud the bright God house
  By eye unpierced or thought.

O face of living flame !
  O hope than heaven more fair !
Thee, nor earth's dirges tame,
  Nor barren love's despair.

With burning words unspoken,
  O passion of my lyre !
Who has thy fetters broken ?
  Who wakes again thy fire ?

Or do I watch the mist
  Above the whispering wave,
Where silent sands are kissed
  By hopeless voices brave ?

VI.

TWIN STARS.

Flow on, flow on, sweet Delaware !
The mountain, mead, and sea .
Delight thy changing song to share,
   And join their hearts through thee.

How many mountain maidens fleet,
   And ocean's rosy daughters,
Have paused to watch their charms retreat
   Beneath thy lingering waters.

But never answering dream has seen,
   Or wakening eye a sight,
So fair has gleamed thy banks between
   On gentle yester night,

When she of beauty born the flower,
   Lay floating on thy wave,
And twilight's fond, enchanted hour,
   To love and music gave.

Above, through parted cloud, love's star
   Reigned o'er the sky alone,
Below, with radiance brighter far,
   A face in beauty shone.

Who once of that cold face of pride
   Had seen the crystal flame,
Not all thy water's swelling tide
   His kindling love could tame.

Who once had drunk the healing balm,
  Her budding lips enfold,
No care would fret his blissful calm,
  Though oceans o'er him rolled.

Flow on, flow on, sweet Delaware,
  Flow on to the deepest sea,
And from thy banks forgetful bear
  The joys love rained on me.

VII.

SILKEN SIGHS.

No god were so supremely blest,
Could I my weary sorrows rest,
Upon thy tender-breathing breast,
           Estelle.

Culling the rainbow's loveliest rays
To deck with brightest flowers thy praise,
The burden of immortal lays,
           Estelle.

Watching thy words in music flow,
Thy frolic glances kindlier grow,
Thy smiles their changing sunshine show,
           Estelle.

Wearing thy soft arms' rosy wreath,
Drinking thy hyacinthine breath,
Through blissful life to blissful death,
           Estelle.

Happy my life's sweet labor done,
To see thy name the proudest one,
That fame has carved upon the sun,
 Estelle.

VIII.

BY THE TIDE.

Fishermaiden, by the sea,
 Dancing on the yellow sand,
Come and sit awhile by me,
 Lay in mine thy sun-browned hand.

Tame thy wayward glances wild,
 Nearer lend thy pearly ear,
What should mermaid's sportive child
 Know of foolish doubt and fear.

Wherefore cruelly from me start?
 Hear'st thou not a wave's sweet song?
Hear'st thou not my heart of heart
 Whisper, " I have loved thee long "?

All unlike the treacherous wave,
 Fickle calm and fatal roar,
Is its pure devotion brave,
 Growing deeper evermore.

Threatened with no single kiss,
 Beauty, thou art lying,
Where fishers loth their spoil to miss,
 For corals red are sighing.

IX.

THE GLANCE.

The shadow of the pansy's dream,
Falling soft on Lethe's stream ;
The mountain lightning's waking wrath,
Cleaving its untrodden path,
Image not the glances hid
Fettered 'neath her fringéd lid.

X.

THE GUERDON.

Soft glow thine eyes, thy snowy skin
With crimson stains ; my lips drink in
Thy beauty's breath ; ah moment sweet !
Proud arms the circle coy complete ;
Denial falters ; fond desire
Melts hopes and fears in one swift fire ;
And all of love's imagined bliss
Imprisoned lives in one long kiss.

XI.

FANCY'S FEVER.

Ungentle love, thy cruel excess
  O'erburdens heart and brain
With wanton wealth of loveliness,
  That turns delight to pain.

Why wilt thou not less fair unveil
  A face, whose fatal charm
My sunken cheek makes ashy pale,
  My pulse with fever warm?

Jealous of every mortal eye,
  Of leaf, of clod, of stone,
To what unknown insanity,
  Wilt thou, Love, spur me on?

Would that to check my wild alarm,
  In hidden dungeon deep,
The only bolt my trusty arm,
  I might my Beauty keep.

That I her light, her food, her all,
  Her saviour thought to be,
Might back to hope her heart recall,
  And fond infirmity.

Last night, within her chamber sweet
  I stole, and round my brow
A crimson garland bound, unmeet
  For eye or ear to know.

A white-plumed moonbeam on her neck
  And blue veined eyelid slept,
But o'er my heart's swift parting wreck
  The storm and whirlwind swept.

Sweet Hudson, whose enchanted wave
  One only face returns,
These homeless rhymes, my joy, my grave,—
  Take thou what Stella spurns.

XII.

EXCELSIUS.

Unhappy Love, ah ! whither art thou fled ?
  To wander lone beside the rocky shore,
  Where mountain torrents answer ocean's roar,
Thou, who wast wont upon the roses' bed,

On Beauty's choice of stolen kisses fed,
  To watch her starry eyes rain golden ore,
  To hear fond fears their wooing whispers pour—
Sweet fears to sweeter joys divinely wed :

Thy nobler mind, edged by adversity,
  Spurs thee to mount the star-crowned crags among,
Beside the lightning's brooding nest to lie,
  Thy bleeding limbs upon the cold rocks flung ;
Nor less, Estella, shall the nearer sky
  Hear beauty's praise in happy numbers sung.

XIII.

THE SANDS OF LOVE.

The Delaware flows by pasture and close,
  The shadows steal over the foam,
The trees on the brink the white vapor drink,
  The cattle are wandering home.
O'ercome with delight, I forget the long year,
And turn fondly thinking Estella is near ;
How faithful my longing, my longing how vain !
What day ever brings the same pleasure again ?

The grass is as green, and as lovely the scene,
  As when, in the morning of May,
She timidly swore by the name I adore
  To love me for ever and aye.
The river, the valley, the sunset are one,
How can I believe that their spirit is gone !
The cold from the mountain creeps over the plain ;
What day ever brings the same pleasure again ?

Soon, soon back to me, from over the sea,
  My vision's love-idol will fly ;
Soon, soon on my gloom her beauty will bloom,
  And heart-beat to heart-beat reply.
But deep through the bliss, that will lurk in each
    kiss,
Alas, there 's a joy that we cannot but miss ;
On love's sweetest rapture will steal the refrain,
No day ever brings the same pleasure again.

XIV.

AN OUTLAW.

The beggar boys make mouths at me,
  And servant wenches flout,
A glance of my coat, without doctor's fee,
  Cures friends of old age and gout.

But grant me a corner in your name,
  A hair to string my harp, ·
I 'll rail no more at churlish fame,
  Or fortune's arrow sharp.

I' ll drive my plow through the yellow sand,
  Between the marks of the tide,
Blackbird and crow, a trusty band,
  My corn in the hill shall hide.

My wine I 'll press from the salt sea foam,
  I 'll glean after vulture and jackal,
The braggart wind I 'll chase to its home,
  And to cloud-built wagon shackle.

But from earth's outlaws will I win
  More wealth than field or town,
And load my Lady's prouder shrine
  With gems to queen unknown.

XV.

UNNATURAL.

Ah ! bid the bee desert the flower,
  Its nest the robin shun,
The parching grass upbraid the shower,
  The blossom chide the sun.

Ah ! bid the sea-anemone,
  Its clinging hand unlock ;
Or constant echo's plaintive cry,
  Forsake the mountain rock.

Ah ! bid the rose forget thy lips,
  The graces rebel prove,
Thy sacred eyes, the dawn's eclipse,
  No more the hurt gods move.

Ah ! bid a wounded captive fly
  From feet, from eyes, from breath,
From all save one sweet face where lie
  Hopes that dare feed on death.

XVI.

THE BARD.

Has not a poet's life a worth
  Above the greedy great,
The larded lords of gold and birth,
  Who steal and strut in state ?

Of what avail is beauty's plume,
　　Or prize of glory won,
Or lovely acts that hidden bloom,
　　And blushing chide the sun,

If he, whom Fame has given breath,
　　Breathe not on them again,
And stoutly snatch from sovereign death
　　The jewels of his reign ?

An immortality, not life,
　　Ill may thine anger slay ;
Cease, Beauty, cease this jealous strife,
　　And kiss my fears away.

XVII.

VIDI.

Let no remorse, Estelle, thy conscience sear,
　　That thy true heart can find no harboring
　　For rhymes that to thy feet their tribute bring
From ocean's waste and sandy desert drear.

I am but avaricious of thine ear,
　　That to its heeding the poor songs that spring
　　Unbidden from my grief awhile may sing—
Last joy from human breast to disappear.

Like shipwrecked mariner, whose glazing eye
　　Beholds a vision rising from the wave,
The beautiful, th' enchantress of the sea,
　　To clothe with splendor his forgotten grave,

Thee have I known and happy yield to die,
Careless of all save that sweet dream to save.

XVIII.

THROUGH LOVE TO DEATH.

Nothing I know except Thee beautiful,
No other object lives within my eye,
My memory is but memory of thee,
My one delight and business but to cull,

With priceless hand that mocks my nature dull,
The winged flowers that peep reluctantly
From thy coy heart, ere heavenward they fly,
Each thought a god, some nobler world to rule.

Misjudge me not if I entreat to sleep
Death's dreamless sleep upon thy gentle breast,
From no ill wish to make my darling weep,
But as a happy child that steals to rest
On roses, that his hoarding fingers heap,
So let me lie with perfumed breath oppressed.

XIX.

LOVE'S MEED.

No more, Estella, will I pine,
Nor on thy heart my passion press,
So Beauty's name immortal shine,
Let torturing wounds my body dress.

The happiness that made me weak
　　Is gone, and wakening with despair
I hear forgotten voices break
　　In madness round me everywhere.

Love is not love that hopes reward,
　　Whisper wild tongues of living flame ;
Love is but love from hope debarred,
　　Its meed is grief, its pride is shame.

Go, Beauty, wheresoe'er thou wilt ;
　　Thou knowest, when thine hour is come,
Thy throne among the stars is built :
　　There, there alone will be thy home.

XX.

THE SANCTUARY.

Beloved, nearer let me lie,
　　Still nearer thy reluctant heart,
Though sooner doomed by thee to die,
　　Though sooner doomed from thee to part.

One blissful hour devoid of fear,
　　On roses sinking to long rest,
With music breathing in my ear—
　　" Ill-fated, yet no god so blest."

Like bee, that of the hoarding hive
　　Forgetful, loads the balmy air
With pregnant germs, of power to give
　　A newer life to blossoms fair ;

That when the night his wing o'ertakes,
  Within the closing petals creeps ;
Whose bier in fresher beauty wakes,
  When deep in death the toiler sleeps.

Thus, Lady, thee my care has sung,
  Thus, Lady, if foredoomed to die,
The lily and the rose among
  Imprisoned, dying, let me lie.

Yet when thy sable locks are gray,
  And dimmed thine eye's wild loveliness,
When burdening years thy step delay,
  And age and grief thy beauty dress ;

Then, when thou knowest thyself more fair
  Than peerless maidens in their prime,
A spirit raining everywhere
  Immortal sunbeams through my rhyme,

Not all unworthy of thy love,
  Perchance thy gentler thought will own
Him, whose despair in silence wove
  A robe of light for thee alone.

XXI.

THE FALLS OF LOVE.

As dressed in childhood's language rise
  Our deepest thoughts, so, Sweet, in thee
My song, that meaner birth denies,
  Embodied, pours its harmony.

" No lesser gift is mine," I said,
  " My soul I 'll coin into rhyme,
With which thy beauty garlanded
  Shall mock the thievish hand of time.

" What are a thousand lives, if one
  Eternal spirit burst in light,
To each new generation
  A living treasure infinite ! "

So spurning other envious care,
  Thine every passion, feeling, thought,
With sacred love that mocked despair,
  To crystal form my study wrought.

And is my recompense to die ?
  Sad flower for gentle love to bear,
Yet shall my dying lips deny
  No word that wrote thee good as fair.

But evil were it for thy fame,
  If foolish tongues in future days,
Not knowing thee unworthy blame,
  Should thus thy noble nature praise.

A goddess has this woman grown,
  A sovereign of the nobler world ;
The slave that helped her to the throne
  Her hand to endless darkness hurled.

XXII.

THE GOD OF TORMENT.

Why starving prisoner doomed to die
With luscious fruits deceive the eye,
Or stretched upon the bleeding rack,
The vanished roses summon back ?
Yet wheresoe'er my sorrow turns,
Oh, Fair and False, thy beauty burns.
Again thine arms around me wreathe,
Again my lips thy kisses breathe—
A madness of embrace.   I sink,
Enraptured on thy heart to drink
Its love note wild, till faint I feel
Thy soul's delight upon me steal.
Thy words of woven witchery,
Beneath their magic spell I lie
A moment—then my tortures wake,
In wounds thy fading kisses break,
A horror thick, compact of night,
Weighs down my straining, barren sight.

Ah, when th' unmocking earth is laid
On love too true to be betrayed,
No more with cheating music sweet,
With fierce heart-longings incomplete,
Th' unfruitful voices of the sky
Will fret thy lover's misery.

XXIII.

THE CASEMENT.

" Again from out the casement shine ;
Again unveil your face divine,
Hear, Lady, hear the matin song,
Whose trembling notes your lattice throng ;
O listen "—like a vacant eye
The silent casement looks reply :
" Alas, forgetful heart, have done ;
This window is but lifeless stone,
That once was quick and glowing frame
Of all thy wildest wish could name."

XXIV.

AWAKE.

I dreamed, Beloved, thou wert true ;
   I clasped thee to my breast,
My lips to lips as tender grew,
   One hope our hearts confessed.

I heard thy whispers : " Minstrel, come
   Where bright immortals throng ;

Oh ! hasten to our starry home,
    That sorrow knows nor wrong."

Light-winged o'er sleeping seas we sped,
    O'er city, hill, and river,
My eyes with beauty's glances fed,
    My soul with love's " forever."

Awake, on parching sands I lie ;
    The sun with lava flows,
My tongue unchains one piercing cry,
    Then thick with horror grows.

My only prayer, the raven's wing,
    That mocks my glazing sight,
Will o'er my eyes one shadow fling
    And stem the molten light.

XXV.

FORSWORN.

A lady by the river walks,
    In veiling beauty wan ;
Through grasses sear and flowerless stalks
    Her footsteps hasten on.

From gray and leafless Palisade   .
    She gazes on the river,
As though with hopeless heart she prayed
    Mute nature to forgive her.

Then climbs a shelving bank, where lies
    A spot in myrtles dressed,
And looks with unforgetful eyes
    On love's deserted nest.

" O loyal soul, unworthy mine !"
    She said.   " Is this the spot,
That knew my hand encaged in thine,
    My vows so soon forgot ?"

No tear she sheds, nor utters moan,
    But swiftly glides away ;
And colder grows the silent stone,
    And darker glooms the day.

XXVI.

THE GATEKEEPER.

Beside a rose-encircled gate,
    That looks on the mountain and sea,
A lady sits in golden state,
    And sings to the hearts of the free ;
With voice that stills the wave's debate
    She sings enchantingly ;
And winds, on beauty's song that wait,
    And bending blossom and tree
Repeat the song, " O brave and strong,
Why struggle and toil in beauty's wrong ?
    Come hither, and joy with me,
    In love's soft bondage free."

But one amid the gathering throng
  Has keener wit to spell,
Beneath the rose what words lie hid ;
  And with voice that falls like a knell,
With pallid cheek and closing lid,
  He tells to hearts aglow,
To what cruel realm of dateless death,
  What house of hopeless woe,
The gate of beauty openeth.

XXVII.

THE COMFORTER.

My love has sowed the barren sea,
  My hopes the Winter wind ;
With ropes of sand, unrestingly,
  My scattered sheaves I bind.

Swift swooping from yon rolling rack
  The tempest spurs its wing,
And fierce before its shadow's track
  The whirlwind's greyhounds spring.

The lightning's hand death-garlands weaves,
  The homestead oak is riven,
The deluged earth its depths upheaves,
  And thunder shatters heaven.

Thou Comforter of sorrow's prayer,
  Staff of the fugitive,
Wilt Thou not visit my despair,
  And lend me strength to live?

THE VEILER.

Ideal divine, thy swift fugitive face
Evermore through the shadows unresting I chase,
Evermore through the shadows I follow thee on,
Tho' the hope and the glory that lured me are gone ;

Tho' from my long struggle I sink faint and sore,
Tho' my foes to my friends have abandoned me o'er ;
Tho' the creatures around me but gibber and jape,
Like mummies that mimic a chattering ape ;

Tho' the star I have worshipped, its wild beauty fled,
At my feet like an eyeless torch lies cold and dead ;
Tho' the kiss from whose passion my life drew its
       breath,
Like a corse on my lips breathes madness and death ;

Tho' hunger and cold are my garment and food,
Tho' my couch is a nest for the scorpion's brood,
Tho' the gods to the furies have left me a prey,
And man may not aid, whom the immortals betray ;

None the less through the storm and the gathering
       night,
Through the spectres that point to my life's lost de-
       light,
Through the treacherous tongues that rain venom
       and fire,
I follow thy voice that bids me aspire.

What is fate to the base is the soul of the proud,
Who rig their wild bark with no sail but their shroud,
And through Heaven's black anger or in death's
   despite,
Pierce the eye of the dawn on the wings of the night.

ELSKA.

I.

DREAMLAND.

Who walks across the purple streams,
That hold the misty isle of dreams?
Who comes, where with embittered moan
Forgotten love is sitting lone ?
Or is it maiden aureole-crowned,
With feet disdainful of the ground ?
Or fairy-idol, passion stained,
By foolish poet fairest feigned ?
Nor saint nor fairy hastens near,
But lovelier and far more dear,
Look from the shadow's fading doubt
How clear her beauty blossoms out.
A presence pure as visions bright,
Undisenchanted of delight,
That, ere our hearts have harbored love,
Across the mountain summits move.
A splendor of soul-swaying eyes,
Stars stolen from Elysian skies,
The sunbeam's spoil, her floating hair,
Her hand, the fleecy cloud's despair,
And hark ! what whisper reaches us,
Low breathing, warm, melodious ?

Oh, sweeter than May music blown,
To cheer the autumn's beauty flown !
For now no more Love drooping weeps,
But with slow wonder timorous creeps ;
Till bolder grown his kisses greet
The swift white marvel of her feet.
" Oh, early loved, late hast thou come
To what far region is love's home ;
Long, long I wearied for thee, Fair,
And made my couch the rose's care,
Till hope forlorn, I laid me down
On flinty rock with thistle strewn,
And sorrowed out the starless night,
With tears of yearning infinite."
Thus he, but she pale love upraises,
And long upon his pale cheek gazes ;
Then swift her snowy neck she turns,
To hide a kiss that tip-toe burns,
With balm and perfume sweet to bring
An end to love's sad suffering.
Nor long with wooing coquetry
Her lips their guerdon rich deny
Till happy now as sometime sad,
With step that makes the meadow glad
Within his myrtle nook he leads her ;
With sunflower's stolen sweets he feeds her ;
Her couch with roses fresh prepares,
Her tresses' golden wealth unbars ;
And as she lies in sunny coil,
Love's victor and love's sacred spoil,
" Oh, welcome, Fairest, to the home,"
He sings, " where fair immortals bloom,

Above the season's chance and change,
Beyond the fire-fanged summer's range,
Untouched of winter's anger rude,
Or autumn's dull decrepitude,
Where fell disease nor wan'despair,
Nor treacherous envy make their lair ;
Where through the even mellow year
The robin's note thrills bright and clear ;
Where minstrels, pupils of the leaf
And wave, unchecked of frost and grief,
Themselves teach joyous mocking-birds
To winnow the wild waste of words ;
And with soft music's echoing rhyme,
Proclaim the fair of every clime.
Oh, not for nothing hast thou given
Thyself to me, and me to heaven ;
And made my bleeding anguish know
How gentle, tender, true art thou,
Of all that will be, or have been
Of fair immortals chosen queen !
Oh, welcome to love's resting place,
Where comes no murmur of disgrace,
Where kings, that mighty empires sway,
A crumb shall from thy threshold pray ;
Where time, that on rich kingdoms feeds,
A servant trims thy garden weeds,
For know, Heart-cherished, thou shall be
Symbol of immortality ;
For ill it were, thy lightest word
By distant ages should be heard,
And her sweet soul that gave it breath,
The prey of cold, unlovely death " ;

So singing in the twilight mist,
Again pale Love and Beauty kissed.

II.

A FACE.

I wandered through the night alone ;
A face from out the darkness shone,
A garnered flame of beauty given
To guide a blinded soul to Heaven.

O lovely face, with ray divine,
Forever on my pathway shine ;
Where'er my wayward footsteps roam,
Be thou my star, my faith, my home.

III.

SINCERE?

Forget awhile, my Lady fair,
　Praise by famous minstrels given,
Forget the words, whose pinions bear
　Thee and beauty's fame to heaven,
And deign a thought to share
　With one, to whom, alas, are known
Music, wit, and language none.

Yet if my song, like floating dust,
　Bear one sunbeam to thine eye,
Or, drop of oil, forfend the rust,

Beauty's best may ill defy,
Or, mote on marble bust,
A hidden charm evoke, in vain
Lofty bards will mock my strain.

IV.

FAME'S FUEL.

A thousand lovely maids less fair
Might from thy beauty's bounty dress
Their fatal charms, the world's despair,
Nor wound thy perfect loveliness.

A thousand poets less divine
Might from thy music's sacred fire,
In borrowed glory proudly shine,
Nor tame one string of thy sweet lyre.

My life's cruel waste and dull decay
Shall feed with oil a lamp of light,
To lead thy name's reluctant ray
Among the stars that mock the night.

V.

AL SERAT.

Think not, slanderers, your cold
Wit my spirit's wing can hold
Prisoned in the raging black
Storm that follows on my track.

If a sunbeam's struggling ray
Through the sable clouds find way,
Quick my soul the path espies,
And mounts into love's cloudless skies.

VI.

THE WIND'S REPLY.

" Alas ! no fagot's flickering fire
Allures from me the winter's ire ;
At hunger's spur my steps I haste,
To glean the crumbs that beggars waste.

" Of books I have or music none
To lend my grief oblivion ;
Nor freedom's charm nor glory's ray
To chase the gathering clouds away.

" My friends are dead, yet still they live
In wounds, no foe had strength to give ;
Each hope a grinning spectre turns,
Each kiss a poisonous ulcer burns."

As, faint with bitter memory,
I fed with tears the barren sea,
And from coward heart my anguish spoke,
In answer brave the North Wind woke :

" Think you proud nature does not own
A charm to churlish books unknown ?
Or need you wealth or friend to blind
With pleasure's cloak the mounting mind ?

" Together from our wingéd home
The wave and I, twin minstrels roam,
The teachers of the tireless voice
That bids the silent earth rejoice.

" If through thy veins resistless move
The currents deep of selfless love,
And thou the courage hast to be
True child of immortality ;

" Pluck from the bird's enchanted throat
The music of its trembling note,
Win from the echo of the shore
The hallowed whisper ' evermore ' ;

" Prick with thy nail upon the leaf
The eloquence of hopeless grief,
Or trace upon the unseen air,
The word that paints thy mute despair ;

" And we will bear to regions far
Beyond the eye of the Northern Star
Thy song, where warmer realms emboss
The sacred sky with the Southern Cross."

VII.

BLAMELESS.

Beneath thy window's hope I lie
In pain that will not sleep ;
Oh, when will laughing eyes reply
To eyes that watch and weep ?

I see thy lattice open steal,
  The skies in music wake,
The frozen flowers love's footing feel,
  In flames the breezes break.
Oh, never blame thy loveliness,
  If something overmuch
Its victim on thy fingers press
  His tender, lingering touch.

Forget to chide thy rosy lips,
  If lured by treacherous night ;
A timid truant from them slips
  To lend my soul delight.
Oh, might I watch thee ever thus,
  Thy fluttering hand at rest,
Thy kindling glances perilous
  Against their lashes pressed.
Oh, never blame thy loveliness,
  If something overmuch
Its victim on thy fingers press
  His tender, lingering touch.

VIII.

HEBE.

The Gods are my vassals to-night :
  Fair Hebe they send from the sky,
With her eye like a well of delight,
  And her ankle so slender and shy.

'T was Venus so sweetly bedecked her,
  And bade her with kisses away,
To bring me a cup of pure nectar
  And all my long watching repay.

May love blow the snow from her breast,
  And plant blushing roses to warm it ;
And perish the feeling unblessed
  That ever approaches to harm it.

IX.

WHOLESOME DELAY.

Kind friend, you must wait till to-morrow,
  I 've really no kisses to spare,
And though I can easily borrow,
  The lenders sad usurers are.

What is there about me to fret you ?
  I 'm sure I can hardly divine ;
Remember, if I should forget you,
  There are lips far more rosy than mine.

Don't press me for kisses to-day, sir,
  Your love takes my heart by surprise ;
There 's nothing like wholesome delay, sir,
  To test lovers' praises and sighs.

X.

A CHANGING LODESTONE.

What ails thee, lovely Lady,
  That thou shouldst prove unkind?
Has beauty's chisel made thee
  Our truant hearts to bind,
And is it meet love's lodestone
  Should change with every wind?

I heard a sweet bird singing
  In the city's desert mart,
A voice of gladness flinging
  Its dream around my heart—
Ah, why must I remember,   .
  When thou forgetful art?

XI.

THE DANCE OF LOVE.

Love, the child of liberty,
Ever ranging like the bee,
Now in the royal rose's flame
Basking, mocks the violet's shame,
Now the ice-plant's blushes wakes,
Now the poppy's slumbers breaks,
Now the water-lily cold
Tempts with gleam of yellow gold;

5

But ever shuns the sacred spot
Gemmed with the blue forget-me-not.
But the lady of my heart,
Mistress of the art of art,
With a thousand strange disguises
Erring fancy's flight surprises.
Now the queen of dance and song,
Glittering knights she shines among ;
Now a pensive nun she flies
The Gods to wound with vestal sighs ;
Now amid the piny grove
Listlessly her footsteps move ;
Poet's idol, gypsy queen,
Fairy shape on moonlit green ;
Every lovely form I woo
Unmasking, proves me falsely true,
And tho' fickle as the sea,
Ever constant, Sweet, to thee.

XII.

SUN AND SHADE.

Well, maiden, mayst thou shun me,
　　Thou innocent and fair !
Whose frolic glances won me
　　To breathe forbidden prayer.
Well, maiden, mayst thou shun me,
　　As the sunbeam shuns the tomb,
For thick the earth-curse on me
　　Lies like the nightmare's doom.

XIII.

DANGER.

Elska, daughter of delight,
Breathing crimson passion white,
The rose's leaf apparelling
The crystal lily's floating wing,
With fond, treacherous flattery,
Beauty's coy, reluctant eye
Lures youth's blind foolhardiness
Where, unseen, swift dangers press.
For, cheated by love's feigning dream,
I saw a peerless diamond gleam,
And reached to clutch the gem divine,
But when I deemed the treasure mine,
Cruel sparks of vestal fire
Punished eager love's desire.

XIV.

DOUBLE OR QUITS.

Maiden, could I once believe thee,
Trust me, all too soon I 'd leave thee ;
But thine anger with such store
Of noble feeling brimmeth o'er,
Like a sunbeam-freighted cloud,
Bending 'neath its golden load.

How can I persuade my mind
E'er to fashion thee unkind?
Summer words that wrought me ill,
Shall I trust their honey still?
Wherefore truer should I deem
Words that grow in winter breme?
Let me both believe or none
Nor, o'erwise, be twice undone.

XV.

MAYTIDE'S MOCKER.

Can Winter linger in thy heart,
  And all the meadows gay
With buds and bells, that kiss and part,
  And laugh the hours away?

Can Winter linger in thy heart,
  And all the woods awake
With birds that through the blossoms dart
  And into music break?

Can Winter linger in thy heart,
  And mock the purple May?
Too fair, remember, Sweet, thou art,
  To keep delight at bay.

XVI.

THE RECUSANT.

Faint at Elska's feet I sank
And, as my soul her glances drank,
Strove to frame the undersong
Of nature chiding Winter's wrong,
Caught from petulant rivulet
Struggling from the Frost King's net,
And with echo musical
Singing Spring's first madrigal.
But vain my veiling music's art
Entrance sued to beauty's heart,
Whose unyielding frigid reign
Rosy love still held in chain ;
Though who saw her glances coy
Lure the dawn with promised joy,
Nor fled, unwise, the oriole's note
Blossoming in her pearly throat,
Ill could guess their passion's rise
From her heart's unbreathing ice,
Ill could guess so tender fire
Played around a frozen lyre,
Ill could guess the crimson wing
On the snow bird wintering ;
Wooing Venus' charms allied
With Diana's marble pride,
Treacherous union never blest
With its own or other's rest.

XVII.

UNDER WORDS.

Hark ! distant feet with music greet
  The sorrow of the night,
Bow down, dull ear, peace, heart, and hear
  Their promise of delight.

Oh, not in vain love's silent pain,
  Fond hope and long delay,
If frozen field and bramble yield
  A flower that mocks the May.

No sight, no sound, above, around,
  Invades the night's repose,
Like lily set in vase of jet
  My lovely Lady shows.

" The winter's cold makes lovers bold,
  Knit close thy heart to mine,
No woven shroud of night and cloud
  Can quench love's fire divine.

" Thy quickening breath has vanquished death,
  The trees of summer dream,
And voices sweet with rhythmic beat
  Stir meadow, bank, and stream.

" The rustling sedge by the river's edge
  Of beauty tells and thee,
And Hudson's wave with cadence brave
  Sings thy name unto the sea."

XVIII.

BEAUTY'S MAGIC.

Proud mistress of my heart's idolatry,
　Less than the highest never deem his aim
　Who sings, fair Elska, thy unstaining name
With echoes borrowed from the earth and sky.

Not unrewarded of Jove's clearer eye,
　Who hopeless feel the spur of generous shame,
　And flocking to the bloodstained porch of Fame,
Close locked in death's embrace unyielding li

But if thy beauty's magic shield my rhyme,
　Know the close-woven ray by poet spun,
Alone, untarnished, mocks the breath of time,
　Fair Helen's glance outbraves Napoleon's sun,
·And thy quick beam shall warm the arctic clime,
　When muffled stars feed cold oblivion.

XIX.

A NOCTURN.

Sleep, Beauty, and of Heaven dream,
　While others dream of thee,
Whose lovely charms awakened seem,
　Sweet dreams from Heaven to be.

Sheathed is thy glance's tender fire,
  Thy voice's music mute ;
No less their touch and warmth inspire
  Love's sad complaining lute.

Dream, Beauty, clothed in gentle sleep,
  So, in his happy nest,
Love dreams and smiles, while others reap
  His harvest's wild unrest,
While treacherous fears light truces keep
  With hope in jealous breast.

XX.

MATINS.

Wake, Beauty, wake ! the morning peeps
  O'er grasses jewel hung ;
Save bats and owls, no creature sleeps,
  The world is turned to song ;

The swallow at thy window-pane
  With twittering note delays ;
The thrasher thrills his trembling strain ;
  The robin pours his praise.

But sweeter sings the voice of love
  O'er daisied meadows playing :
" Wake, wake, and all the pleasures prove
  Of hearts that go a-Maying."

Thy steps I 'll lead where roses grow
  To deck thy golden hair,
And burn on whiter neck than snow
  The kiss no lover dare.

Wake, Beauty, seize the sunbeam's wing.
  While clouds hold short debate ;
Retard no more the happy spring,
  Thy lover 's at thy gate.

XXI.

MAY MORNING.

The wind is still on lake and hill,
  The leaves are greener growing ;
The fields are bright with blossoms white,
  And brooks to the brim are flowing.

From rocky steep the sunbeams leap,
  The dewdrops gem the grass,
And fast away, like wizards gray,
  The trembling shadows pass.

" Pee-wee, chir-chir, more wet, kill deer "
  Hark, all the jarring chorus !
While cloud and sky in harmony
  Are bending gently o'er us.

XXII.

MARSYAS.

'T was in the merry month of May
When nature takes its holiday,
Across a meadow wandering,
With oaten pipe that plumed its wing,
I met a maid, who nothing said,
But with her glance the daisies fed.
" Sweet daisies," said I, " happy ye
That with such banquet nourished be."
Then seated by the fair prude's side,
Her ear with idle praises tried ;
Telling her the grasses bent
Beneath her beauty's blandishment ;
Telling her new sunbeams woke,
At each word her music spoke ;
Telling her her tiny foot
Wooed the budding leaves to view it ;
Telling her Murillo drew
From such a face our Lady true ;
With a thousand voices more
Beating on a barren shore.
For I no other answer had
Than " Poor creature, he is mad."
Till at length all power forsook
A tongue, that ill such praise might brook,
And pride held each awakening word
In its sullen tomb interred.
Till the maiden smiling, said:
" Tell me, why was Marsyas flayed ?"

XXIII.

START AND FINISH.

Comanche's bow never shot so trim,
Nor rifle the brag of the prairie,
As two bright eyes, whose arrows dim
The glances of elf or fairie.

Who touches a lady's finger-tips,
I 've heard great sages tell,
May come at last to her pouting lips,
If his method please her well.

And if to arrive at that sacred spot,
To patient love 't is given,
No monarch but will kick at his lot,
And grudge his thanks to Heaven.

XXIV.

COUNTERPARTS.

CAMEO.

What instrument, by skill divine
Directed, gentle Elska knew
From stubborn stone to woo
This cameo-chiselled hand of thine,
That, on thy breathing breast,
Like novice nodding at her shrine,
Devoutly sinks to rest?

INTAGLIO.

Dark ruffian dangers round thee lurk,
Bright gem, yet mark how nature's care
   Defends her treasures rare ;
See how this horny palm, her work,
   Is hollowed out to fit
Thy beauty, and from Jew or Turk
   Securely shelter it.

XXV.

SNOWFIRE.

They call thee Snowfire, lovely maid ;
   But never word so fair
From angel's lips unguarded strayed,
   Could paint thy beauties rare.

Thy tangled locks with sunbeams dight,
   Thy neck that rubies wound,
Thy glance's brave bewildering light
   That melting, meets the ground.

Thy trembling lips with music warm,
   Thy chiding finger fine,
The moulded marvel of thine arm,
   Thy glowing waist divine,

Thy hand that yields reluctantly,
   Thy flash of angry pride,
Thine eager no, thy tender sigh,
   Thy kiss long, long denied.

Ah, ever fairer blooms the rose,
  When thievish touch is near,
And sweet and ever sweeter grows
  My love-song in thine ear.

XXVI.

WIZARD NIGHT.

When with tell-tale glance and blush
  Close beside me Elska sits,
Strive, as strive it may, my brush
  Beauty's features never hits ;
Together rose and lily run,
And face and portrait are as one.

But, when far from Beauty's eyes,
  Wistfully I wander on,
Weighed upon by starless skies,
  Hoping, hopeless, and undone,
The deepest corner of the night
Reveals my lady's picture bright.

XXVII.

THE TRUANT.

Have you seen my flitting gold-hair fairy,
  Where hide her wayward feet,
Whom now decoy her glances wary
  And words as music sweet ?

Her subtle hand in knitting swift,
　What task employs its skill,
What woven charm, what faithless gift,
　To win you to her will?

Turn, foolish youth, oh, turn aside,
　To weeds his business runs,
Who follows beauty's plume of pride,
　And sober counsel shuns.

As snowdrift in the mountain's arm,
　That mocks the noontide's ray,
The fairer breast your prayers would warm
　Will freeze your life away.

XXVIII.

THE ELFQUEEN.

Beside a mountain well I lay,
Drinking June's enchanted ray,
Listening the solemn oak-tree teach
Harmony to the graver beech,
And the long sustaining sigh
Of the pine leaf's melody,
Lingering lead the silvery lay,
Wakening from the pensile spray
Of the white birch hovering
O'er the rivulet's beating wing,
While darting trembling leaves among,
Like shuttles of a woven song,
Feathered ministrels ceaselessly
Idle love's long labor ply.

Yet sadder far than merry they,
A sullen mote in stainless day,
Listless I lie forgetfully,
And with indifferent glance espy
Treacherous sunbeams slily creep,
Where maiden mosses cloistering sleep.
For ill the heart is nourishéd
With beauty when its soul is fled,
And she, whose ambush glances bright
Spurred churlish winter to delight,
With absence' bitter irony
Pierced Summer's painted forgery.
Thus bound beneath the double chain
Of former bliss and present pain,
Cruel nature's joyance threw the dart
Of ill-timed mirth to aid my smart.

So long I lay in dull despair,
The thievish birds pecked at my hair,
And round my feet the martial ant
Began his colony to plant ;
When suddenly a tongue of flame
Whispered the sorrow of my name,
And bursting through earth's prison mould
Like jewel dropped from garment old,
A vision shone, whose loveliness
Ravished my brooding heart's distress ;
A maid, whose charméd bravery
Might well Orion's belt outvie ;
A golden tress with daisies starred,
A foot with emerald grasses barred,
An ivory shoulder, from which snowed

A robe, whose zone with roses glowed.
Then I, who in her presence mute
And tuneless grew as broken lute,
The folly of the sensitive soul,
Whose idle dreams the will control,
Saw fairy elves on colored wing
Between the sunbeams glistering,
And heard their mingled voice repeat
With veiling art her praises sweet.

XXIX.

PERILOUS CHARMS.

Lovely maiden, walk with care :
   Prudence' kind alarms
   Grow with beauty's charms,
Thousands flock to make thee rare.

Lovely maiden, dress with care :
   Let each golden tress
   Veil its loveliness ;
Weave not nets yourself to snare.

Lovely maiden, look with care :
   Let the ground employ
   Eyes of dalliance coy,
Harmless, but when fettered there.

Lovely maiden, rest with care :
   Let no thoughtless, sweet
   Slumber seal your feet ;
Beauty sleeps in danger's lair.

Lovely maiden, shine with care :
  Shun the cloudless, bright
  Day, nor less the night ;
Sun and star betray the fair.

Lovely maiden, hear with care :
  Let no failing, faint
  Lover breathe his plaint ;
Lovers die, but ne'er despair.

Lovely maiden, dream with care :
  Let no false tongue poet
  Approach your ear to woo it ;
Well can pearl of flattery spare.

XXX.

TO-MORROW.

To-morrow, sweet to-morrow,
I 'll bid farewell to sorrow,
And welcome, but you may not tell,
Fond heart, the name your pulses spell,
The fairest, coyest, merriest maid
That ever lover's hopes delayed ;
Ah, Beauty, cruel the hours have been,
And days, that thrust themselves between
Thy lover's prayers and one too kind
To wish his eyes with weeping blind ;
Swift hand, and foot in dancing light,
And lips that thrifty bee invite,
Clear eyes, that veil their modest fire,

And all unwilling wake desire ;
Soon, Sweet, no bloodless dream shall guess
The secrets of thy loveliness ;
Soon, fettered to thy lover's side,
Thy golden tresses loose untied,
Reluctantly shalt thou confess
Each smile that made my treasure less,
Each word to lucky stranger given,
Each step that parted me from heaven ;
And think not, Beauty, light her fine,
Who robs me of such joys divine.

XXXI.

LOVE, AS PRIEST.

Ah ! who can tell how love is born,
    From gentle touch or word,
Or feigning glance of winning scorn,
    By which the pride is stirred ?

Divine the love that sudden springs
    From maiden's glances coy,
And its auroral splendor flings
    O'er youth's swift-changing joy.

Divine the love by pity fed,
    Fair child of parent fair,
That crowns the homeless wanderer's head
    With flowers the angels spare.

But love a source more sacred knows
   When, sprung from tears and sighs
Of mutual grief, its blossom grows
   To Flower of Paradise.

Pure soul with soul in music wrought,
   Transfused with fond desire,
Thought woven upon answering thought,
   One word, one hope, one fire.

XXXII.

BEAUTY'S BENISON.

No longer is my soul untenanted
   With hope, Elska, since that celestial hour,
   Of immortality the whitest flower,
When thy clear eye its saintly pity shed

Upon the tomb, where with the living dead
   My fettered life in learning's thorny waste,
   In labor's sloth, and noble aims misplaced,
Festered, and with deep inward anguish bled.

But evermore soft wings of music chase
   The sunbeams, and from night's transparent sky
Fair visionary shapes of breathing grace,
   Beckoning, unlock the stars' sweet minstrelsy ;
And, wooing to no mortal resting-place,
   Bid me to sing of Heaven, that lives in thee.

XXXIII.

UNSEEN DELIGHT.

When love is at its purple prime,
Or waits to hear its vesper chime,
  How soft its trembling rays !
But love at burning noontide height,
What eye can bear its crystal light,
  What tongue repeat its praise ?

We look upon the waving ground,
We watch the rivulet's mazy round,
  And seek in flower and leaf
To figure forth our ecstasy,
As lightning keen, as glow-worm shy,
  A joy akin to grief.

XXXIV.

BEAUTY'S DEPTHS.

Companion of my iron days,
  Whose braver faith makes danger sweet,
And plucks the lightning's fatal rays,
  To point a path for wandering feet.

Let others praise thy silken tress,
  Thy hand's unstaining ivory,
Thy languid neck's pale loveliness,
  The music of thy wayward eye.

Let others praise the eloquence fine
In which thy gentle feelings speak,
As through the golden crystal wine
The budding sunbeams laughing break.

Indifferent to me the prize
Of cunning Time's cruel sovereignty,
When in thy deeper beauty lies
A charm to mar his mastery.

XXXV.

THE ARCHER.

On a bed of roses laid,
In the sunflower's constant shade,
Far from toiling day's unrest
Deep I lie in revery blessed.

But when sunset mists are born,
My arrows I tip with the rose's thorn ;
Lightly from my couch I spring,
And joyous spread my purple wing.

When the twilight's languid hour
Masking breathes mysterious power,
From shadowy ambush flies the dart,
That, unseen, fires the gentle heart.

XXXVI.

WOODCRAFT.

Oh, loth to wet her faltering feet
  Was my dainty little maid,
As nearer came her cheek of flame
  To the forest's trembling shade,
As near the forest Elska drew
  With step of startled fawn
And eye as wistful, strange, and true
  As ever earthward shone.

Let others lay, by toiling day,
  Foundation, wall, and roof,
For lover's sleight, the fire-fly's light
  Is lantern good enough ;
And moss and leaf, for board and lath,
  His cunning hand suffice
To build a room, whose corner hath
  The charm of paradise.

Oh, loth to wet her faltering feet
  Was my love at set of sun,
But drops of dew on her ringlets grew,
  When the stars through the purple won ;
The dew-drops hung from ringlets long,
  And from her lips a rose,
And from her ear the sweetest song
  That guileless maiden knows.

XXXVII.

HOMEWARD.

Three months of sunless sorrow,
From Beauty's face remote,
" Ill day and worse to-morrow,"
On prison walls I wrote.

I toiled, I pinched, I hoarded,
My food a stolen bean,
No miser half so sordid,
No beggar more unclean.

The grave relented, Darling,
Again my feet are free,
As from its cage the starling,
Thy captive flies to thee.

XXXVIII.

COUNTRY DANCE.

Beside the shore of the waving wheat
In Autumn's yellow prime,
My step the prairie voices greet,
I hear the cowbell's rhyme,
And watch the crescent's crystal feet
The cloudy stairway climb.

Oh, early come, and tarry long,
  Sweet maid of prayer and sigh !
I hear the twilight's undersong
  Win through the grasses high,
And hopes and fears, a breathless throng,
  Betray my Beauty nigh.

The golden-rods make room for us,
  She smoothes her russet gown,
My touch her auburn hair undoes,
  The ringlets tumble down ;
What court or Castle Dangerous
  So fair a face has known.

Her prudish eyes she may not lift,
  Each timid favor grows
A beggar for the sacred gift,
  The heart of heart bestows ;
Across the moon the shadows drift,
  The wind on tiptoe goes.

But, hark ! across the field is borne
  The distant dancers' din,
Round lighted barn the martial horn
  Pursues the violin,
And, perched on boxes, phantoms warn
  The swaying shapes within.

Not long for Moorhead's truant belle
  The weary waltzers wait,
Yet subtly village gossips spell
  The hid decrees of fate,
And soon the marriage bells will tell
  The fruit of love's debate.

XXXIX.

THE PASSENGER.

At the hawser tugs my rhyme,
Wind and wave are beating time,
Hasten, Lady, step aboard,
Sail and rudder wait your word ;
Fear not, though the tiny boat
Tremble at your slender foot,
Staunch it is and stiffer than
Giant ships that plow the main ;
These, though ribbed with English oak,
Rock will rend or thunderstroke ;
But the dainty craft that bears
Elska's name and beauty's wares,
Will the rolling billows fret,
When the proudest flags have set,
Safe, through hornéd tempest gore
Ocean's wastes from shore to shore.

THE LAST AVATAR.

Our gentle Lady Bountiful,
  Fruit of the barren sea,
Thy liquid grace, thy changeless soul,
  Breathe nature's harmony.

All gods and goddesses in thee
  Their golden centre find,
The elemental energy
  Lives in thy shaping mind.

Dawn nestles in thy waving hair,
  The stars thy glance obey,
The floating clouds thy fancies are,
  The wind thy whispers sway.

Spring wakens at thy happy smile,
  Thy breath the Summer warms,
Thy bounty honors Autumn's toil,
  Thy pride cold Winter arms.

The lilies wear their sacred charm,
  The shadow of thy breast,
The royal roses crimson-warm
  Are in thy kisses dressed.

The heart-born God his bow has bent,
  Thy fatal eyebrows' curve,
His quiver is my bosom rent
  By darts untaught to swerve.

MUSIC'S DARLING.

Will music's Darling longer strive
To hide her picture fugitive
From fancy's eye, that watch and ward
Untiring keeps for faithful bard ?
Can she forget the witchery
Of music gives the blind to see ?
Forget how rarely numbers fail
To draw the vestal from her veil
Of modesty, and crown with praise
The fair, who walk in hidden ways ?
Not now my prayer, that fancy may
On Beauty's charms sly finger lay,
Or guess what magic marvels lie
Beneath her maiden mastery,
Or sing her casting glances bright
With modest joy's exuberant light,
The sorcery of sequestered smiles,
The look that misery's heart beguiles,
Her cheek of roses never bare,
The sunbeams snugging in her hair,
The gemfall from proud lips, her throat
Of pearl, where wingéd roses float,
The bracelet on her lithe wrist shining,
Like glowworm round a lily twining,
The ribbon clasping shapelier waist
Than Venus' girdle ever graced,
White arms to circle paradise,
Wise hand that all approach denies,
Her gracious movement and the beat
Of swift invulnerable feet,

Conclusive of delight ; enough,
My song demands not web nor woof,
That weave the pictured cloth of gold,
That idle poets sacred hold.

A homelier task, sweet fancy, thine,
A homelier task, but more divine,
For thou must Beauty's charms forget
In music Beauty's life to set.
So must thou lurk in the shadow of
The Maiden coy, whom many love,
And deftly from the husk of home
Lure lovely labor's blushing bloom ;
Oft, ambushed, watch at peep of day
Her whiter hand the white cloth lay,
The toast and coffee brown prepare,
Twice happy, who such banquet share,
Or note the moistened tea-leaves strewn,
The turban grim, the rusty gown,
And Amazon with martial broom,
Who gars the dust fly round the room.
Unmasked, in olive bunting dressed,
With ruffles that outbrave the best,
Her foot encased in slipper neat,
Perish the eye would wish to see 't !
She sits demure with eager look
Unravelling a mazy book,
Or Tennyson's painted classic line,
Or Hugo's rampant rage divine,
The songs that Sigurd's sorrow weep,
Or Darwin's linkéd reason deep.

Anon, in russet ulster dight,
Her leggins buttoned out of sight,
The dimples in her cheeks aglow,
Breadwinning through the driving snow,
See trips to teach the tuneless ear.
The measured notes to neighbors dear.
Returned, she strives the crippled meal
With merry mien and words to heal,
Or spreads rich store of dainties sweet
To lend a stranger welcome meet ;
High effort then to counterfeit
Her stories spiced with kindly wit,
Of purse-proud spite, or service kind,
Of churlish pride, or heart refined,
Or, theme perverse, of homage paid
By youth too apt to flatter maid :

The dinner done, and dishes bright,
And shining student's lamp alight,
Before the ivory keys she sits,
And music's tangled tissue knits,
Suggestive notes, that far and wide
In various paths the mind divide,
With interludes, that alternate
With parent strains in fond debate ;
Till echoing rise, in choral charm,
The chimes that nature's spirit warm,
The chords that bind the fond complaining
Of summer seas with surges straining
Beneath the lash of winds, that sweep,
In stormy chase, along the deep.

Or plaint of mountain rivulet
Escaping from the frost-king's net ;
Or, rich with awful prophesies,
The sounds from cavern deep that rise,
Like murmur of rock-faring folk,
Who tireless seek earth's golden yolk ;
Or song from robin's throat that wins,
When beauty's springtide war begins ;

And look, the morning's budded beams
Surprise the mist of silent streams,
And, footing slow, wayfaring day
Approaches wrapped in garment gray,
From slumber's fetters labor breaks,
And life's contagious business wakes,
The goodwife bustles round the house,
To school toil urchins dolorous,
Through tangled roots the ploughshares strive,
And laden carts to market drive ;

Now round us waves of daisies beat
Against the speed of laughing feet,
As Beauty flies in loveliness
From urgent lover's fond caress,
Till gracious to his pleading praise
Reluctantly her step she stays,
To rest upon a covert seat,
Where briery rose and grasses meet,
A perfumed gloom still quivering
With frightened bird's escaping wing,

Where pine leaves prick the lazy wind
To music, and warm rays unbind
Belated buds and leaves ; but she,
In maiden's simple surquedry,
Upbraids the hand, whose touch undoes
Her lustrous hair, that tumbles loose
Round bending neck and prudish waist,
That ruder touch would deem misplaced,
Till, white within the rippling gold,
A breathing picture never old,
Beneath a shower of blossoms gay,
She smiles, the Sweetheart of the May.
Ah ! why with wind and wave and wing
The chosen words rewinnowing,
Has never fond face-fancier
Had subtle skill to pencil her,
Fair, fair, as visions bright that bloom
And fade on slumber's mimic tomb !

Alas ! in one o'er music's glass
Joy's spring and sorrow's winter pass ;
The beckoning light of Beauty's eyes
No longer wooes me and denies,
No more with roseate delay
Loved lips my timid heart-hope sway,
New cadences with sober spell
Of parting pleasure toll the knell,
For as in Beauty's bower I wait
To watch from sunset's closing gate
The twilight steal, like truant nun,
And do her sober habit on,

In trust the frolic fire-flies may
With sly revolving lamp betray
The masking face of danger nigh,
And home my prudent footsteps hie,
Woe 's me ! unheralded the night
Across her stealthy footprints light
Her trailing mantle draws, and loud
O'er soughing sedge, through branches bowed,
The hurtling sword-winds press and fierce
All shields with sharpened edges pierce,
Till, wild beneath the lightning's goad,
Of light and sign they sweep my road
And drown the prayers, that piteous
Besiege each blind sepulchral house,
Till, love and faith and friendship lost,
Like slave from laboring vessel tossed,
Far, far on the drift of the wild world's tide,
Alone, with compass lost I ride,
Alone, with sorrow measureless,
Whose bitter fountain none may guess,
Hope barren, dumb, forlorn of light,
Downtrodden by misfortune's might,
Oft wondering what new hands unknown
With adder's teeth my couch have strewn,
Until through tears of blood I see
The faithful friends who torture me.
Oh ! spawn of base ingratitude,
By greed and treacherous envy wooed !
Accursed ! not my hand shall smite you,
But unforgetful fate requite you,
Stern fate, beneath whose veiling eyes
Truth lives and justice never dies.

But hark ! what voicing memories
Responsive greet the sounding keys !
What madding Phrygian measures wake !
What nobler griefs my bosom shake !
Relentless war's hoarse horror thrills
The solitude of crested hills,
The rifles crack, the cannon roar,
The streams run red with human gore,
And grappling close the dire debate
Resounds, till death has silenced hate,
And crimson sets the troubled sun
On dateless glory lost and won.

Soon changed, the drum's forgetful roll
Steals sorrowfully on the soul,
The mourners pass in seemly guise,
And slow the laureate dirges rise :
Weep, warriors, weep, your hope is gone,
The night has swallowed up the dawn,
The Hero-youth rests on his bier,
His name no more, a hope and fear,
Along the resonant battle-ways
The doubtful cast of fortune sways.

But now upon my trembling ear
Steal old, old airs supremely dear,
Old strings are touched, whose charm divides
The cloud, that softer pictures hides.
Within a homestead gray appears
A woman bent with pain and years,
Upon whose consecrated face
Who will may earthly beauties trace ;
6

In thoughtful quest with motion slow
From room to room her footsteps go,
For long untaught herself to spare
She strives the household tasks to share,
To trim the fire, replace a book,
Arrange a shelf, or prompt the cook.
All faces at her coming turn
Her wish or purpose kind to learn ;
His ear the lazy setter pricks,
Well taught what hands his dinner mix ;
The veering chicken cackling flies
To peck the meal her dish supplies ;
Her lame steps spare the busy ant,
Whose nests the sandy pathway haunt ;
Her simple heart too well is known
To youthful vagrants many a one ;
And, little skilled her gold to nurse,
Each plaintive peddler shares her purse ;
Much counsel wise has she to give
Home-keeping youth or fugitive,
And now her smiles of welcome greet
The prattle soft of little feet ;
Her children's children round her stand
To win a blessing from her hand—
Alas ! how ill can words express
Of age the garnered loveliness.
Oh, Thou, whose voice was life and fame,
Oh, loved beyond all other name,
My Mother !

But again I feel
New magic o'er my pulses steal,

Quick tremors, that through every sense
Magnetic urge art's eloquence.
Again the Maid of mysteries,
Unwinding woven harmonies,
Before me sits, fulfilled of grace,
Enchantment breathing from her face,
With clearer eyes than mountain lake,
Where sunbeams steal their thirst to slake,
With listening lips, that seem astir
With thoughts too sweet to meet the ear,
And changing look, as when our eyes
Ourselves behold in nobler guise,
Her subtle finger questioning
The heart of each accordant string,
Whose notes far wandering enchant
Coy elves, who hide in hallowed haunt,
That, swift from hillside, cave, and dell,
Their fairy shapes, half visible,
Around her throng, their finer voice,
Rebuking life's tumultuous noise,
Angelic speech, at war with all
Base customs, that our hearts enthrall

And still the fair Musician plies
Her task that ever forward flies,
Her glance in joy of music glowing,
Her cheek its vermeil favor showing,
, And now her rapid fingers chase
A thousand notes, that headlong race,
Now with th' impatient vocal keys
She mingles soft breathed silences,

Sweet music gone, sweet music coming,
Fond space for fancies soft to bloom in ;
Until her truer touch has found
Of melodies the master-sound,
The key-note of plain common things,
Of stocks and stones the hidden wings,
A spell informed with sacred power,
Familiar and yet strange as our
Own souls, an influence that sways
With gladness all our linkéd days,
And joins the dulcet cradle laughter
With age and all we hope hereafter.

But look through music's parted veil
The Player's face shows passion-pale,
Like lily raining lovely light
Upon the fragrant lap of night,
Or Naiad, when Apollo's call
Wins through the white-winged waterfall ;
Till peeping from her body's dream
Strange eyes and other features beam,
And fair as star-born shapes that try
With doubts the sleepless lover's eye,
Shines forth in beauteous disarray
Her soul, whom all sweet sounds obey.

The while forgetting thought and will
The listeners sit, as hushed and still
As heart of bride beneath her zone,
When falls the priest's last benison,
And watch the Maiden's higher art
O'ermastering her impetuous heart,

The wayward graces growing less,
The chastened charm, the stormy stress,
The note that follows, flies, or lingers,
The music dropping from her fingers,
The prouder poise, the lightsome eye,
The look that bids the world good-by,
As, gained the difficult delight
Of selfless music's classic height,
She pauses on the strenuous steep,
Where art has ear for rapture deep,
When high her dominant pinions soar
To realms unvisited before,
While echoes exquisitely sweet
Of other worlds our hearts entreat
To joys beyond the wing of hope,
To scenes beyond our human scope,
Where beauty's rhythmic laws control
Of love the universal soul.
Fair Sorceress, no eyeless hand
May mortal's spirit so command,
And as those thralls of melody,
Fond fancy and true memory,
Have won these visions dark and fair
To paint themselves on unseen air,
Till from divided aims have grown
Sweet sounds and words in unison,
May music, fame's high instrument,
With kindred thought divinely blent,
Forever in resplendent rhyme
Your picture guard from envious time.

A SCHOLAR'S WOOING.

Forgetful words, where'er ye bide,
In the surge of the forest or tide,
Or in caverns that house ye and hide,
   Diviner voices gather near :

Ye, whom Athena's touch unbound
From the citadel violet-crowned,
   At whose echoes of rapture and fear
The vales and craggy hills resound ;

Or ye by Kalidasa won,
   Whom the "Roof of the World" bends to hear,
That with brightness unborn of the sun
O'er springtide's early blossoms run.

   Approach, and whisper in the ear
Of my Lady grown silent and cold
All the passion and gladness untold,
That swayed the gentle heart of old.

If still my Lady deaf remain,
To the crystal delight of your strain,
To your aid call the tender refrain,
   The Celtic woe to music gave.

And, breathing memory's fondest verse,
Of Sir Tristram the trial rehearse,
   And of Guinevere's champion brave ;
Or sing the tales of Dante's nurse,

The tales Provence untimely sung,
That lay hushed in a pitiless grave
With the nightshade and myrtle-leaf hung;
Or songs from root more worthy sprung,

That love's unfettered ear enslave,
That from Laura and Beatrice bore
To the brow of the pale Leonore
A chain that crowns them evermore.

If Beauty's frowns your suite requite,
Send the " Tongue of the Unseen Delight "
To subdue her with mystical might,
The hymnal wine-stained Hafez taught

To far Mosalla's rosy ways,
Whose enchantments the lover obeys,
As the dervish its reason inwrought;
Nor slight the ringing Norland lays,

The love-lore of the changeless free,
That like flower from the wilderness brought,
Or a spark on the mist-shrouded sea,
Betrays the heart unwittingly.

And add the transports fancy-fraught,
That awoke from the lyre of the morn,
When the veil from old ocean was torn,
And wonder-worlds to beauty born.

If scornfully my Lady turn
From the praises around her that burn,
From the homage one only could spurn,
Her arrogance nor coldness blame.

But call the singers unafraid,
Who with earthquake and hurricane played,
    When the nations awoke out of shame,
And France and Freedom's call obeyed.

Or science' thievish wing let fly
    To the mansions ill guarded of fame
'Mid the stars, where with lack-lustre eye
The gods beside their jewels lie.

    Each truant thought with bolder tame,
Till a languor untaught by the spring
To the nest lure the wanderer's wing,
And love forget to watch and sing.

THE PORTRAIT.

"The portrait of your gentle aunt inspire
My touch to draw, fair Comrade, will you not?
My brush, I fear, its cunning has forgot,
Since forced by penury to toil for hire.
    Rest where this sacred laurel leaf embays
    A mossy seat, safe from the noontide rays ;
    Why should you haste while beauty's wing delays?

"Beneath our feet the dimpled ocean smiles,
The mountain's cloudy crests behind us rise,
Whose brooding shadow laughing streams surprise,
Whose chiding song fond fancy's flight beguiles ;
    Save the light smoke from yonder fisher's hut,
    By winnowing sunbeams into silver wrought,
No mortal stain the crystal scene defiles.

"Your aunt is tall and lithe, a nameless grace,
An inborn music ever seems to play
With wayward charm about her joyous face ;
    Small is her hand and foot, the ladies say,
If somewhat fuller breathe her moulded bust,
None will reprove my thrifty art, I trust ;
    Why should not time a little backward stray?

"What fairy hands can I entice to steal
From underneath the tired sun's chariot wheel
    The roses' dye to wound her finger-tips,
    Or stain with crimson her half-listening lips?
Alas! so foolish anger wherefore feel,

That I time's ravages would mitigate,
And nobly struggle against evil fate?

" How shall I paint her fond, reluctant eye,
Commanding with sweet careless witchery,
    Coy as a Naiad's glance, that hides beneath
The lucid waterfall's chaste bridal veil,
When thro' the mists of some enchanted dale
    With treacherous lamp the moonbeam wandereth,
    Luring the traveller on to blissful death?"

" A portrait painter is but born to lie,"
The Maiden cried, rising indignantly.
    " My aunt is fifty, not a moment less,
You must have known her long before your birth,
    What are you painting now, a low-neck dress?
A hardened conscience is of priceless worth,
    Such wickedness what mortal mind could guess!"

" Hideous is beauty uninformed with mind,
    And always fair, whom noble thought inspires;
All cannot have both gifts in one combined,
    Where passion the proud chiselled marble fires;
Yourself be charitable; I must live,
    Unless my breath your ear's compassion tires:
Why not a little prudent pleasure give?

" See how the dimples waken in each cheek,
That fashioned seems in music sweet to speak,
    While from their nest the wingéd blushes peep,
Or wandering fret the beauty of a breast,
Where gentle love, with balmy joys opprest,
    Enchanted lies in dreamless, blissful sleep,
    While still his fingers pale the lilies heap."

" Better to earn with brave perspiring shovel
Your corn and pork in some unsightly hovel,"
  My Critic said, " than shine by flattery.
  What have we next ?—a lover by a tree ;
  Now comes the silly Moon most naturally ;
And, Mary guard me ! look, a half-closed lattice ;
Could any thing be quite as flat as that is ?"

" Awhile," said I, " forbear your honeyed praise,
Whose cloying sweetness my swift brush delays.
  Portraits are honest, if you but draw near ;
  Would that their subjects might such honor share !
My task is almost done.   Do you recall
Those lines that madcap poet wrote last fall ?
  Your aunt has often quoted them, I fear.

" How shall I paint their gentle thoughts aright?
' The pitying sunbeam, that delays its flight
To bless the tortured Inca's dying sight ;
  The lily on the holy Virgin's breast,
  In the white dream of saintly martyr drest ;
How vain so feeble images to express
Her ivory neck fretted by golden tress ! ' "

" The work is almost finished, is it not ?"
  Then she ; " oh, marvellous ! what a transforma-
    tion !
No Pelias boiling in the sterile pot,
  But really an entirely new creation ;
One touch alone your genius has forgot,
  The veil fair Venus round Æneas threw
  To shield her hero from the Grecian dew.

"Yet there is something which I must admire ;
  What breathing life speaks even in her dress !
Her foot, lips, eye, languid with music's fire,
  Seem eager hesitation to express ;
The lattice is as eloquent as a lyre."
  "Thanks, Lady," cried I then, exultingly,
  "I knew my soul would paint beneath your eye.

"Observe the proud hand swiftly loitering ;
'I will not, shall I ?' archly questioning ;
  This way and that our eager mind divides,
While vain imagination spurs its wing,
  In clouded fate the masking issue hides :
Mankind will dogmatize the torturing doubt,
And worship what it never can make out.

"What wakes the double world to ceaseless strife,
  Bidding the right hand waste, the left hand beg,
Of sov'reign motion the true inward life ?
  Doubt is the fruit of Truth's immortal egg,
  True art stands always on one yielding leg ;
The stolid bull that rests upon all fours,
The dreaming Hindoo not the Greek adores.

"Stay, shall I not a little larger paint
A tiny ear half hidden from the view,
  Of wandering music's soul the secret lure,
That heedless from wan sorrow's pleading plaint,
  Or passion's prayer averts its beauty's cure ;
Nor e'er will know its own sweet praises true,
Until a hundred cannons whisper ' You ?' "

" I," cried the Changeling with a sudden start,
" What have I done, alas ! what have I said?
Too well I see you understand all art ;
It is too flattering ; I 'll not allow it ;
What would it injure just to erase the head?
If not, at least I 'll surely disavow it.
How could you do so treacherous a deed?"

" It is the brush my guidance disobeys,
That vainly would its thoughtless step restrain ;
Alas ! that senseless wood, in beauty's praise,
Should hold true honest labor in disdain ;
And, careless of its toiling master's food,
Its homage rash on timid charms intrude,
Ill worshipper before thy sacred fane.

" You see a brush is troubled with no debts ;
No velvet-footed dun its long ear frets
With whisper poisoning the balmy air ;
It toils nor spins, nor knows love's cheating care,
With colors bright its happy fancy fed
Wooes not that flitting phantom called a bed,
Sweet hope that lurks in cruel housekeeper's lair.

" But never shall a meaner task profane
An instrument that once your service knew ;
Look, how I snap my gentle brush in twain ;
So breaks a heart beneath your glance divine ;
Away its spirit flies to Bolotoo,
There still to paint an unsubstantial You,
And teach the pitiless gods to peak and pine.

" But if the copy you should fairer deem
  Than its original, perhaps we might—"
Our heroine, ere I finished, gave a scream,
For creeping from the hill, a cat'spaw stiff
  Whipped off her hat, whose careless pinion bright
A moment hovered o'er the churlish cliff,
  Then, glancing downward spurred its rapid flight.

" How can I in such sorry plight alive
Return ?" she cried ; " what reason can I give ?"
  Then swift her heedless footsteps forward spring,
  As eager from the height the maid to fling,
Winged she skims along the pointed rocks ;
Her slender hand in matted rootlets locks,
  Adown the cliff in act of clambering.

" Stop ! stop !" I cried, " you 'll surely break your
    neck ;
  Your hat in safety on the dry sand lies " ;
But when did idle words e'er woman check ?
  The sliding pebbles with her foot she tries,
  My careful hand with prudish pride denies,
And blindly from the bush withdraws her hold ;
In vain, for stronger arms her own enfold.

Then woke the splendor of her angry eye ;   •
  " Unclasp your villain touch ! how dare you, sir !"
Then I : " Liege Lady, all your prayers are vain ;
Forever in these fetters you shall lie,
  Unless you promise never hence to stir."
" Never !" she cried.   " Your folly is my gain."
" I promise," said she, and again was free.

Then down I bent my prudent footsteps true,
For well the mountain craft my boyhood knew,
　And with the truant hat soon backward hied ;
" Forgive me," said her faltering accents kind ;
　" More easily than forget," my glance replied ;
" But let us haste some sheltering cave to find ;
See what a storm comes rattling on the wind."

For now behind the secret rampart hills
　The sullen clouds their troop are marshalling ;
The voiceless lightning nature's pulses thrills,
　While dark battalions spread their boding wing ;
　Awhile the winds in silence weave their shroud ;
　Then breaks the deepening thunder's terror loud,
And wounded Earth and trembling Heaven fills.

Then I, to calm the blushing maiden's fear,
　As safe we sat beneath a shielding rock ;
" Will not your favor this my poor coat wear ?
　The door that laughs at penury's fearful shock,
　Will never yield to thunder's gentle knock."
Then happy at her wayward ear in chain,
I framed a song to suit the tempest's vein.

　　" Across a mead with daisies pied
　　A maiden led her happy swain,
　　When suddenly a summer rain
　　Around them poured its drenching tide.

　　" In trembling hope her dress to save,
　　And life, the prudent maiden fled
　　To rest, where wide with branches spread
　　A pasture oak asylum gave.

' ' Ah ! foolish maid, to rest secure,'
  Her lover cried, ' at danger's gate !
  Know, ere, kind Heaven ! it prove too late
A tree is lightning's quickest lure.

" ' But here beneath this shielding cloak,
  With wiser footstep swiftly hie,
  And all indifferent defy
The fury of the pitiless stroke.'

" Mid blushes pale the maiden stood,
  While modest death and bolder life
  Within her breast woke doubtful strife,
Till louder roared the thunder rude.

" The oak still braves the winter's rage ;
  The swain prays daily Heaven to send
  A friendly thunderbolt to end
A wound no healing arts assuage."

Then she : " Interpret me this leaf, that fell
Into my room from hand invisible :
  See here 's a fire beneath the forest's lid,
With squaws and feathered warriors seated nigh,
  And here, half 'mid the waving grasses hid,
A youth seems whispering a maid good-by,
And here 's a headless eagle soaring high."

" I drew it," said I, " as you well might guess,
  Who know me in my humble Indian guise,
Unskilled in pluméd words my thoughts to dress ;

Nor wiselier taught the charm of classic art,
　At whose cold touch wild fancies crystallize,
But one, that sings like bird in dell apart,
　Or paints, as flower that hid in forest lies.

" The leaf repeats a tale of years ago,
　A passion-flower from root of danger sprung,
An Indian maid, who taught love how to woo,
And nature's soft but transient joys to know,
　Though tomahawks about their pathway hung ;
The eagle is my tribe, though loth I see,
My neck has lost its continuity.

" The gentle pair met, kissed, and died as one,
　And yesternight, as brooding long I lay,
　And thought of ghouls with weasel eye that prey
On spendthrift youth, a face to hope unknown,
　Like nature's darling, seemed on mine to turn ;
' Twice happy they, who do not die alone
And into solitary cinders burn ! '

" I cried, nay frown not on a theme forbidden,
　Though angel voices lure its flight away,
My fancy's wing shall linger on bed-ridden,
So rather hear a kindred song that made
　The background of our portrait of to-day,
A thrifty task, that all my debts had paid,
Had thievish Beauty not my brush waylaid.

　" ' To-morrow forth thy lover goes,
　　To swell the battle's steely wave,
　　Nor other hope nor solace knows,

  Than one cold glance thy bounty gave ;
  A torch to light him to his grave,
   Fair Flower of Baltimore !

  " ' Light slumbers seal a maiden's ear,
   Whose dreams a lover's step divine ;
  Sweet dreams awake to hope and fear,
  When sorrow's soft complaint draws near,
   Too near the heart of Ermaline.
    The Flower of Baltimore !

  " ' From snow-white couch a moulded foot,
   Creeping, a timorous touch obeys,
  And holding its wild music mute,
  In fleecy sheath and sable boot
   Reluctantly its pride arrays,
    Fair Flower of Baltimore !

  " ' Then o'er her shoulders' fairer charm
   A silvery silken robe she throws,
  That swift with jealous fond alarm
   Downward with gathering beauty flows,
   Till rich with borrowed grace it shows
    The Flower of Baltimore !

  " ' Backward the golden hair, that gowns
   Her ivory breast, her quick hand flings ;
  Its waves with shining crescent crowns ;
   The while her waist a girdle rings,
   That close with chiding finger clings ;
    Fair Flower of Baltimore !

" ' Then to the casement soft she creeps
  With step of brave infirmity,
And through the masking lattice peeps
  With glance of wayward witchery,
  Half fearing what she hopes to see ;
    Fair Flower of Baltimore !

" ' Beneath the constant oak tree's leaf
  A pale face breathing silent prayer,
A pleading face of hopeless grief ;
  Kind angels, make thy soul their care,
  Tho' lovers die, they ne'er despair !
    Fair Flower of Baltimore !

" ' A shadow on the window lies ;
  Slowly the casement open slides,
A faltering " Nay " her voice replies,
  With lightsome step her lover glides,
  With bashful art her face she hides,
    Fair Flower of Baltimore !

" ' A rose-leaf clothed in moonbeam cold,
  Such love alone her fancy knows,
But now no painted flames enfold
  A breast, that to such rapture grows,
  The passionate air with crimson glows !
    Fair Flower of Baltimore !

" ' Without the room a sleeping death,
  Her rebel kinsmen's fatal pride,
Within, a tender balmy breath,
  The kiss with wooing smile denied ;

Suppressed delight intensified ;
    Fair Flower of Baltimore !

" ' The soul acquaint with bitter woe
    Alone this deepest truth can spell ;
The Heaven of Heaven that mortals know
Lies hidden in the heart of h—l,
A truth thy beauty teaches well,
    Fair Flower of Baltimore !

" ' "Take thou this girdle ; may it prove
    To thee no traitor," faltered she ;
One kiss their trembling sorrow wove ;
Bleeding, her lover tore him free ;
The dark wind echoed heedlessly ;
    Fair Flower of Baltimore ! ' "

" Is not the halting tale a little long ? "
    The Maiden said, with an ungentle frown ;
    " Alas ! have women so forgetful grown,
That they can thus their modest nature wrong ?
Some latitude must be allowed to song ;
    But don't you think the fancy rather shocking,
    That would idealize a shoe and stocking ? "

Then sullen from my side a pouch I drew,
    A sacred pipe to people from its store,
And as the purple circles round me flew,
Their airy wing upon the wind I blew,
    That to the storm king gentle tribute bore ;
" The spirits love," then I, " this perfumed breath,
That paints the soul after the body's death.

" It is a charm I learnt of Beaver Tail,
　The wisest medicine man among the Sioux ;
Its potent influence hardly knows to fail,
　If you but proper time and patience use ;
Look, while I speak the parted clouds avale,
　And fairy fingers swiftly press to tie
Hope's glittering girdle round the beamy sky."

Then forth we passed into the crystal air,
　That vocal grew with many a hidden note,
　That on the new bathed sunbeams joyed to float,
The robin's voice, the thrasher's music rare,
　The blackbird whistling to the merry jay,
　The sparrow's mirth, the cuckoo's virelay,
Choiring the beauty of the closing day.

For now beneath a gorgeous baldachin
　The royal Sun sinks down to blissful rest, ,
With softer light his flattering glances shine
　Thro' low-hung clouds in living crimson drest,
Till lessening wave, hushed wind, and lustrous tree,
　By twilight's charm-compelling finger pressed,
Own gradual its mystic sovereignty.

Then glimmering thro' the purple of the west
　The tremulous evening star in beauty grew,
Fugitive as the one unguarded glance
Of Dian chaste, faint as in maiden's breast
　Of sweet first love the image vainly true,
That backward starts at its own countenance,
Yet unforgotten lives thro' life's mischance.

Then I : " If to thy guardianship I give,
  In lieu of yellow gold or jewels rare,
  The sacred cord binding this wandering star,
That thou forever in its song may live,
  When silent dull earth's lessening voices are,
May I not from thy beauty's milder reign
A boon solicit for love's wasting pain ? "

" I thank you," said she, " for your priceless gift,
  Entailing though it may no little care ;
I 'm glad my finger is so long and swift,
  An instrument not easy to repair,
Should it discover any serious rift ;
  A master marvellous and steady practice,
  Surely the touch needs ere it quite exact is.

" Your royal bounty how shall I return ?
  Stay, here 's an honest glowworm in the grass ;
Fear not, the truthful Cupid would not burn,
  Were you inflammable as country lass ;
Your Bible open when your home you reach,
The brilliant preacher with one word will teach,
  What in its bag your future fortune has."

" No other gift my treasury bare can find,"
Then swift my touch her chiding hands unbind,
  And o'er the mead with printless foot she flies,
Until an oak, with purple brambles twined,
  Her further flight with threatening dart denies ;
There by a rock the maid unconquered stood,
When down her foot sank in the treacherous mud.

A heroine's dainty foot incased in mud
Is not in form, I know it well enough ;
I would have made it different if I could,
But when a meadow borders on a bluff,
The rains delay, and often treacherous spots,
Unwelcome darker-eyed forget-me-nots,
Surprise us like a sudden pinch of snuff.

And my dull halting brain lacks skill to invent
A story, plot, or simplest incident ;
Bright fancy's glittering wing long since has fled,
O'er happier hearts its purple charm to throw,
And sent to me a prudent priest instead,
The only voice, whose flattery soothes me now,
A poor, plucked, palsied, practical carrion crow.

Besides, I was brought up, as few have been,
'Mid lawyers, doctors, gentle clergymen,
Who wisdom loved, and often would extol her,
Except on state occasions now and then
They only lied to earn an honest dollar ;
Lying is such a precious commodity,
A sportive lie were an outrageous oddity.

So, unallured by hope's enchanted wand,
Snail-like I follow truth along the sand,
Noting such facts as fix my curious eye,
Careless, though oft by treacherous voices fanned,
The rising waves engulf my task and me ;
When they subside, again I trudge along,
Though lingers in my ear the ocean's cheating song.

Truth for its own sweet sake I first was taught
  To love with passion, by some railroad men ;
There is no better method to be bought ;
    The way, though costly, speedy is and plain ;
    But I digress, though eager is my pen
To draw one fire-proof saint in sweet particular,
Who boldly laid his track quite perpendicular.

I left our heroine in no gentle mood,
  And hardly dare return. " Look at your work,
  Ungenerous, cruel, you wicked, wicked Turk ;
I hate you, sir, was never brute so rude ;
No, don't ! " she cried, and crimson-staining stood,
  For, bending down, I kissed her miry foot ;
  Ah ! roguish Love, how could you make me do 't !

Then on a rock with scented grasses strewn
My ancient coat, a guardian brave, I spread,
Rejoiced again the rebel queen to throne,
  Whose beauty holds all loyal hearts in thrall,
That, weeping, mourn a kingdom banishéd,
  And strive with gentle prayer continual
  To empire's care their sovereign to recall.

Around us grew mosses and pencilled ferns,
  The golden-rod, whose wealth brave poets steal,
Sole guerdon that their toiling madness earns,
  The foxglove, skilled the heart's disease to heal,
Asters, wild larkspur, rabid gueule-de-loup,
And flowers, whose thick leaf sheathes rich blossoms
    blue,
With many more that at her feet I threw.

Then in the azure of the deep-blue sky
The choiring stars unveil their melody,
    While closer fleecy clouds their pinion fold,
    And noiseless rise, from caverns deep that hold,
The purple mists, the perfume of the sea,
    Of charm its wailing voices low to heal,
    That like forsaken lover's far reproaches steal.

But I, enraptured, gazed upon a face,
That might an angel's loveliness disgrace,
And had unpeopled half the bending sky,
To follow a new-found divinity,   ·
Had it uplifted its proud, languid eye ;
That, breathing beauty in the sober shade,
A gleaming isle of soft enchantment made.

Let others measure life by linkéd days,
    Or stretch the world out with far wandering feet :
Around one spot my heart of heart delays,
    One hour of joy makes all my memory sweet,
One hour, of toiling time the crowning praise,
    Through pregnant cycles framed to be the eye,
    That lights the forehead of eternity.

Forever sacred shines the house that guards
    The heavenly Presence hid in human ties ;
    The father's care, that impulse high supplies,
The mother's smile, that failure's tears rewards ;
    So happy lot cruel fate to me denies ;
My only home is one enchanted thought,
By music's touch to mystic beauty wrought.

Long on the Maiden's face my silence fed,
　Proud, passionate face in pity beautiful,
　That breathing seemed a truth infallible,
An inward light through vase of crystal shed ;
　Then my heart's whispers drew my pale lips nigher ;
　" Is what I hoped a gem, a sacred fire,
　To which no touch of mortal may aspire ? "

I said, and hearing gentle answer none,
　" Fair Maiden," added, " lend thy chiding ear
　Awhile from thy poor suitor's grief to hear,
What from thy bounty his hurt soul has won,
　Too costly gifts to deck thy lover's bier ;
Ill task it were a sceptre to bestow,
On whom thy sentence in the dust lays low.

" For when thy lovely face upon me beamed,
That like an unforgotten vision seemed
　Of boyhood's year, deep sunk in wasting pain
My soul was buried, of sweet hope devoid,
　Indifferent to joyous pleasures vain,
Nor less with strenuous thought's proud purpose
　　cloyed,
　So blind the struggle seemed, so small the gain.

" For I my youthful years could never bring
　To love or hoarding gold or vulgar place,
Bright ribbons that to tattered bodies cling,
But with my pilgrim staff went wandering
　Through cities proud and still forgotten ways,
With footstep light, in glowing hope to find
The sacred truth that shall redeem the kind.

" ' The world's forgotten soul, where lies it hidden ? '
  Eager I asked of every passer-by ;
  At which all stared in strange perplexity,
And crouching some by their own shadows ridden,
So.ne filling empty words with ancient dust,
  As guiding light their answers loud supply,
As torches dead in empty sockets thrust.

" Till answered one that shone of countenance high,
  And nobler, seemed to scorn his company ;
  ' What seek you, youth ? Ourselves your God have
    ta'en,
  And with our deeper cunning subtly slain,
To sway the world with easy mastery ;
  Doubt you the truth ? behold the church, his
    shroud,
  That wins us tribute from this hoarding crowd.'

" At wisdom's lie earth's honey-garnering moulds
  With death bees filled : noisome from out the sky
  The burnt stars dropt, and such a bitter cry,
As when a slowly lessening wall infolds
  A prisoner, broke from my dumb agony,
That rooted Death forgot his masking dance,
And in his own heart drove his opiate lance.

" Yet in my misery an impulse brave,
  Such legacy high aspirations give,
Spurred me my life from vices base to save ;
  ' Though nothing true in man or nature live,
  My soul,' I cried, ' shall in my soul believe,'
And 'mid my mouldering friends in silence stood,
A hermit in Gehenna's solitude.

"But when I drank the lustre of thy face,
And knew its beauty born of hidden grace,
  A sudden meaning blossomed in the Sun,
And with sweet music flooding dusty ways
  The joyous Earth again its life begun,
As love to fire awoke my frozen youth,
That knew in love the secret soul of truth.

" Then promised Fame to make thy name a song
By English maids the hawthorn buds among
  Whispered, or where Niagara's torrents roar,
  Or Western cornfields lap the horizon's shore,
Or where just judges India's nations tame,
Or far Australian hunters track the game,
  Or Hudson's waves earth's gathered riches pour."

As one that hears forbidden suitors speak,
  My Charmer sat with half-averted eye,
So eloquent grew the witness of her cheek,
  ' So wistful-loth her hand, half poised to fly ;
" Ah ! bitter blossom, sprung from honeyed root ;
  I may not grant what I cannot deny,
I would not have you plead, yet cannot wish you
    mute."

"My happy youth with visions bright was blest
  Of holy martyr brave and wandering knight,
Who, spurred by secret love in faithful breast,
  Ride forth the helpless and opprest to right,
And, proud in self-forgetful courage drest,
  Their bodies heedlessly to torture give,
  So their high souls in deeds immortal live.

"As deep for lives like thine my sympathy,
So deep I hate the lot to women sent,
Who feed with comforts the soul's discontent,
And, leaving life's ennobling charity,
On narrow household cares their thought bestow,
Losing the little their dull masters know,
Like lessening apes that into shadows grow.

"Reproach me not, nor altogether blame
The selfishness of this forgetful hour,
That, bound by gentle thoughts in golden frame,
Around my soul its sacred balm will pour,
When I, a distant, half-remembered name,
In foreign clime invoke delightedly
Its reawakening joyful mystery."

"Enchantress, breathing beauty infinite,
Other reproach than praise inadequate
Fear not from him, whose glory were to write
Thy name of joy upon the direful gate,
Where wretched mortals doomed to torture wait ;
A hope to law nor cruel religion known,
Whose changing empire mocks man's changeless
groan.

"Farewell the heart-beat whispering, 'It is she,'
Farewell fond walks beside the laughing sea,
Farewell the golden thread of woven thought,
Farewell bright glances into fancies wrought,
Farewell the chiding of the evening-star,
Farewell to all save memory's prison-bar,
Farewell to all save one sweet face afar.

"Welcome the strength from bitter misery born,
　Welcome the soul purging from earthly stain,
Welcome true love in secret bounty shown,
Welcome dear care for kindred souls forlorn,
　Welcome the ideal's ̇self-forgetful reign,
Welcome the glory of thy beauty known,
　Welcome one hope that whispers Thee again.

" Proud solace of the painless infinite,
　Unknown of him, whose pleasure-cloistering eye,
　'Mid blushing roses painting Heaven too nigh,
Delays to drink the sacred difficult light ;
My soul shall nurse upon the unseen height
　A selfless love, germ of a nobler world,
　When dead the Sun lies in its banner furled."

The Maiden's face, bright as a thought unspoken,
　Mastered my words with silent sympathy ;
Then, with a sigh from fetters half unbroken :
" Mother would die, for, in her changeless faith,
The heretic's belief is the soul's death ;
　Mother would die, mother would surely die ;
　Mother would die, mother would surely die."

" Fettered," then I, " shall be my sleepless tongue,
　Though half earth's charms beneath its silence die,
For ill can beauty by itself be sung,
　And hers the least, whose veiling modesty
　Reluctant meets the crystal fountain's eye ;
Yet am I, too, a Catholic in a fashion,
And love you with a universal passion.

" The idea is charitable as the soul ;
God's love its source, God's love its equal goal :
A careless tale, a foolish friend once told
  My heedless ear, not ill the deep truth shows
How art itself, with silent finger cold,
Invites the evil to its marble fold,
  And over all its sacred mantle throws.

" He loved a girl, none fairer, so he said,
  A boast that marred a gentle tale, else true,
  For well my sorrow charms more fatal knew,
He loved her, and, perchance, his love had wed,
Had he on other food than cold words fed ;
  But in this country, generous, brave, and free,
  That steals its thoughts, he died of poverty.

" Unknown they loved, unknown the lovers met,
  For ill can haughty parents' prudence brook,
  Rich heiresses on poets' rags should look ;
Unknown they met in some forgetful street,
  Where poverty alone and misery speak
Discord, that grew as heavenly music sweet
  Beneath the rose-songs breathing from her cheek.

" One evening, by the Hudson's wintry tide,
They rested on a huge iron wheel that lay
Rusting upon the pavement ; on each side
  Huge factories stood remote in empty yards ;
None but a madman to such spot would stray ;
  The very thought my palsied tongue retards,
Such tales of river thieves about it play.

" A nameless corpse from out the river picked,
The morgue, the merry students' lottery,
For legs, arms, trunk, and head a little nicked,
   And into science rapidly we pass ;
Our absence wakes the papers' warring cry,
' Absconded,' some say, some the charge deny,
   And kindly dub us drunkard, fool or ass.

" But little thought they of cruel danger's care,
   In that one hour, when, sunk in blissful rest,
   Her head lay pillowed on her lover's breast,
Whose pale lips hovering over roses rare,
Sweet boon, till then ungranted to love's prayer,
   In sacred scarlet clothed his first-born kiss,
   That beggared heaven and filled the earth with bliss.

" The dull street blossomed into paradise,
   Forgetful time in rhythmic music sped ;
When, glancing up with languor-drooping eyes,
   The maiden sees an ominous spectral head
Above the wall behind them slowly rise ;
   A lurking eye, like an assassin's knife,
   Aiming its treacherous point against her life.

" She paler grew, but with a gentle smile,
   As happy in her lover's arms to die,
   Whispered his careless ear the danger nigh,
He rising, said aloud, ' Wait here awhile,
   I will return ' ; the head sank noiselessly ;
Then by the hand he led the silent girl,
While Fortune breathless gave her wheel a whirl.

" For suddenly forth from a neighboring cart,
With warning whistle, two dark ruffians start ;
While o'er the wall their angry comrades climb,
To aid with rapid tread the hideous rhyme ;
Our friends lend wings to unreluctant feet,
And, shadowed by pursuers still more fleet,
Reach just in time a thickly peopled street.

" Later, for poets will their soul denude
And pawn its clothes to give their fancy food,
   My friend asked me how best to introduce
Into a fancy sketch this spectral head ;
   ' So picturesque a thing is hard to lose,
Yet not less difficult to find the thread
By which a murderer to art is wed.'

" Then I : ' the background of a surface tale
   Your worthy friend would admirably grace,
A coal-black head, a maiden lily-pale ;
   But worthier you, should you from distance trace
The mystic curving lines of good and ill,
   Their meeting the immortals' starting-place,
Cradle of heroes' heaven-descended will.'

" ' Ah ! gentle murderer,' exclaimed my friend,   •
' Where'er your chainless mounting footsteps bend,
Or whether, housed in thoughtful chamber bare,
You make the idle law your studious care,
In wise delay to thrash the barren air,
How happy I to hang your lips upon,
And learn your morals and religion !

   7

" ' Then shall I weave from deadly serpent-rays
A living darkness round one guileless face,
 Whose purity informs the pregnant slime,
 Till heroes born of demons heavenward climb ;
Sweetheart ! mankind shall live but by thy grace,
 And worshipping beauty and Thee divine,
 See God's own eye from h—l's black centre shine.'

" So ends the burden of a tale ill told " ;
 " But he ! " cried Beauty, with an eager glance,
That seemed the story's broken thread to hold ;
 " What happened ? I am sure no evil chance
Could well befall so true a lover bold ;
 Though so wild actions our reproof must move,
 One needs must listen ere she can reprove,

" And if she listen—" " She, she married well,
A man whose value one who runs can spell,
A millionaire they called the yellow dwarf,
Rich in all virtues save a dangerous cough,
(Pardon the rhyme my ear 's a little off,)
And now, a queen of good society,
She gladly lets forgotten follies die.

" A letter fell into her mother's hand,
 Who by mistake the document untied,
Then at her child presenting it cried : ' Stand !
 Deliver ! or you shall be crucified.'
 The girl confessed her love with generous pride ;
Vainly the mother stormed : ' Is she not free ?'
Urged the wise father ; ' let the matter be.'

"Then later hired a girl, all innocence,
To be her servant, she on some pretence
  Her secret to her trusting mistress breaks ;
My friend had wronged her with cruel added blows,
Witness the arm her kind reluctance shows,
  For well the eloquence of a thing that speaks,
The wise old judge from long experience knows."

"But he ? " my Listener echoed with a sigh,
"What business else should the poor poet try ?
  A homeless soul, that knew no resting-place,
  And half in love seemed with his own disgrace,
That that, where all succeed, the skill to die,
  Sequestered far from feigning friendship's eyes,
  Hid in the potter's field his lean mould lies.

"How oft to sell his tales and poetry
About the streets my hungry footsteps fly,
Though all cried excellent, no one would buy ;
'American,' they said ; 'yes, yes,'t is true,
But how can we waste money upon you,
When nothing need be paid for English thought ?'
And truth, a thing is cheaper stolen than bought.

"Well, I recall the dying scene ; he lay
  Delirious on a miserable bed,
The fever's flame, the frozen ashes' ray
  His warmth, till at the last raising his head ;
'Thou, Heaven, and I were all alone,' he sighed ;
  'Give me one kiss ; darling, where art thou fled ?
Darling ! darling ! darling !' he gasped and died.

" So passed his soul up to the blissful skies,
  So died his country's immortality,
  A name beneath cruel envy's obloquy,
An unseen sun above his country lies,
His beggared country that its gods denies,
  And its diviner mind starved and forgot,
  Aspiring to be thief, turns idiot.

" Kinder to them had been the murderer's knife
  Than mother or than country. Who can tell
The purposes that underly our life,
  Or what divining mind can rightly spell
This good, that evil?" Soft the Maiden sighed,
  And from her downcast eyes began to well
Sweet tears, that sweetly to my tale replied.

" The last song that he wrote, this wizard place
  Suits well : the treacherous rocks to slumber kist,
  By the pale fingers of the wandering mist,
The moonlit sea, where beauty's trancéd face
Through shrouded wave breathes melancholy grace ;
  I will repeat, since so you urge the song,
  'T is quaintly written and not very long.

    " ' Silvery net, silvery net,
    Woven with care, warily set,
    Lier-in-wait, thief of the sea,
    Win from the deep treasure for me.

    " ' Faint on the marge, weary and sad,
    Fed with the mist, misery-clad,
    Long have I lain, sorrow-begone,
    Mocked of the stars, scorned by the sun.

" ' Ripples the wave, still though the wind,
Watcher unseen, what dost thou bind ?
Hasten my hand, hasten my oar,
Soon shall the prize bloom on the shore

" ' Heavy the spoil, fisherman bold,
Diamonds or pearls, what dost thou hold ?
Tho' with strong hand back draw the tide,
Swiftly my boat, more swiftly glide.

" ' What on the wave glooms shuddering,
Dark as the wild night raven's wing ;
What 'mid the weeds glimmers so fair,
Deep with delight clothing the air ?

" ' Thee have I won, luminous maid,
Ivory-limbed, beauty-arrayed ;
Fleece of the cloud, flame of the sea,
Fatal to all, captive to me ?

" ' Cold are the drops, that from thee drip,
Colder thy cheek, colder thy lip,
Cold is the ice, swift streams that rims,
Colder thy still crystalline limbs.

" ' Gentle the arms round thee that twine,
Tender the lips melting on thine,
Creep, Beauty, creep, close to my breast,
Cold is the bird, warm is the nest.

" ' Opaline glance, steal from thy sheath,
Roses again wake from your death,
Violet veins swift through the snow,
Bear to my heart love's overflow.

" ' Slumbers too deep, joys too divine,
Round the fond heart coil serpentine ;
Fortunate love ill vigil keeps,
Forth from sweet dreams cruel Beauty leaps.

" ' Forth from wild dreams madly I start,
What like a sword pierces my heart?
Am I awake ! ah, misery !
Loveliest one ! why dost thou fly?

" ' Look how the rocks shield her white feet !
Look how the waves rise her to greet !
Down she has leaped into the sea,
Look how she turns piteously !

" ' Arrows of love dart from her eyes,
Piercing the mists round her that rise ;
Hark to her song, summons of fate,
Whispering low : " Why dost thou wait ?

" ' Knowest thou not, he, who hast kist,
Once my pale lips all joy has missed ?
Linger ye on hopeless, alone,
Memory's mock, corse on a throne ? "

" ' Echoes my soul, short my delay,
Beckoning shape, thee to obey :
Into the storm, into the sea,
Vision divine, gather thou me.' "

I finished, and the Maiden's face of pride
    In trembling hands its wayward beauty hid ;
" Forgive me," through her blinding tears she sighed,
    As I her passionate sorrow vainly chid ;
" Alas ! has love so fatal potency ?
Promise me, Sweetheart, that you will not die ;
Promise me, Sweetheart, that you will not die ! "

Then, through the sorrow of a brooding heart,
    That knows the depths of human misery,
    And thoughts unconscious in the soul that lie,
And motive mystery of each hidden art,
    A word gleamed golden on my ravished eye,
Unheard, unknown, since through the forming earth,
Thrilled the deep impulse of its sacred birth.

Veil, veil thy sight, each faintly beaming star ;
    Be still, wild wave, and fond, impatient wind ;
Keep, mortal eye, thy gaze profane afar ;
    Be nature's swift inquisitive senses blind,
    Banished the inward vision of the mind,
That thought within its range may never hold
The word, that sways love's starry kingdom old.

BALLADS.

ADA.

Fair Ada in the hammock lay ;
   I watched her beauty pale,
Her glance as blithe as wave at play,
   Her motions graceful as the sail
That frets the waters gray.

No costlier gem the city wore
   Than winsome Ada fair,
And I was but a teacher poor,
Who begged his way from door to door,
   Dull folly's alms to share.

But now my heart recalls the time,
   One little season gone,
When, listening to the billows' rhyme,
   Twin footsteps, she and I alone,
The sandy ridges climb.

Fair Ada whispers her desire
   That I shall sing to her,
And from her eyes a tender fire
   Outbreathes of power to minister
To love's forgetful lyre.

Then, as a fated prisoner
  With double vision sees
The dimpling brook with reeds astir,
  The flowers made fair to woo the bees,
Till tears the prospect blur.

With look of longing hopelessness
  I gazed in Ada's face,
And strove with music's wing to dress
  A tale, whose words of sober grace
Had moved my heart's distress.

THE LOVERS.

In high Montclair the daughter fair
  Of pious widow grew,
Her rector's creed, her mother's prayer
  No other books she knew.

As rosebud at the chapel door,
  That scoffers stop to bless,
As freely from her beauty's store
  She gave, she could no less.

An earnest youth, a neighbor's son,
  Who shared with heaven her heart,
To distant school long since had gone
  To learn the healer's art.

At first the maiden heard with pride
  Her lover's larger speech,

And with her mind on tiptoe tried
  His lofty thoughts to reach.

But when his bold and trenchant jest
  Her rector's creed attacked,
A deepening sorrow unconfessed
  Her tender bosom racked.

At length, with her small words, as one
  In fetters close who wrought,
She strove with soft persuasion
  To charm the spectre thought.

Short truce, when faith and reason meet,
  And soon, with eager eyes,
A fever dogged her faltering feet,
  And leaped upon its prize.

Her lover by her bedside knelt
  And heard her dying prayer,
Ask not what keen remorse he felt,
  What anguish and despair !

When o'er the South that summer swept
  A fever naught could stem,
When mothers from their nurslings crept,
  Nor turned to look at them ;

The young physician thought of one,
  Whose prayer lay near his soul ;
He sought the tainted Southern sun,
  And found the martyrs' roll.

Together now in churchyard green
  The hapless lovers lie ;
And rude the foot that steps between
  Or hastens careless by.

Their names, what profits it to know ?
  Are loyal souls so rare ?
As gentle natures round us grow,
  That fame nor fortune share.

Though love no more with spur and spear
  The lord of battle rides,
His changeless empire far and near
  In human hearts abides.

RECIPROCITY.

" You helped my husband from his horse,"
  The Richmond widow said,
" And I might farther.fare, and worse
  Than with such comrade wed."

Next week, at Newport, as the bride
  In her languid hammock swung,
And watched the dimpling sunset tide
  And the sails from the welkin hung,

" When the day," she sighed, " is laid on its bier,
  And the stars peep after the sun,
My listless ear delights to hear
  Of crimson laurels won.

" The flashing sword, the forward word,
    Red stream where armies meet,
And heroes brave, o'er open grave,
    Who press with eager feet.

" And tell me of my former Love,
    Whom you lifted from his horse,
When your brown blade's wrath cut a double swath,
    And parted corse from corse."

" Strange fires will rise in beauty's eyes,"
    Then he, " my true heart's purse,
When you learn at length by what quaint device
    I saved your husband's horse.

" That dreadful day, when Early's brave,
    From the forest stealing forth,
Like surging ocean's shoreward wave,
    Swept over the sleeping North ;

" I saw in our hour of sorest need,
    At turning tide of the fray,
A grizzly chief on a coal-black steed
    Strike fire through the ranks of gray.

" My eyes along my rifle glare,
    One crack, and on we bore ;
I found the saddle red and bare,
    What need to tell you more ?

" Close not your eyes, fair rebel prize,
  Shall beauty know remorse ?
A boy in blue may well outwoo
  A graybeard on a horse.

" Close not your eyes, fair rebel prize,
  To your heart this comfort take,
No mortal soul to heaven hies,
  Unless it earth forsake."

A frown, a smile my Lady gave,
  " No more of him or his horse,
Whom once this hand, but now the grave
  Has taken for better or worse.

" The bargain was out of the common course,
  But not so very wide ;
You helped my husband from his horse,
  He helped you catch your bride."

RUTH.

" You shall not marry Madelaine,
  By my child's head I swear ;
Look not upon her face again,
  Remember and beware."

Stern grew the rector's mouth, and dark
  His gathering brow : beneath,
From sullen eye shot fiery spark,
  Like sword from clouded sheath.

" Let not thy grief to guilt o'ergrow,
    The wedding-day is set,
Forget our love of long ago,
    Forgive, if not forget."

The rector's voice was soft as one,
    Who knows of woman's mind,
Each door by which persuasion
    Its subtle way can find.

So shrill a laugh her answer was,
    The raven's note were mild,
Like nail upon the creaking glass,
    Its edge the copses filed.

" And must we live a nameless life,
    Our little child and I,
And Madelaine your happy wife?
    Oh, give your words the lie !

" I never wrought you, Herbert, wrong,
    You never knew to fear,
That I would lend a treacherous tongue
    To scandal's greedy ear.

" The guilt was ours, the punishment
    I wished to bear alone,
I loved you so, I was content
    By thee to be undone.

" But Madelaine alone of all
    The world my heart who knew,

And loved herself my friend to call,
  Shall she rob me of you ?

" Or are you hungry for her gold ?
  Gold cannot joy the heart,
Nor match with love that grows not old,
  Tho' years of sorrow part.

" Last night beside the Delaware
  I left our little child,
And, Herbert, at your name I swear,
  The sleeping darling smiled.

" This ringlet "—" Foolish Ruth, have done,
  Why nurse a sinful sorrow, .
To wound with cruel contagion
  His heart who weds to-morrow ? "

Like dove to savage eagle turned,
  Fierce grew her heart's despair ;
" Learn thou," she cried, " what I have learned,
  Remember and beware."

Black grew the rector's face, a stone
  Beside the pathway lay, `
A moment, and the deed was done ;
  He kneeled, but not to pray.

Beside the fainting form he bent,
  A gleaming dagger drew,
Swift, swift, its point unswerving went
  Her trembling body through.

Within the forest's secret grave,
    The guilty work he bore,
And deep, with branch and leafy wave,
    His victim covered o'er.

How short, from kiss to dagger's thrust
    Of human love the span,
What foolish maiden still will trust
    The lips of lying man?

The rector from the whispering wood
    To church has sped, and soon
His people's sins with holy blood
    Has washed out every one.

But in the wood poor Ruth awakes,
    Her eyelids open wide:
"Oh, Herbert, how my bosom aches!
    Come kiss me, Love," she sighed.

But as she spoke a ruddy stream
    Forth from her lips there burst;
" 'T is true, 't is true, that fearful dream,
    Thou fiend forever cursed.

" Ye merry birds that sweetly sing,
    Is there not one to dip
His wing in the water wan and bring
    A drop to cool my lip?

" Is there no bird in the leafy wood,
    Of all that charm the air,

Will dip his feather in my blood,
　And my sad message bear?

" That I am foully, foully slain,
　And who the deed has done
Will wed the lovely Madelaine
　Ere sets to-morrow's sun.

" My child, my darling child," she cries,
　And as to greet it leaps,
But on her lips her sorrow dies ;
　She falls, she gasps, she sleeps.

Now merry wakes the morrow morn,
　Still shines the Easter sun,
And like a rose-bud newly born,
　Shows sweet Maud Livingston.

Her coy star-beaming eyes she veils
　Beneath their lashes long,
And swift the color blooms and pales
　· Her dimpling smiles among.

The joyous wedding guests are met,
　Laymen and clergy proud ;
Her mother's cheek with tears is wet,
　Her father's head is bowed.

" Dearly beloved," with vacant voice,
　The bishop bland began,
When suddenly a plaintive noise
　Down from the tree-tops ran.

A robin from a hawk in chase
   Darts thro' the window wide,
And, like a suppliant seeking grace,
   Drops down before the bride.

With tender hand the lovely maid
   The little bird caressed,
And pressed its fluttering wing afraid
   Upon her snowy breast.

But whence that sudden shriek, why glare
   The bridegroom's fearful eyes?
Upon the maiden's bosom fair
   What bloody witness lies?

Each guest is frozen to the ground,
   The bride has swooned, the groom,
His altered face half turning round,
   Flies from the haunted room.

To Milford town he went and sought
   Ruth's unbefriended child ;
Around his neck it clung untaught,
   And on its father smiled.

He brought the child to Madelaine,
   " Oh, guard it as your own :
My face you 'll never see again,"
   He whispered, and was gone.

The tangled woods of Tarrytown
   To deeper green had turned,

And, summer's living beauty flown,
With autumn's splendor burned,

When, in the forest's hidden heart,
A school-boy chanced upon
Two corpses that had grown a part
Of mouldering clod and stone.

THE LADY OF LOST DELIGHT.

" Push off, push off your heedless boat ;
This spot is haunted ground ;
And swiftly down the river float,
Nor once again turn round."

The swirling wave flows swiftly by,
My toiling oar is tired ;
Awhile in beauty's nest I 'll lie,
And drink its air inspired.

" Oh ! hasten, foolish youth, unmoor
Your boat from off the strand ;
And stoutly ply the laboring oar,
Nor lift your eyes to land.

" It is the Lady of Lost Delight,
Who in this covert weeps ;
Beneath the coming of the night
How soft her footstep creeps.

" Dark arrows ambush in her eyes ;
   Dark tresses veil her breast ;
Where, living on sweet kisses, dies
   Sad cloistering love unblessed.

" With mournful music's witchery
   Our souls she mastereth ;
Till faint beneath the spell we lie,
   And life discern nor death."

Forbear, my timid friend, forbear ;
   My heart unwounded is ;
I've known a thousand ladies fair,
   But never spot like this.

Secure the buds and bells among
   I 'll watch the sun go down,
I never wrought a woman wrong,
   Why fear her idle frown ?

His boat beside the Hudson lay,
   All painted white and green ;
But though they searched for many a day,
   No more was Edwin seen.

THE MERMAID.

A mermaid in a mossy cave
Stealing from the laughing wave
Its music, clothes with witchery
Wooing voice and languid eye.

A mariner by the double note
Won, upon her pearly throat
Paints a rose leaf, gentle sign,
Sealing human love divine.

The purple morning's herald ray,
Spurring o'er the mists its way,
Sees the mermaid's golden hair
Playing with the wanton air ;

Sees a corse with eager hand
Clasp a wealth of yellow sand,
And the eagle hovering
Nearer with its hungry wing.

EDITH.

Upon the frowning Palisades
    A cottage nest is hung ;
There to sad evening's gathering shades
    Fair Edith, dying, sung :

" Farewell, dear rocks, to me not rude ;
    No more my steps shall climb
To hear your sacred solitude
    Return the church bell's chime !

" Farewell ! far sweeter echoes heard,
    As holy and as pure,
When Walter's lips, by music stirred,
    My fainter answer lure.

" Farewell, dear Hudson's silvery stream ;
  No more by thee we rove,
With woven hands and hearts, to dream
  The sweet, swift dream of love.

" Ah, might I in the gateway stand,
  His violets on my breast,
And feel again my loving hand
  By hand more loving pressed.

" His lips the sunset rose's beam,
  His voice the robin's call,
His eye like azure mountain stream,
  His strength a shield for all.

" Cold is my hand and pale my cheek,
  My sight grows dull and tame,
In sighs my faltering whispers speak,
  Yet still they move his name.

" Ah, parting sunbeam, travel fast
  To Walter's cruel camp ;
Tell him I loved him to the last
  With love death cannot damp.

" Tell him my last heart-beat shall kiss
  The leaves of laurel green,
With which, that day of saddest bliss,
  He decked his forest queen.

" Ah, cruel Heaven, canst thou not spare
  From thine eternity
A moment to my sorrow's prayer
  My lover's face to see ?

" The autumn wind, with changing plume,
  No more recalls the spring ;
It bears the shattered rose's bloom
  On summer's bier to fling.

" What muffled phantoms eager press
  Between me and the light ?
What wizard shapes, in fitful dress,
  Mock my fast-fading sight ?

" Farewell ! dear sister, mother dear !
  Ah, woe ! my lover brave,
Death shall to thee my spirit bear,
  Thy heart shall be my grave."

LINDA.

A lady at Jamaica lives,
  Who utters word to none,
But evermore in silence grieves,
  And, turning from the sun,
  Walks on in pride alone.

" Now, Linda, do your golden hair ;
  Friend Griswold comes to-night,
And you and Clara school-mates were,
  So let no thoughtless slight
  Disturb the swain's delight."

Then paler than the lily grew
  The lady's cheek so fair,
But as, who knows no other care,

Around her wrist she drew
    Her jewelled bracelet rare ;

" Dear husband, welcome Griswold Vaughan.
    Thou wise of husbands, who,
Between the sunset and the dawn,
    Hast wit enough to know
    A friend from secret foe."

Then smiled the haughty Linda fair,
    But in so cold a way,
'T were better smile were wanting there,
    Than round her lips to play,
    And mock her heart's despair.

Oh ! young and fair was Linda Brent,
    Brave were her glances keen,
Like eagle's beak her eyebrow bent,
    And haughty as a queen,
    But winsome was her mien.

Great wealth had Linda's husband proud ;
    A railroad lord was he ;
And princely merchants lowly bowed,
    And crooked their rusty knee
    To greet him servilely.

The toiling years make riches grow,
    But love has other root,
And soon the nicest ladies know,
    How ill a costly boot
    Repays a pinching foot.

Proud Linda did her golden hair,
  And brave the mirror shone,
That glassed her arm and shoulder bare,
  And jewels many a one,
  That shimmered like the sun.

Then fair as cheating fancy moulds
  A faithless charmer's face,
To one who evermore beholds
  The strength of goodly days
  Decay in hope of grace.

Among her guests, in loveliness,
  She moved like vision strange,
Whose haunting beauty none may guess,
  So swift, with wider range,
  Fair charms for fairer change.

Of gentlemen, than Griswold Vaughan
  More courtly was there none ;
His tender glance as eye of fawn,
  His harder heart than stone,
  Knew many a maid undone.

There 's danger in the meadow gay,
  Or on the smiling wave,
A falling leaf has power to slay,
  Or spider's web to save
  Our footsteps from the grave.

" Dear Griswold, pluck for me a rose,"
  Said haughty Linda Brent ;
  And, with a look of blandishment,

Within the leafy close
  Her lightsome step she bent.

"Oh, let me see the pretty ring,
  That makes your finger shine ;
You promised once that any thing,
  Or human or divine,
  I asked of you was mine."

Then suddenly the golden ring
  She from his finger drew,
And, with a glance deep questioning,
  "Dear Griswold, is it true,
  This story told of you?"

"Oh, give me back again my ring,"
  Too eagerly, he cried.
"Alas, what need of quarrelling
About so slight a thing?"
  The lovely Linda sighed.

"A year ago, but let that pass,
  You swore you loved me more,
Than ever woman fabled was ;
  But how swift frost and hoar
  Love's blossoms covers o'er.

"Yet if you value so your ring,
  I dreamed of valiant knight,
Who clothed himself with raven's wing,
  And scaled the window's hight,
  To win his love's delight."

When haughty ladies stoop to woo,
   The bravest well may fear,
For pride is evermore untrue,
   And foolish is the ear,
   That shall its pleading hear.

But Clara Jones owned land in fee,
   Of Hempstead half the town,
And loth was Griswold Vaughan to see
   A prize so near his own,
   In needless jeopardy.

" She shall not have him," in her heart,
   Said Linda bitterly ;
But all so well she played her part,
   No keenest eye could see,
   How deep her treachery.

The sky is hung with sable pall,
   The trees are laid asleep,
Or wake to touch funereal,
   As fitful breezes creep
   Across their shadows deep.

A shadow with the shadows blent,
   An eye no shadows blind,
Alone, alone sits Linda Brent,
   As one, who of the wind
   Its secret path would find.

What footstep trembles on the air ?
What stealthy footstep slow ?

And who so ready as Linda fair,
  The lattice wide to throw,
  And whisper welcome low?

" Has love forgot its cunning, Sweet?"
  The lovely Linda sighed;
"One hour of happiness complete,
When hearts in music meet,
  Whatever ill betide."

Then richer than the perfumed press,
  That holds the blood-red wine
Her lips compact of loveliness
On lips as eager press
  Their honeyed wealth divine.

" Now give me back again my ring,"
  Her foolish lover cried.
"Alas, what need of quarrelling
About so slight a thing?"
  The lovely Linda sighed.

" Why, Linda, shine your eyes so bright?
  What sudden flames they dart!
What depths of wonder and delight,
What darker fears than night,
  They waken in my heart!"

" Be still, be still, my lover brave;
  What danger is to fear?
The house is stiller than the grave,
  And love keeps vigil near;
What more could monarch crave?"

Then like a careless child at play
　　Among the summer flowers,
Her lover cast his fears away,
　　Nor asked the weaver hours
Their colors dark or gay.

Then Linda from its scabbard's lair
　　Drew forth a dagger sharp ;
Between his neck and shoulder bare
A stroke she struck so fair,
　　It made his body warp.

No woman's work of useless blows,
　　One nervous flash and swift ;
From neck to heart the weapon goes,
　　And ere his lids uplift,
Again in death they close.

With many a loud and piercing shriek
　　Ran Linda to her lord :
" Oh, haste," she cried, " your vengeance
　　wreak,
Help, help, I cannot speak,
　　Strange horrors are abroad."

" Woe worth the day, woe worth the thought,
　　Brought thy false footstep near ;
What sorrow has thy coming wrought,
　　What sorrow long and drear,
　　Thou comrade once so dear ! "

" My maid who wept her youth betrayed,"
To Clara Linda said,
" This ring that your initials bears,
With many bitter tears,
Upon my table laid."

Full Clara was of joy and youth,
Her cheeks as red as cherry,
And from her lovely, dimpled mouth,
Like music of the south,
Came laughter warm and merry.

But now her cheek is pale as lead,
She wanders to and fro,
And ever lower droops her head,
And sighs from heart of woe,
"Ah! would that I were dead!"

A MINSTREL'S ALMS.

It fell on a day in leafy June,
When ladies tender been,
Blithe Harry with his flute a-tune
Went lightly down the glen.

A hundred maids, there were no more,
A minstrel may not lie,
At window, garden-gate, and door
Repressed a rising sigh.

A Cripple blocked his way to ask
A copper he might see :

" Lag not behind, be that thy task,
 Thou shalt not lack a fee."

They saw Squire Acres swollen sit
 His daughter and wife beside,
" Now, Cripple, try thy nimble wit,
 Well may it thee betide."

Then he : " Give alms to charity,
 Twofold will Heaven repay."
" Tempt not my soul with usury,
 Thou limping loon, away."

Then Harry : " Squire, your heart you wrong,
 The proof will soon appear."
He pressed his lips to his fairy flute,
 And blew a whistle clear.   .

" I 'll play a tune, and we 'll agree,
 If shut remain your eyes,
Myself will pay the Cripple's fee,
 If not, I name the prize."

The first note merry Harry plays,
 The daughter's glances drop.
" What thief my foolish heart waylays ?
 Oh, gentle minstrel, stop."

She listened, trembled, blushed, and sighed,
 Then bent her timid knee,
" Oh, minstrel, spare my maiden pride,
 And pay your court to me."

The Squire's eyes open wide. " My wife,
  My horse, my land be thine ;
But Isabel, my more than life,
  My darling child resign."

Loud Harry laughed, the Cripple took
  A large and shining fee ;
From tender hands the minstrel broke,
  And leaped walls two or three.

THE INDIAN SUMMER.

Great Manabozho laid aside
  His bow and tomahawk,
And strewed afresh his fragrant couch
  With leaf and yellow stalk.

The shaking spring long since had passed,
  And passed the summer's toil,
And bending bough and wigwam groaned
  With field and forest spoil.

He stooped beneath his wigwam door,
  Drew forth his sandstone pipe,
And looking at the scarlet trees
  Exclaimed : " The year is ripe."

Exclaimed, " My beaver dams are full,"
  And stroked his painted breast,
And gazed upon the giant lakes,
  Outstretched to north and west.

" Well have ye thriven, earth and seas,
  Beneath my shaping hand,
Ye that were drop of water once,
  And thou but grain of sand.

" And well my shining lamps are trimmed,
  That measure night and day,
And well my countless children fare,
  And none my will gainsay."

He fills his pipe, and on its mouth
  A lighted pine-cone lays,
And smokes till hill-side, field, and lake
  Are clothed with purple haze.

At length, on softest deerskin sank
  The hero-god to sleep,
Nor wakes till through the russet grass
  The wind-blown blossoms peep.

IADILLA.

" No longer, father, bid me fast,
My hope forboding visions blast " :
  Iadilla spoke, and lay
  Mute, awaiting yea or nay.

The glede within the wigwam glowed,
His head the dusky father bowed,
  Looking on the prostrate form,
  Pallid cheek and wasting arm.

S

" Despair not now, my patient son,
Eleven hungry days are gone,
  Ere to-morrow's lamp has set,
  Famine's pangs thou wilt forget.

" A name beyond the proudest brave,
A guardian god to slay or save,
  Thou wilt win and bless the word,
  Thee from failure base deterred."

The fagot blazed upon the hearth,
The faster's head sank back to earth,
  With one gentle glance and true
  O'er his face his robe he drew.

The sire upon the morrow stands
Without the tent with laden hands,
  Pushing on with vacant stare,
  Sees the sacred wigwam bare.

But from the ridge-pole steals a voice :
" My father, grieve not, but rejoice,
  Fast and prayer were not in vain,
  Freed from earthly care and stain,

" The bird-soul of the human kind,
Your son a robin redbreast find,
  Tchee re lee re lee re lee
  Father, sorrow not for me."

LELINAU.

With pensive brow dark Lelinau
  Within her wigwam stands,
Lips no longer falter no,
  Listless fall her hands.

" Delay the marriage rite to urge,
  So thee may fairies keep,
Father, till the pine-leaf's dirge
  Lays my grief asleep.

" Again through whispering spirit-wood
  O'er haunted hill and hollow,
Let your child, in happy mood,
  Fairy footprints follow."

In dusky hand a piny plume,
  Her hair with wild-flowers dight,
Through the forest's gentle gloom
  Stole her footsteps light.

And hears she not her friends and kin
  Around her wigwam gather ?
Maidens decked with rabbit-skin,
  Braves with eagle's feather ?

In vain they 'll watch ; the groom in vain
  Around his wigwam glower ;
Never will they see again
  Maiden, plume, or flower.

But fishers on the giant lake,
  Beneath a cloudless moon,
Hear a voice of gladness shake
  Forest, mead, and dune.

And see at times her slender form,
  A plumed prince by her side,
Followed by an elfin swarm,
  O'er the hillocks glide.

Dance, fairies, dance on Manit-wac,
  Between the pine and wave ;
All gifts be yours, that mortals lack,
  All pleasures mortals crave.

WINONA.

Wan worshipper of wave and leaf,
Yield no more to hopeless grief,
  No more pride's purpose keep ;
Come again for love and rue,
Where tender eyes and true
  Watch for you and weep.

" From Minnewakon's reedy shore,
Brother, never, never more
  My footsteps wander may ;
Chained to living wave and bough,
I read their whispers low
  Day and night and day.

" A year, a month, a day is gone,
Since love-lorn I wandered on
  Across the golden west :
Fence and furrough backward fled,
Till rippling round me spread
  Seas in verdure dressed.

" Remote from Mammon's multitude,
Grass for couch and gun for food,
  Forgot all other care,
Till in hope with deer to meet
One night my careless feet
  Through this covert fare.

" The harvest-crescent pricked the cloud,
Branches by the breezes bowed,
  Around the breathing lake,
Spirit-voiced, for rhythmic feet,
Swaying shape and pinion fleet
  A mystic circle make.

" As on my soul the lovely scene,
Glooming wave, and starry sheen,
  Its mirrored beauty threw,
Look, what deer athirst or maid
Through parted linden shade
  Rustles into view ?

" Was never deer with step so light ;
' Hail, enchanting vision bright ! '
  I whispered, stealing near ;
' Veil not from me eyes, that shake

A splendor o'er the lake ;
  Wherefore shouldst thou fear ? '

" She turns her head with native grace,
' Look not on Winona's face,
  Or look forever more ' ;
O'er her face, as o'er the book
Of life, with tranced look
  Silently I pore ;

" At gaze till night, to purple mist
Melting, frames in amethyst
  A fairer form than praise ;
Limbs of veiling loveliness,
And eyes, whose star-beams guess
  Sorrow's hidden ways.

" The twilight gleams ; at blush of dawn
Nature's darling child is gone,
  But not the promise sweet,
When the star of evening glows,
Again in rapture close
  Heart to heart shall beat.

" Rapt hours to mortal never given !
Fire of noon and calm of even,
  And have you fled away ?
Hark ! is it a diver's cry   .
Or voice of agony
  Wakes my soul to flay ?

" A month has passed, since fell despair
In my heart, as in a lair,
  With sleepless tooth has lain ;
Since with lightning's vivid lamp
Through forest, brake, and swamp
  Long I searched in vain.

" Nor know if she be fairy-child,
Gypsy, or the daughter wild
  Of dusky savage race,
Slain by jealous hand, or torn
From lover's prayers and borne
  O'er the pathless ways.

" But chained to Minnewakon's wave,
Phantom hands my forehead lave,
  And from each haunted spot
Music-laden echoes creep
Of dreamless death, or deep
  Bliss by man forgot."

JACK.

Up, clouds, and pack !   My name is Jack,
　My home the sunny South,
Let all who wish a dainty dish
　Approach with open mouth.

My mother was an Indian maid,
　My father was a rounder ;
The tale would be too long delayed
　To tell you how he found her.

Ere I had lived a year, a year,
　A year, but barely three,
They died, and left my title clear
　To a House of Charity.

Ere I had lived a year, a year,
　A year, but barely ten,
I fled away from Sisters sere,
　And sought the haunts of men.

When times were good, in merry mood
　I sported in the sun ;
And soft the bed and rich the food
　My wits' five fingers won.

When times were hard, and I could beg
  No bed from door unkind,
I hung my body on a peg,
  And wavered in the wind.

Already many parts I 've had,
  I 've been an Indian doctor,
I 've been an honest country lad,
  I 've been a college proctor ;

I 've been, I fear, a little fast,
  A masking, wayward elf ;
But now my floating years are past,
  'T is time to fund myself.

No more at folly's board I 'll sup ;
  I 'll take a lovely bride,
Surrender up the flowing cup,
  And fling the cards aside.

OLD-TIMERS.

Catch on, catch on ; away we go
  Across the prairie wide ;
We 'll get there, we 'll get there,
  Whatever else betide.

We 'll hold our quarter section down,
  In spite of blizzard's boast ;
For sturdy western men are we,
  And lords of mud and frost.

We 'll boom our town, the only town
    Possessed of every good ;
No shoeless cobblers there you 'll find,
    No tailors wholly nude.

Though 'hoppers come with hideous hum,
    We 'll swear o'er our poker dice,
That Mammon for the view alone
    Would pawn his very eyes.

Catch on, catch on ; away we go ;
    Why should old-timers fear ?
Erelong we 'll meet with tenderfeet,
    And ease them of their gear.

BLINKY JACK.

"Boys, liquor up, two on the trey,
    And ten fish on the case ;
Come, Cæsar, spry, that rock and rye !
    Or I 'll whitewash your face.

"Poor Blinky Jack 's at Stillwater,
    Supported by the State ;
'His case ?' Why, friend, you can't have come
    From prison very late.

"The cards had been a little frisky,
    And Jack had lost his pile,
And a glass or two of lightning whiskey
    Had made his ivories smile.

" The morning sunbeams shuffled by,
    As we left the Bug-Trap's door,
When whom should we see but an onary cuss
    A walking on before !

" It may have been his black silk hat,
    A great oath Blinky swore,
' Now by what right does an onary cuss
    Stalk on the boys before ? '

" He ran, and with his pistol butt
    Assayed the stranger's crown,
' For God's sake stop, I 've done nothing,'
    The man began to groan.

" ' Then why on earth don't you hurry up
    And do something ? ' cried Jack ;
' Go heel yourself, you onary cuss,'
    And he fetched him another crack.

" We thought the matter had been fixed,
    But some one bribed the judge ;
We raised the bid a hundred birds,
    Old Baldhead would not budge.

" ' Live ? ' Why the rascal lived, of course ;
    They played him for a wreck,
But a silver plate soon made his pate,
    As strong as a frozen deck.

" Jack's fears were true, a milksop crew
    Old Fargo now infest ;
With gun and pack, 't is time to back
    Our steeds and rattle west."

TERSE AND TENSE.

" I look," Belinda cried, " with scorn
  On ladies city-bred,
A week after my boy was born,
  I wed the onion bed."

And was your reputation healed,
  Or were your neighbors nice,
Or was the tender fault concealed
  In fashion worldly wise?

She answered still : " I look with scorn
  On ladies city-bred,
A week after my boy was born,
  I wed the onion bed."

THE TIME TO SPEAK.

My watchful mother bade me pick
These damson plums that hang so thick,
But, soft, I promise, if, before
My fingers half my basket store,
A lover sue, I 'll ease his pain,
If later, kings shall sigh in vain ;
Drop ! drop ! drop ! drop !
Twice fortunate, who bids me stop !
Half full ! I 'll add a quarter to 't,
Forgetful youth, why art thou mute?
Three fourths ! Well, here 's one quarter more,
Now, lover, speak or rue it sore ;

All full ! ah, why should I annoy
The lads, by seeming cold and coy ?
I 'll play no more at hide-and-seek,
'T is now the very time to speak.

A FOND DAKOTAN.

Remote from men, Belinda Fenn
  Sat musing on her lover,
Before her spread a grassy bed,
  Behind a basswood cover.

Of western maids of various shades
  Unmatched was fair Belinda,
Her step was light as pleasure's flight,
  Her heart as warm as tinder.

O'er blade and bud the shadows strode,
  The wood-duck sought his nest,
Pee wee, chir chir, more wet, kill deer,
  The birds sang east and west.

Belinda sat, the hour grew late,
  Had Bijah proved untrue !
She stamped her foot ; " The heartless brute
  This trysting-tide shall rue.

" But peace my heart, too swift thou art,
  His step steals down the hill,
In silence greet repentance sweet,
  ' The still sow gets the swill.' "

No more she frowned, with eyes on ground,
  She softly sighed to feel
Around her waist two warm arms haste
  A presence to reveal.

"Oh, hug me close, your arm is loose,
  I fear you 've lost your grip ! "
She turned, oh, rare, a grizzly bear
  Stood by with pouting lip !

The grizzly blushed, his hopes were crushed,
  The iron had pierced his soul,
He slunk away, like a shadow gray,
  And hid in a gopher's hole.

Now lovers all, both great and small,
  This counsel do not miss,
Who hopes to snare Dakota's fair
  Must learn to hug and kiss.

THE RIVAL.

Beware ! beware ! my lover,
  Of a rival word as sweet,
As language can discover,
  Or tender lips repeat :
A word to every human ear
Peculiarly soft and dear,
And chiefliest to woman,
Who 's rather more than human ;
A word, whose charm unmettles
  The boldest rake and flash ;

A word, that wraps in nettles
  The poet's raving trash ;
A potent word that settles
  An absent lover's hash ;
. That siren word, my lover,
  No other is than cash.

AN OPPORTUNIST.

The wheat was stacked, the grass was cut,
  The sharpened plows were stirring,
At Woodlawn church the parson's horn
  Our souls to heaven was spurring.

I sat beside the fair Jeanette
  With scanty hope of grace,
And with a sigh of pleasure glanced
  From ankle fine to face.

Unpressed her hand beside me lay,
  But hark the thrilling news !
The parson stops, the church is bare,
  " A whirlwind has broke loose ! "

With proud Jeanette I homeward fled,
  Our farms lay close together,
The swallow drooped in passing hers,
  It cleared mine on one feather.

Through open ways and forest maze,
  By lindens tempest-arched,
By prostrate pines centipedal,
  And oaks with branches parched,

We passed, and came to Dead Horse Hollow,
 And climbed the Giant's Chair,
But looking north and west I saw
 Of whirlwind hide nor hair.

But " Hark Jeanette, oh, look ! " I cried,
 And round the maiden's waist
The fondness of an errant arm
 Forgetfully misplaced.

" What means this ruffian touch ! "—" Oh, see,
 The whirlwind's smoky crest !
Fear nothing ; never blizzard's beak
 Shall tear you from my breast ! "

On fairy feet, in cadence sweet,
 The breezes round us played,
Till twilight's chiding finger cold
 Was on my shoulder laid.

We found on reaching Beauty's home
 The whirlwind was no myth,
Its breath had snapped the homestead pine,
 And drawn out all the pith.

And from the well the water sucked,
 Two ministers will swear,
That dry as Jeroboam's hand
 It answered stare with stare :

Of romping grindstones four or five
 About the garden posed,

Two helps had from their shoes been blown,
And one was half unhosed.

But that ill-wind that others wrung,
  To me was music sweet,
And led the sweetest maid that breathes
  A captive to love's net.

A WIDOW'S ANSWER.

The partridge plumps into the net,
In vain for cautious plover set,
A blushing maiden whispers yes,
A widow's humor who can, guess?
" I 've heard these furnace sighs before,
On promises I set no store,
Experience by hope misled
Of evil's virtue robs the dead :
Yet, gentle youth, be not less bold,
Nor fancy all coy widows cold."

MY OWN MORTGAGEE.

Why, really, you frighten but please me,
  I feel like a babe in love's hand ;
Nay, sir, do not offer to squeeze me,
  ' T is more than decorum can stand.

How often my pupils I 've taught
  From penniless lovers to flee,
But I never once cherished the thought
  Of wedding my own mortgagee.

Since fancy my horoscope cast,
   I 've stored all its dreams on my shelf,
And now that my green days are past,
   What pleasure to husband myself !

Yes, really, you frighten but please me,
   Twice happy our marriage will be,
For then you 'll both bind and release me,
   My darling, my own mortgagee !

A WESTERN IDYL.

Of all the loyal compass points,
   I only love the west,
A woman must be hard to please
   To find life here unblessed.

At first, ours was a harder lot
   Than idle girl would wish,
We ground our wheat in a coffee mill,
   And dined from a single dish.

My brother tumbled in a slough,
   But they saved our good milch cow,
She helped us on till a golden year
   Brought us a Berkshire sow.

Of husbands I 've had four or five.
   The first ? well, let me see ;
The Indians took a slice of him,
   When they came a courting me.

The next was by a blizzard caught,
When home the neighbors brought it,
It had flown up a mile or two,
Good Lord ! who would have thought it !

Another by the fever bit,
On his way to Deadwood town, .
Had one road agent hold him up,
And another shoot him down.

Last night ! ah, me, the ways of Heaven
Are much involved in doubt,
As you yourself are well aware,
My goodman White winked out.

He fought the ' hoppers day and night,
I set the world by him,
He left our homestead farm unpatched
And our cabin shingled trim.

My friend, this is your second call,
Out here we travel quick,
And to speak plainly you must wed
To-morrow, or cut stick.

THE BROKER.

What ! have you drunk this bottle dry,
And left it here in mockery ?
You wretch, of servants all, the worst
That master's patience ever cursed,

This night, you wine-skin, I 'll maroon
Your soul upon the thirsty moon ;
No more your wily wrinkle's smile
My mind from justice shall beguile.
Was 't not enough, when I my old
Dress coat bequeathed you, that you sold
My Poole's, and left my beauty bare
For prudish maids to wink and stare?
Was 't not enough that, yesterday,
You robbed me of a whole month's pay?
Due you a year?   Wretch ! nothing 's due
To such unthankful knaves as you.
What is the hour ?—past five o'clock ;
At eight precisely mind you knock ;
I must be early at the board ;
To-morrow, havoc waits my word ;
A ring 's been formed to break St. Paul,
And down the list goes rattling all ;
A hundred thousand, make or break—
Be sure you see me wellawake.
Take back this note to Lottie : say
My father's death called me away,
Or mother's—any thing you please,
The girl has grown a frightful tease,
And yet she is the prettiest witch
That ever made one's fingers itch ;
But marriage claims a victim soon,
So what the deuce is to be done?
Already I 've begun reform,
To-morrow, tho' the season 's warm,
Pull off this sermonizing boot,
Be careful how you twist my foot,

Quick, hurry, knave, it 's getting late,
Remember, wake me just at eight.
What 's in my coat, a roasted quail ?
Will Heaven's bounty never fail ?
Raymond 's a brick, and such a wife !
A peep at her 's well worth a life ;
Too soon must trusty Edward King,
An altered bird, unplume his wing.

A FIFTH AVENUE BELLE.

Oh, Harry, how can you so wickedly jest,
   With the sermon still warm in your ear,
Have I come from the Church of the Heavenly
    Rest
   To be tortured and bothered so here ?

You said I ought never to walk in the park
   With David or Robert alone,
That all men were very unsafe after dark,
   With the modest exception of one.

My lover 's a banker, and you are, alas,
   As poor as a poor Nihilist,
And matters would reach a most dangerous pass,
   If Julia untimely were kissed.

I 'll not kick at a walk, at a concert or ball,
   But a kiss, never ask me for that ;
It would break mother's heart, and that is not all,
   I 'm afraid you will spoil my new hat.

POCKET GUIDE-BOOK.

Philosopher and ignoramus
In search of shoes to pique and shame us,
Will find in Boston lasts to suit
Titania or Vidar's foot.

Connecticut his weight must bear,
Who on the shad of shad would fare ;
For fish the seas and rivers over,
There only shad are sweet as clover.

But, who of wives the fairest seek,
Our Empire City must bespeak,
For none can match in beauty's pride
With girls, who bloom by Hudson's side.

TO A MOTH.

Pretty Moth, with silver wing,
Round my candle hovering,
Beauty's dainty satellite,
None dare call thee parasite ;
Though thy tongue delights to eat,
From the purple of the great,
Royal banquets of a cost
That had beggared Sheba's host.

Thee the careful housewives fear,
And as summer days draw near :

Towel-capped and brush in hand,
By the curtain ripe they stand,
Till with frenzied glance they spy
Thy deft finger's tracery,
Then around the chamber spring,
Threatening death to every thing.

Thee the widowed faithful bless
As their martyr-year grows less,
And in carnal robes they find
The chastening working of thy mind ;
Wicked husbands down below
Laugh to see real tears flow,
And the pirate's flag unfurled
Warn again a trusting world.

Evil earth hates thee like truth,
That arch corrupter of our youth ;
And thee in Holy Book 't is told
Heaven itself denies to hold ;
So, too, was never poet blest
In this vile world with blissful rest,
And many urge, and clearly show it,
Heaven 's closed against a poet.

Gently, then, my erring brother,
Let us deal with one another ;
Think not this poor chamber 's graced
With garments to thy toothsome taste ;
In bare columns movable
Poets charge the sov'reign dull.

From my window guide thy flight,
See I point thy wing aright ;
Make of Astor's coat a sieve,
But my trousers modest leave.

A FIRESIDE POET.

Like worshipper of Zoroaster,
  With midnight lamp a-burning,
There stood a ragged poetaster,
  His half-baked verses turning.

In velvet dress and shining gear,
  His wife sat by complaining,
And called him madman, thief, and bear,
  Her warm tears fast down raining.

That half he wished her cool and still,
  Remote from Cupid's bower,
On Malabar's mysterious hill,
  Within the silent tower.

NEAR.

Who calls the Yellow River wide,
When Beauty smiles on the other side ?
A bamboo reed will bridge me o'er ;
  A moment, and I 'm with her,
And in her trembling bosom pour
  The love that lured me hither.
Who calls the Yellow River wide,
When Beauty smiles on the other side ?

Who says Pekin is far away,
When Beauty bids me not delay?
Though countless miles our feet divide,
  On tiptoe I can see
The city of celestial pride,
  That holds none fair as she ;
Who says Pekin is far away,
When Beauty bids me not delay?

A SONG OF CH'ING.

Enchanting youth, unbar one loving look,
I 'll lift my dress, and wade across the brook ;
  And fancy not, if you refuse me,
  A wiser lover will not choose me.
I 'm young, but not too young to grow,
Nor surely you too old to know,
  You foolish, foolish, foolish fellow,
  Unripe will mend, but not too mellow ;
Enchanting youth, unbar one loving look,
I 'll lift my dress, and wade across the brook.

A CELESTIAL ANNEX.

The twinkling stars how faint they grow,
As from my husband's side I go ;
As swift with face in starlight wan
I fly th' approach of early dawn ;
Our prouder sister, she alone,
Can call our husband all her own.

Orion and the Pleiades,
How brilliant those, how timid these !
I muse as through the twilight gloom
I bear my couch back to my room ;
Our prouder sister, she alone
Can call our husband all her own.

TO THE TRADE.

My foolish friends, have done
  With petticoat and rhyme ;
Quick from the charmers run ;
  Waste not your purse and time ;
No girl beneath the sun
  Is worth a pewter dime.

Go, plant the fallow main ;
  In sheaves the sunbeams bind ;
With spider's woven chain
  Enslave the spendthrift wind ;
Pursue the paths of gain
  With unperverted mind.

THE LITTLE WORLD.

IDLE HOURS.

Enchanted hours of idleness,
What busy fairies round you press
With hands unseen your wealth to bless?

If but the muse unweave the light,
And spread before our dazzled sight
Her glittering store of rainbows bright.

Or whether on cold winter's tomb
The purple hyacinth perfume
The saffron crocus' tender bloom;

When, through the languor-melting frame,
There steals the coy, delicious flame,
That blushes at its own sweet name;

Or stretched beneath the pines we lie,
And hear the melancholy sigh
Of waves complaining to the sky;

When Sirius' kingdom has begun,
And through our veins the smouldering Sun
Provokes its sullen rage to run ;

Or waste we autumn's golden age,
While mazy rounds our feet engage,
Enclosed by bearded barley sage ;

When mellow with the new-press'd wine,
The roguish Genius of the vine
Repeats his perjuries benign ;

Or winter's hand the bare nest rocks,
Or drives with stinging lash his flocks,
Or champing rivers' fury locks ;

When Pity's nursling first forsook,
For freezing storms his sunny nook,
Beguiled by Beauty's pleading look,

Who, breathing sighs of deep distress,
While laughing eyes the fraud confess,
Her empire won by helplessness.

MARGARET.

'T was in the joyous month of June,
When rivulets their voices tune,
And amorous insect tribes commune
    With whispering leaf and wind ;
When birds are singing on every spray,
When buds and bells make meadows gay,
And strange vicissitudes waylay
    The heart that loves its kind :

Wandered May Margaret, frolic maid,
By many a backward glance betrayed,
Where stoops the mead with daisies laid
    Beneath the fringéd wood ;
While some unseen divinity,
Ill seems ungentle chance might be
Such guide, advanced my footsteps nigh,
    To mar her solitude.

" The raven's wing were white, I guess,"
Then I, " if matched with the silken tress,
That throws its shadowy loveliness
    Upon thy face divine,
And black upon thy breast of snow,
Where vestal thoughts to music grow,
The foam-and-cloud-nursed gull would show,
    Would such disgrace were mine !

" But let thy thoughts my guidance learn.
Thy soul shall with such rapture burn,
All Mammon's bribes thy hand will spurn
    The hidden charm to win ;
For, like the central fire-beam's blaze,
Thy name, high theme of minstrel's lays,
Shall grow, till Time's own consort prays
    To bask its shadow in."

The maiden stayed her printless feet,
Surprised that artless truth too sweet
For flattery's guile to lurk in it,
    Could so enchain the ear ;

Yet deemed it prudence not amiss
To send one simulated kiss,
Wise scout to pierce this threatening bliss,
    And glean its secrets dear.

Brave martyr kiss not idly sown,
The fruits from thy life's bounty grown,
On barren earth till then unknown,
    To paint were task profane ;
Each thought within its hoarding shell,
Like pensive nun in holy cell,
Retired delights its joys to spell,
    And half forgets its pain.

BARBARA.

" When shrunken flowers are drooping low,
When rankest weeds reluct to grow,
When road and path with dust o'erflow,
    And springs are dry ;
When wind and cloud in fetters move,
When youthful hearts are closed to love,
When fancy's wing forgets to rove,
    And joy to fly ;

" What wiser, Barbara, than to rest
Upon this hay-cock's sun-burnt breast,
And watch the sun's wheel sloping west,
    Unbending, while
The plaint of the thirsty rivulet,
Or woodpecker's stirring castanet,
Like rhyme to murmurous music set
    The hours beguile ?"

With cruel denial and delay,
And many a hint to haste away,
And learn how far advanced was day,
    The maiden spurned
My touch, then poised in act to fly,
With swift caprice of coquetry,
She on the grass sank suddenly,
    Her head half turned.

In simple lawn and lace arrayed,
From beauty's cloister never strayed
A more enchanting, colder maid,
    Fond eyes to greet,
Than she, who from her veil of pride,
By curious hand half drawn aside,
Looked on the spot, where ways divide
    And lovers meet.

Awhile her serious lips and coy
Of sacred words the charm employ
To win my hopes from earthly joy
    To regions bright ;
When suddenly the silken braid,
From which a golden ringlet strayed,
By careless touch unbound, displayed
    Its hoarded light.

Then flashed her fear-compelling eyes,
Where crystal passion's armory lies,
And glances of severe surprise
    Upon me threw ;

Nor less rebuked the heedless haste,
That did not deem the hope misplaced,
That circled half her glowing waist,
　　Rich kingdom new.

But artless beauty soon relents,
When homage, wed with penitence,
Robs justice of her last defence
　　'Gainst mercy's prayer ;
And she, whose heart all gentleness
And pity seemed, needs must confess,
Not wholly wrong it were to bless
　　Her slave's despair.

Then I, as one who hopes in fear,
" Less cruel remorse my soul would sear,
Could I but kiss away the tear,
　　That gems thy cheek ;
Grant me this grace, and poesy
With laureate immortality
Shall crown thy generous spirit high
　　And courage meek.

" For I have built a sov'reign rhyme,
That holds imprisoned Father Time,
And reigns beyond each changing clime
　　Or ether's tide ;
And Beauty's name shall rooted cling
Around earth's foaming caldron-spring,
While stars among its branches sing
　　With nobler pride."

Then she, in crafty Indian mood,
Who bids his host foretaste his food,
Before he dare pronounce it good,
    Thus praised my rhyme :
" Who wove the idle words may read,
And if his tireless step succeed,
Myself will o'er their slumbers tread,
    Some other time."

On tender lips such nettles grew,
As she her captive hand withdrew,
To fall where lay concealed from view
    A dying rose,
That, jealous of its rival's reign,
Strikes its keen spur's revengeful pain,
Where lurks snow-bound a light blue vein,
    That crimson grows.

In terror gazed the maiden round,
For where should gentle leech be found
To draw the poison from the wound,
    At dear life's cost ?
When I—ah ! could no wiser friend
To thoughtless ear true counsel lend,
As o'er the pleading stain I bend,
    My soul love-lost.

Thenceforth o'er barren mountain peak,
Whose hungry cave the wolves forsake,
Or where the ocean's thunders shake
    The desert shore,.

9

Roaming with dark bewildered mind,
I breathe her vestal name unkind,
To wandering wave or homeless wind,
    Forevermore.

ADELAIDE.

The billows breaking on the rock
    Their motion's warmth impart ;
And wilt thou ever colder mock
    The prayers that urge thy heart ?

Oh, wayward is fair Adelaide,
    As crest of dancing wave,
With sidelong glance, she smiling said :
    " What would my lovers have ?

" Do you not see this pearly shell,
    That owns each breath's control ;
But wooed however long and well,
    Yields not its perfect soul ?

" Do you not see this frolic flower
    That twinkles on the air,
Though thousand painters try their power,
    It still will show more fair ?

" O foolish bard, I was not born
    To shine for one alone :
So look no more, all love forlorn,
    But make my beauty known."

RE-RISEN.

Saintly maiden, crystal fair,
  What angel rays are shining thro' thee,
Guiding crippled faith to prayer,
  Luring sorrow's cry unto thee,
  Teaching sorrow's voice to woo thee !

By no torch of mortal fed,
  Gleam thy glances golden bright,
As love, wakening from the dead,
With trembling breath and veiling head,
  Turns again to beauty's light.

Churlish winter's reign is past,
  On each bough the birds are singing,
  Showers of music round them flinging,
" Ada, Ada, Ada, fast,
Timid love to Ada haste."

THE PENITENT.

Wearied with his former folly,
Idle Love grows melancholy,
Till to vestal vows he turns,
And like a holy candle burns.

Now his bravery cast aside,
The Church's unexpected bride,
Shut within the convent wall
He lives in prayer continual.

But to penance never born
Pale he grows and matin-worn,
And his fading roses tell,
How hard his task who worships well.

Gentle Pity, pensive nun,
Faltering in her órison,
Vainly checks the fearful sigh .
Lest the pretty novice die.

ORISON.

Dainty sister, ill it were,
Pious ear should silence prayer ;
Ill that music's voice should spurn
Echoes true, that home return.

Love, who made thy breast his home,
Vowing never thence to roam,
But beneath thy crystal eye,
Passionless on lilies lie.

Feels, alas ! his pulses beat
Feebler from the holy heat,
And his dimpling roses fade,
Till they match the lily's shade.

Till, at length, his fancies stray
Where the myrtle shadows play,
And the sacred angelus
Wakens dreams forbidden us.

Till he half forgets thy heart
Only brooks his colder art ;
And his pleading orison
Whispers to forget the nun ;

Whispers from the freezing north,
Led by him to wander forth ;
Seeking some fair island, where
Changing flowers the seasons are,

Where, Christina, thou wilt fear
Man's rebuke nor danger near,
And if heaven angry be,
Learn that heaven dwells in thee.

THE HUMMING-BIRD.

Beneath a trailing woodbine's shade,
  I saw a tiny nest,
Whose conscious thread to music laid,
  The builder's care expressed.

Around it many a scarlet flower
  A humming-bird had twined ;
To lure within his gentle bower
  His mate's inconstant mind.

Bright gem of pluméd beauty's pride,
  The Muses' ornament,
Soon will thy misty, glancing bride
  At passion's call relent.

With careful joy a wooing nest
I, too, have woven fair,
And its half-hidden portal dressed
With roses fresh and rare.

But, deaf to music's flattery,
The heart's entanglement,
My mistress mocks the plaintive cry
Of love's fond discontent.

CARPE DIEM.

Let us pleasure while we may,
Let us drink the purple day,
Foolish who sweet love delay ;

Soon will fade love's rosy dream,
Freezes soon love's dimpled stream
At the touch of winter breme ;

Or perchance, ere summer 's past,
Skies with wasting storms o'ercast
Beauty's flower untimely blast.

Seize, then sieze the golden day,
Bind the sunbeams ere they stray,
Let us pleasure while we may.

GRETCHEN.

Coy Charmer, often watched, and long,
Come fill my glass with wine ;
You cannot speak our English tongue,
Nor know I aught of thine.

Yet whisper Beauty's eyes to me
  The sweetest English spoken,
A tender, wistful melody—
  My heart is almost broken.

Fair Gretchen, fill my glass with wine,
  And whisper me again
The language of your eyes divine,
  Its mingled joy and pain.

THE NEEDLE.

What, Gretchen, are you looking for,
  With hand and eye engrossed ?
Or have you dropped upon the floor
  Your heart, or thimble lost ?

A glance like darting arrow sped,
  On snowy cheek a blush
Unfurled, like banner floating red
  Above the battle's hush.

"I had my needle in the hand,
  A moment she is gone ;
What are you for a man to stand
  And make a foolish fun !"

Abashed, her errant hand I took,
  And with it felt around
In many a crack and hollow nook,
  Where needles most abound.

Fair maid, of rips and holes the bane,
  Your fruitless search forego,
Your needle never will again
  On fairy finger glow.

Too well I know its hiding-place,
  Its thirsty point how sharp,
And soon will he, on whom it preys,
  With pain and anguish warp.

Will pity's touch the wretch reprieve?
  Nay, Gretchen, do not start ;
Your gentle touch may chance relieve
  This needle in my heart.

So full of life, so full of charm,
  Alas, she would not stay,
But with a cry of swift alarm
  Broke from my prayers away.

ABECEDARIAN.

" Your English I shall never know,
  Our time we vainly spend,
Your words all run together so,
  They seem to have no end."

Each teacher has his method wise,
  No studied plan have I ;
But looking in fair Gretchen's eyes
  I quickly made reply :

"Fair skeptic, smooth your troubled face.
    There is a cure I wis,
Before each word I 'll deftly place
    A little pause like this."

I kissed my pretty pupil once,
    She blushed and turned away ;
"Alas," she sighed, "I 'm such a dunce,
    Let us no more delay."

Oh, happy task is it to teach,
    And happy task to learn,
How sweet is our true English speech,
    And how sweet kisses burn.

Again indignant from me turned
    My pouting pupil fair,
My gentle touch with anger spurned,
    And cried in fond despair :

"Your English I shall never know,
    My time I vainly spend,
Your pauses run together so,
    They seem to have no end."

CAROL.

The floor of the frost is broken,
    The sloughs are edged with green,
The winter's farewell is spoken,
    The sky is warm and sheen.

Awake, for the birds are keeping
   Shrill school by beauty's bower,
And morning with gems is heaping
   Each spreading leaf and flower.

Awake, for no dream is telling,
   Camille, how fair thou art ;
No dream but a carol welling
   From faithful minstrel's heart.

A LITTLE WHILE.

A little while in pity smile
On him, whom fortune knows no more,
A little while, Camille, exile
   My soul from sorrow sore.

A little longer let the gleam
Of hazel eyes bewilder me,
A little longer let me dream
   Of what can never be.

Not ill I may thy smiles repay,
Nor fail of praise and linkéd rhyme,
That shall outlive the judgment-day,
   And mock the file of time.

THE MARBLE-MAID.

Beneath thy whiter breast than snow
   There beats a colder heart,
Camilla, that will colder grow
   The lovelier thou art ;

Till lip and cheek of roses bare
  Are marble as thy brow,
And thou with breath unchanging part,
  Immortal grown as fair,
And watch the generations bow
  Beneath love's tireless dart,
That pricked thy lovers to despair,
  But glanced with idle blow
From Beauty's breast untaught to care
  For mortal weal or woe.

INFLUENCE.

'I 'd liefer die than yield to love
  My vestal lips," Camilla cries ;
Then I : " May Vesta potent prove ! "
  For other guardian is there none,
But round us silvery birches rise,
  With voices eloquent of May,
And at our feet the waters moan,
And subtle shadows round us play,
And beauty's finger wreathes our seat
  With fragrant blossoms many a one,
And elves with mischief in their feet
  Blindfold the sunbeams on the wing ;
I know of nothing said or done,
  But ere the chiding cowbells ring,
Camilla sighs : " I would not miss
Of love's sweet store a single kiss."

THE BRIDGE.

Above a snow-hung bridge a gray tower stands,
  The russet hills around are winter bare,

The trees no longer join their tender hands,
  No voice of tuneful birds delights the air ;

O'erhanging rocks frown on a sullen stream,
  Whose leaden feet creep halting either way,
The grasses shudder in the frozen gleam
  Of spectral suns, that mock the dolorous day.

Why wakes the memory of this dreary scene ?
  Why thrills my heart with sudden ecstasy ?
Beloved, know, where Beauty's steps have been,
  The grave of death looks beautiful to me.

HIDDEN CAUSES.

Thou hast forgotten, Lady,
  Long since forgotten me,
And those swift hours that made me
  Forget all things but thee.

What have I thought of, Lady,
  Save one proud face divine,
And of the true love, Lady,
  I fondly dreamed was mine ?

Ofttimes I sit and wonder,
  What chance or felon fate
Our twin hearts smote asunder,
  And changed thy love to hate.

From me thou never, Lady,
  Hadst thought unkind or word,
Thy glance alone delayed me,
  Thy voice alone I heard.

Ah, has it never pained thee
  To think of the sacred vow,
The false oath that unchained thee,
  And holds me captive now?

THE PROPHET VOICE.

Frosty winter's ungentle reign
  Holds the pride of the leafless tree,
Sowing deep its unfruitful grain,
  Icy harvest of surquedry.

Dead the joy of the crested sod,
  Hushed the oriole's liquid note,
Spent the wealth of the golden-rod,
  Mute the rivulet's chiding throat ;

But defying the winter's rage
  Answers shrilly the pine-leaf brave,
Ever green in its lusty age,
  Prophet voice from the silent grave.

THE GOLDEN MAIDEN.

Between the mountain mists and sea,
  A sunny land and fair,
Sequestered, veils resplendently
  Its magic beauty rare.

The hoarding hills forget their greed
  To deck the ocean's bride ;
The rivers scatter golden seed,
  Nor tame the cornfield's pride.

But richer than old ocean's dower
   Or field of double gold,
In beauty's native land one flower
   Garners a wealth untold ;

A maiden of the wandering race
   To timid man that gave
Gods, and the gentle hope of grace
   To mount above the grave.

Her glance is winsome as the ray
   That makes the hill-tops glad,
But pensive smile and mien betray
   A lofty spirit sad.

For not unskilled is she to guess
   The heritage to her given,
The long and bitter loneliness
   Of children dear to heaven.

Past, past is many a weary day,
   And I have seen her not,
But many a year will fade away
   Ere her face be forgot.

THE STRANGER.

Maiden of the sunny glance
Tell me what divine mischance
Led the child of wine and song
Snow-bound hills and fields among.

Purple clusters of the vine,
Heavy with the stored sunshine ;
Lovelorn winds on violets fed
Still their fragrance round thee shed.

Many a true heart breathes a sigh,
Moist is many a tender eye,
That their queen of love is gone,
That the west has stolen the dawn ;

But though dear as summer day,
To the fond hearts far away,
To the cold hearts that are near,
Doubt not that thou art far more dear ;

Dearer than the ray of light
That first unlocks the polar night,
Where in double prison lie
Leaden travellers doomed to die.

LAURA.

Thy words are lame, thine acts have wings,
Whose flight as sacred perfume flings,
As follows angels' visitings,
                                        Laura.

What sunshine on thy cold lips beams !
How gracious thy coy courtesy seems !
What fire in thy proud glances gleams !
                                        Laura.

Reluctant, eager, cold, aflame,
The lightning's pride, the violet's shame,
What madness wakens at thy name !

Laura.

Though thy disdain has turned from me,
No self-born base infirmity
Shall check the worship due to thee ;

Laura.

Nor time nor absence thy sweet face,
Though reason lose her thronéd place,
From sorrow's heart shall e'er efface,

Laura.

I bring a gift of little worth,
Except to show what flowers have birth,
When love smiles on the frozen earth,

Laura.

The slave is happy who has seen
The rose he won from winter keen,
Make lovelier proud beauty's queen ;

Laura.

Thy praise, the Muses' sacred trust,
Their care shall guard from soiléd rust,
When earth shall crumble into dust ;

Laura.

THE ASTER.

Brave Aster, autumn's daisy thou,
Though hardier thy mien and brow
Than summer's fickle blossoms know.

Undaunted little sentinel,
No rustling fears thy courage quell,
Though falling leaves of winter tell ;

Yet spring nor summer's favorites own,
Nor other climes have ever known
The gorgeous splendor round thee thrown ;

When scarlet oaks and maples twine
Their flames around the fragrant pine,
Like giant growths of eglantine ;

For our brave year, untaught to yield,
With its rich life-blood stains the field,
Like Spartan borne upon his shield,

Or royal dame in castle old,
Who from her jewelled mantle's fold
Fronts threatening death with eye as bold.

Nor own'st thou less serene delight,
When richer moons with arrows bright
To silvery day turns sable night ;

Watching where fair Titania leads
Her elfin troop across the meads,
That blossom with the gold-shod steeds ;

Their mystic shade the oak leaves fling,
Light dancers o'er the greensward spring,
With laughter shrill the copses ring ;

The squirrel answers from the brake ;
From lurking socket peeps the snake ;
The owls their strange flight homeward take

But ill it were thy constant eye
Should see the swallow southward fly,
Or faithful robin frozen lie ;

So happier in thy sacred death,
Go thou to join the joyous wreath,
That dies to live in beauty's breath.

SOUL-SONG.

Thy foot is on a nameless grave,
  But well thy sorrow knows,
O'er whom the cypress branches wave,
  The dew-strung brier grows.

A love untold grows never old,
  And he, who slumbers here,
In silence chained to marble cold
  A voice for beauty's ear.

And this imprisoned soul of song,
  Whose echo stirs thy heart,
And with the grave's uncheating tongue
  Betrays how fair thou art,

Will often sway thy wayward pride,
  That scorns the state of kings,
And win thy secret steps aside,
  Where death to beauty sings.

PLAYMATES.

How well do I remember,
  Could Lethe well forget ?
My winsome cousin Genie,
  And Liza, nature's pet !

The romping games, the struggles,
  The truce or rapid flight,
The pouting lips that slowly
  Repeat their long good-night.

May Time, who burdens others,
  Make light their golden hours,
And steal from every garden
  To strew their path with flowers !

INDIRECTION.

What willow branch is swinging
  Against the window pane ?
What rose-bush round me flinging
  Its buds like crimson rain ?

Is fitful lightning breaking
  Upon the troubled night ?
Or cheating fancy waking
  My dream with beauty's light ?

Oh, face that envy praises !
　　Oh, haunting form divine !
Who on Elise once gazes
　　Must slumber's joys resign.

ELIZE.

Fair face of many a gentle heart the bane,
　　Forget the sighs that round you breathe,
Forget, Elize, the crown of pain,
　　That beauty's fingers wreathe.

If you must grieve, is it not cause enough
　　That future years will miss a face,
No goddess old gave promise of,
　　And time cannot replace ?

With faithful pencil day and night I sit
　　Unheeding other thought or care,
So may I by art's counterfeit
　　Save ages from despair.

IMPERSONAL.

" Who broke the vase ? " a lady said ;
　　Her child, with dripping dress,
Hung down her curly, little head :
　　" It broke, mamma, I guess,"

That night another daughter fair
　　Beside the window stood,
Forgetful what fond lovers dare,
　　What foolish feats and rude.

"You foolish girl," her mother cried,
" Why did you not resist ? "
My Beauty hung her head and sighed :
" Mamma, mamma, it kissed."

SORROW'S SWEETHEART.

Has your fancy now and then
Wandered to the season when,
Sorrow's Sweetheart, day on day
Love-bound in your bower I lay ?
Since those hours of morning bright
I have vanished into night,
From the were-wolf begged my bread,
Warmed with adder's breath my bed,
Living seen the thief and knave
With dishonor brand my grave ;
Yet how gladly would I add
Ill to ill and worse to bad,
Could I from misfortune's hold
Win my pretty playmate old ;
Could I fashion pathway meet
For the footing of her feet ;
Feet too small to tread alone
Dusty road and flinty stone,
Framed like Ate's soft to walk
On the heads of men, or talk
With the blossoms silken field
Or enchanted hill-side yield.
Kindly wishes, that remain
Wishes, are not all in vain,

Or the truth ambiguous
Changing fortune teaches us ;
Light and shadow come and go,
Ill from good, and joy from woe
Spring, and soon, as morn to night,
Grief shall lead you to delight,
Ellen, such the gentle prayer
Wings its way to heaven, where
Prayers, 't is whispered, sometimes find
Patient ear and answer kind.

SMILE AND SIGH.

Pensive Ellen, sitting lone,
Listening to the grasses' moan
Is this the gentle girl I knew,
Who bashfully to beauty grew,
And like rosebud, reluctant to bloom,
Filled with perfume the cloister of home ?

Love for beauty's eyeless feet
Baits his trap with promise sweet ;
Relentless love, that fair and young
Forgives not, bound you with his thong,
And your heart, torn with grief and despair,
To the beak of the tempest laid bare.

Flower to far Wisconsin blown,
Seated in your room alone,
What ails you, that with glad surprise
You press your heart, uplift your eyes,
And with glances expectant and bright
From the window look into the night ?

Sunken years and miles across,
Laughing blossoms round you toss ;
The salt air tingles in your vein,
Your island days come back again,
And the meadow, the pathway and tree
Re-awake at the voice of the sea.

Double love is double pain,
Slowly joyous pictures wane,
Your cold Lethean footsteps creep,
Where dimpled jailers careless sleep,
And you look with a smile and a sigh
On your children, the prairie and sky.

BOS.

I wandered o'er the daisied mead ;
Bloomed never spring so fair ;
My steps on perfumed grasses tread ;
The birds rejoice the air.

Beneath an oak tree sinking down
Soon fast asleep I lay ;
I dreamed I won a golden crown
And fairer queen than day.

An honest, worthy ox passed by,
And placed its foot upon me ;
Now crushed in bleeding pain I lie,
And all good people shun me.

A RECALCITRANT BARD.

To-day the sainted Washington
Was born, and glistening in the sun,
The broker, trader, bootblack, thief
To bursting purses grant relief,
From bar to groaning table fly,
Shark-gulleted and desert-dry.
And must I, life's poor counterfeit,
With broken pencil rhyming sit,
Or from my bare-bones of a room
Watch velvet dress and nodding plume?
Cruel Muse, put out thy cheating spark,
An angel guide to dungeon dark.

THE POET.

Who with truer eye has won
A beauty from the skeleton?
Who with touch of gentle hand
Drawn water from the thirsty sand?
Who from midnight's cavern deep
Lured the morning rose to peep?
Who from evil misery wooed
The spirit of a higher good?
Who with royal faith would light
The sleeping ocean's fiery might,
In honor of a sacred name,
Wrapping the baser world in flame,

Yet with careful tread o'erpass
A glowworm lurking in the grass?
Much of love and more of sorrow,
His unthinking heart will borrow.

THE HOUR.

It is the hour, it is the hour,
Of hoarding time the crowning flower,
When my lady's loyal feet
Promise their poor slave to greet ;
She is coming, fairer queen,
Than mortal eye has ever seen,
Moving form of majesty,
Clothed with light from Venus' eye ;
She, whose slightest glance to gold
Turns my mouldy chamber old,
Turns to joy celestial
A heart that sorrow holds in thrall ;
See, upon the table stand
Flowers impatient for her hand ;
Five sweet roses Bonzaline,
Mirror of her lips divine ;
Violets that the florist says,
Blossom but twice seven days ;
Gentle gift to one, whose love
Twice seven centuries will prove ;
Fair flowers that all my breakfast be,
For poets banquet thriftily.
It is the hour, it is the hour,
With hopes immortal brimming o'er ;

Soon swift arms will interlace
In one passionate embrace ;
Soon the dainty joiner kiss
Will unite two hearts in bliss ;
Soon will lips love burdened stain
Snowy neck in crimson grain ;
Soon, twin blossoms of one sun,
Soul and soul will melt in one ;
Peace my swiftly beating heart,
How importunate thou art !
The hour is come, the hour is gone,
How slow each minute loiters on ;
Harsh upon my nervous ear
Grate the footsteps drawing near ;
Hateful grows each form I see,
Cheating my far straining eye ;
With sudden pang my heart is fed,
Is my sweetheart sick or dead ?
Or has she grown, ah, jealous fear,
Indifferent to her lover's tear?
Armed doubts around me steal,
Stab on stab their poignards deal ;
Has she heedless grown of one,
Who drinks delight from her alone ?
Faint my knees grow, mute my heart,
From each pore the blood-drops start ;
Lifeless with despair I lie,
Weltering in groan and sigh ;
Kind Heaven ! thee my anguish prays,
Spur cripple Death, if Love delays.

THE LAST SIGH.

I loved a maiden,
  Fairer never seen,
Beauty-overladen,
  Nature's peerless queen.

From her honied breath
  Life itself I drew,
Dreaming not that death
  'Mid her kisses grew.

- Lifeless now I lie,
  Love- and hope-forsaken,
Cannot love's last sigh
  Memories fond awaken ?

APRIL-HEARTED.

More constant than a woman's eye
The leaf that frets the winter sky,
  Or foam on mountain stream,
Or shadow flitting fitfully
  O'er haunted midnight's dream.

The golden sunbeams level flew,
The grass was wet with morning dew,
  I looked in Beauty's face ;
She swore : " I love but only you
  Through honor and disgrace."

But ere the bending grass had dried,
Or on her ear my foostep died,
   Forgotten was her oath ;
Upon another's breast she sighed :
   " I cannot love you both."

Go, get ye gone, ye womankind,
For who so foolish hopes to find
   Of all fair charmers one,
Whom love, however true, ean bind
   From morn to setting sun ?

LAMIA.

Thy softer glance than soft starlight
   Shines ever pure and true ;
Thy lips are roses joyous night
   Has freshly bathed in dew ;
Thy breast like sacred temple shows,
With pity heaves, with feeling glows ;
But in thy heart half dead with cold,
There lurks a wrinkled serpent old.

THE CYNIC.

" Within each human heart there lies
   A germ of beauty infinite,
That with awakening power replies
   To him, who feeds its growth aright."

I said, and heedless of return,
   My substance, thought and action brave
To all, who cared the truth to learn,
   As brother unto brother gave.

The friends I honored held my trust
  Their profit and a fool's deceit,
For who would trust us surely must,
  They argued, be a simple cheat ;

Thenceforth in honors ripe they grow,
  Still gather rain from others' drouth,
Still gather bliss from others' woe,
  Still gather food from hunger's mouth.

And as they bless with thievish hand
  The name of gentle Charity,
Their flattered victims round them stand
  With grateful heart and bended knee.

But I, to flatter the great herd,
  The gilded and the naked swine,
Have taught a philosophic bird
  To sing : "Enjoy your sty divine."

VAULTING PRESUMPTION.

Unwholesome tank of lying breath,
Aspiring to be saved from death,
And, lodged within revengeful verse,
Immortal grow beneath my curse :

Yourself, my viper friend, must be
Of your own infamy the trustee ;
The force, your ingrate slander spends,
To crystal heights my fancy sends.

GRATEFUL.

No troubles of my own I had,
When I was young, to make me sad ;
And were a friend but ill at ease,
I crawled upon my hands and knees
And begged I might his humor nurse
With helping hand and open purse ;
But now that care has found me out,
And all my hopes in utter rout,
My grateful friends, with faces black,
Have clubbed and hired for me—a rack.

THE MOURNER.

"At our own father's funeral,
    In gay attire, with griefless eye,
In insult of the sable pall,
Is this my brother's voice I hear?"
    Then I : "Weep not for those who lie
    In silent death's long dreamless sleep ;
The cypress and the mourner's tear
    The living claim ; for them I weep ;
    I weep for youth's high hope betrayed
By masking law and lying seer,
    For love on wanton's bosom laid,
    For simple faith from fireside flown,
For fetters cheap and freedom dear,
    For honest labor lackey grown,
And living men their worshippers,
Whose very thoughts are sepulchres."

A REVERT.

Five years and more a friend of mine
Waxed famous as a broad divine,
All worshipped him, although his creed
Was nothing more than greed, greed, greed ;
Had he in Judas' shoes been placed,
He would have felt himself disgraced,
And why, because he asked no gold,
And all too cheap the Saviour sold.
His church, his pockets and his flow
Of words grew opulent, when lo,
A miracle ! this soul-destroyer
From priest repented into lawyer ;
And then, O shame, when he became
No hypocrite, he lost his fame.

MY HOST.

A poet's fancy chanced to glint on
The great unclassified John Swinton ;
And strove to find, if find it could,
Within the chaff a grain of good,
And found, what priests may well abhor,
John little cares for th' abstract poor ;
But with the beggar loves to share
His purse and dish no less than prayer ;
Prefers, believe it those who can,
A broken to a flawless man ;
Would rather far an outcast know
Than whom the flies of fortune blow ;

And tireless prods the wise and good
To leave their selfish solitude,
To see mankind with human eyes
And turn this earth to paradise.
These marks are homely, but they make
The very gates of heaven shake,
And Peter's self begin to doubt
The policy of barring out.

A DENTIST'S TEAR.

What tongue will praise the poor and old?
What muse her peddler's pack unfold
   To deck their silvery slips?
Our mawkish verses can but speak
Of ringlet brown and vermeil cheek,
   Bright eyes and rosy lips.

To-day, before a sun-burnt house,
Begirt with buzzing linden boughs,
   I saw a wrinkled dame
With ague-stricken needle strive
From time's deep wounds to keep alive
   A garment none can name.

A dentist I, and toothless she:
" Good dame," I cried, " well met are we ;
   Will you not buy some teeth?"
She turned her head a little, then
Attacking her forked task again,
   Replied with scanty breath :

" 'T would take it from the childer, sir ;
'T is not for long I shall be here,

My life is almost spent ;
'T is true I 've lost full many a bite,
The boys have often argered it,
 But I will not consent."

I smiled to hear her quaint reply,
But from my heart-root rose a sigh,
 I vainly tried to smother.
Dull men, I thought, love maiden's charm,
The slender waist, the rounded arm,
 But angels love a mother.

M. W. H.

A shipwrecked mariner I roamed
 Beside the shingly beach,
The creeping breakers hungry foamed
 Their prisoner's flight to reach.

Sadly I mourned a gentle friend,
 Whose parting form I saw
Snatched from the wreck by mocking fiend,
 And hurled to ocean's maw.

When from a cave beside the sea
 I heard a silvery voice,
That swayed with royal melody
 The billow's soulless noise.

There by fair Circe's music lulled,
 His brow with myrtle bound,
On roses from the sunset culled,
 My happy friend I found.

10

" Sweet sorceress, was thine the charm
   That swelled the masking wave,
Compelling to thy kisses warm
   This truant from the grave ?

"And thou, my friend, whose prouder thought
   With mine close woven grew,
And night and day to beauty wrought
   Truth's changeless figures new,

" As brave thy youth so peaceful be
   Thy generous manhood blessed,
While changed to true Penelope
   Fond Circe soothes thy breast.

" Though I, upon the crested foam,
   Again with tempests ride,
Forever in my heart thy home
   And its sweet song abide."

NIGHT.

The tangled grass my footstep bars ;
   The fire-fly blinking wooes its mate ;
Above me shine the constant stars ;
   The new moon gems its eastern gate ;

But never ray of heaven-born light,
   Nor earth-love's kindling beam shall bloom
Upon the endless, joyless night,
   That wraps my heart's forsaken tomb.

J. B.

Your voice, fair Lady, thrilled an ear
  Unused to words of praise,
And breathed the soft enchantment dear,
  I knew in happier days.

The words, engraved on heart of stone,
  Endure when others fade ; ·
And still I read each thought and tone
  By sorrow's ear waylaid.

A FRESH INK-STAND.

Five miles, with unabated breath,
We 'd stepped from red Elizabeth,
A slender nymph, as blithe and gay
As sunbeam dancing on its way,
And I a God-forgive-me-creature
Distingushed by no special feature.
At length, we heard a waterfall,
And careless followed music's call ;
An inch the cascade leaped ; " Oh, where,"
My charmer cried, " are scenes so fair ?
Awhile forget cold culture's art,
And dip your pen in Nature's heart."

L'ENNUYÉE.

I sat within a house of gold,
A room adorned with pictures old,
And furniture of choicer kind
Than gilded idlers toil to find ;
Proud carvings rare, and cushions deep,
Might charm the Argus gout asleep ;
But never sign of printed thing
Its friendly features offering,
And mused : '' What poverty of mind
With riches evermore we find ! ''
But on the sofa chanced to look,
And saw with larger eyes a book
Myself had written ; infinite
Remorse confused with fond delight
Awoke at knowledge of the wrong
Unweeting done my friends and song,
And tired of caustic argument,
I rose and toward the window went ;
There, pricking the rich curtain thro',
A sunbeam my attention drew,
Sad witness, with what careful craft
A mining moth had sunk his shaft ;
'' Brave moth ! '' then I, '' thy thievish name
Has power to heal the shuttle lame ;
And why, if starving workmen bless
Thy labor, should my song do less ?
Thou brilliant little socialist,
Thou bright, untamed misogynist !

And yet, like poet thou at last,
In beauty's flame swift ending hast."
I sighed, but heard an answering sound,
As music's wing had kissed the ground,
And felt a presence sweet as dawn,
When twilight's vail is half withdrawn ;
Yet needed eye nor ear to tell
The step fond memory knows so well,
Within my heart such echoes dear
Proclaim my lovely lady near ;
And teach me on my face are bent
Her eyes of beauty redolent ;
Then, as my hand her touch delayed,
I showed the moth's ungentle raid,
But watching saw no muscle stir,
And thought : " Alas, what aileth her ? "
And eager questioned her upon
Her frolic step and laughter gone,
Or caused by pretty spaniel strayed,
Or lover forward or afraid.
My Beauty then with languid air
Unbosomed all her heart's despair ;
The ball and concert tiresome grown,
And stupid visit never done ;
Her life to dull proprieties
Addressed, and fashion's witless lies.
" Oh, might I break convention's chain,
And to my studies turn again,
And every precious moment give,
With widening aim inquisitive,
To learn the shaping powers that deep
In heart and nature hiding keep."

Then I : " Coy April maiden bright,
To music moulded of delight,
In me the charms of cheating sense
Awaken but indifference,
But who the philosophic mind
In beauty's darling hopes to find ?"
" And must I, then, as dull become
As those dull friends that haunt our home?
Yourself know all life's wandering ways,
The censure of mankind and praise,
Yet some mysterious wisdom hold,
That makes you in misfortune bold,
And careless, save to find the thought,
That has your good or evil wrought.
Teach me that subtle spell, for I
Am tired of dull prosperity."
Then urging many a glance invasive,
With whisper wistful and persuasive,
She forced me take a golden lyre,
That trembled with her beauty's fire :
From beauty's hand the lyre I took,
With fearful joy my bosom shook,
Till, as who bold with terror fly,
Where thicker dangers round them lie,
With glance uplifted swift upon
Her beauty's inspiration,
I looked, the strings with ardor pressed,
And to her soul my soul confessed.

SAIDA.

Oh, loved for other charms than those
    That mould thy faultless face ;
Oh, fairer than the mystic rose,
    That o'er thy bosom plays !
Sweet maid, whose soul in beauty breaks,
As amber light the water wakes.

Not mine the joy that others know,
    Who drink thy loveliness,
Or wrapt in music languid grow,
    Beneath thy song's caress ;
Not mine through every vein to feel
The trembling flame of passion steal ;

Yet, Saida, who of all the throng,
    That whisper thee divine,
Would dare so much thy spirit wrong,
    As match his love with mine,
Who know no other Heaven than thee,
Yet never hope that Heaven to see ?

Perforce with sorrow's subtle art
    Each cloistering feeling pure,
Each hidden thought that moves thy heart,
    Within my night I lure,
Until, through mist of blinding tears,
Thy sacred self of self appears.

Oh, airy step, as burdensome
　　As morning's budding beam
To hopeless haunter of the tomb,
　　Again into my dream,
Enchanted vision, creep again,
And look in sorrow on my pain.

PASSING.

I saw her face, its look of grace
　　To fancy's eye is near,
Though circling days their shadows chase,
　　And year succeeds to year.

Her breast of snow, with joy aglow,
　　The touch of her winged hand,
What miser but would beggar go,
　　Could he their wealth command!

It might not be, her footstep free
　　In music died away,
And left me but a memory
　　To haunt me and waylay,

THE FAKIR.

Wherefore art thou sitting lone,
Dumb as monumental stone,
Beard and hair knit with the dust,
Soul and body cased with rust,
Heedless of the rival throng
Love and business pour along?

" Stranger, trouble not my gloom,
Truth in silence seeks its home,
Mix your spirit with the clod,
Thus alone you worship God."

HOW LONG !

I wake with music in my ear,
Alas, alas, he is not near ;
My stricken bosom bleeds anew
To think how kind he was, and true ;
Alone I weep, I weep alone,
And pray for day, till night is gone,
And pray for night, till day is past,
And wish each moment were my last.
I look upon my youth and sigh,
It takes so long to live or die.
Around me stand with rooted wing
Fair mournful shapes unpitying,
Fond Memory with averted eye,
Forgetful Hope and Constancy,
And silent Love, with smiles as bright,
As those that fed my soul with light ;
O husband, stretch through sorrow's door
Thy hand, and bid me grieve no more !

ITS MATE.

When first I saw your face, alack !
My hair was braided down my back :
I met you as this stream you sought ;
I saw the silly fishes caught ;

Ah, simple girl ! well might I then
Have known the subtle craft of men ;
But no, for I was of your kind,
And where in nature will you find,
Excepting man, the good and great,
One creature preying on its mate ?

INDISCREET.

With listening step my lady creeps,
Through door and hall, where silence sleeps ;
Within her lover's chamber stands,
And breathless gropes with eyeless hands ;
Her warm lips press his laggard ear ;
"Stone cold !" she shrieks with heedless fear,
Upon the guilty pillow falls,
And on her murdered lover calls :
Poor heart, could none this counsel give,
Though lovers perish, scandals live.

DISENCHANTMENT.

I sat me down at a Christmas feast,
  With rosy wine cups crowned,
And like a garland many a guest
  The noble banquet bound.

A raven on a sheltered bough
  A moment stayed its flight ;
"All love," it sang, "is but the glow
  Of mouldering bones at night !"

I turned to every loving friend,
  Dear as the realms above,
To bid them mock the ghostly fiend
  With words of holy love.

Where knights and blooming maidens shone,
  What horror meets my eye?
In every seat a skeleton
  Is grinning vacantly.

Ghastly their eyeless sockets stare;
  Their teeth together make
A sound at which the frozen air
  With palsy seems to shake.

A sudden madness seized my brain;
  I fled into the night;
Lives there a voice to win again
  A lost soul to the light?

LILY.

Unseen, I watched a little maid,
  Of sportive grace untold,
Around whose head the sunbeams played,
  And mingled gold with gold,
She looked her name, a Lily fed
  By golden-rod and rose;
But hark! how fast o'er coral bed
  Her sober prattle flows.

"O Dolly, what a fearful fall!
  What shall I, shall I do?

I 'll run and Doctor Gimcrack call ;
   He 'll cook a pill for you.
Look, Doctor, at her broken head,
   Her legs how mighty weak !
' Put Sukey Doughnut quick to bed,
   And tell her not to speak.'

" Now let this be a lesson, Miss,
   Don't clamber up the shelf ;
Well, never mind, Love, there 's a kiss ;
   I once was young myself.
Don't, Sukey, look so dead afraid,
   You 've often heard how I,
On mother's bed was fainting laid,
   Not many months gone by ;

" They painted me with iodine,
   And day and night and day
My mother's eyes were fixed on mine,
   Like stars that watch and pray "—
Thus deep in biographic lore
   The child her tale began,
When glancing from the darkened floor,
   She saw a stranger man.

With elfish scream, through door and hall
   And kitchen Lily sped ;
The cook her startled knife let fall,
   The blade half through the bread,
And followed fast, till on the stairs
   They found us one and three,
All screaming, though the cook declares
   Earth holds no braver she.

The bread was cut, the tale alas !
 Unfinished must remain,
Though but half-told a power it has
 To make me young again.
Fair daughter of as gentle race,
 As sports beneath the sun,
Soon from your charms that grow apace
 The bravest youth may run.

THE SANDS OF DEAL.

Oh, say have you seen the lady,
 Once seen forever loved,
Whose gentle glance betrayed me
 To sweet hopes unreproved,
 To sweet hopes unreproved,
That I could not all conceal,
 As in beauty's light she moved
Across the sands of Deal ?

I looked on the sacred shore
 And the breakers rolling high,
I heard their angry roar
 In veiling music die,
 In veiling music die,
Till their echo sadder grew,
 Than aught but the broken sigh,
That bade my queen adieu.

MUTE.

Would, Lady, thy poor servant might
　Thy beauty's worth express,
But all the long and sleepless night
　No words love's longing bless.

The gifts are thine of gentle birth
　To noble nature wed ;
A grateful pride by modest mirth
　And vital feeling fed.

But as beneath thy voice's sway
　To life all objects grow,
Mute lies the troubled heart that may
　Too well its sentence know.

MY REMNANT HOPE.

Cruel Love, why rob me of my sleep,
　My remnant hope, that dreams may lend
My Lady's face to eyes that weep
　Unhallowed absence without end ?

The moon's empurpled loveliness
　Infolds each sleeping leaf and flower,
And ministering angels bless
　With silvery touch the sacred hour.

But these dull eyes, whose fatal sight
　Beheld the veil of heaven withdrawn,
Inherit now the night of night,
　The ashes of a golden dawn.

THE WRECK.

"Oh why are your lips so pale,
  And your eyes so far away,
Like one who watches a sail
  Dissolve in the ocean gray.;
Who watches a shadowy sail,
  Till the sky and the waters meet,
Till his famished glances fail,
  And his heart forgets to beat?"

A little month has gone,
  Since far from the busy haunts
Of men I wandered on,
  As pleasure's call might chance ;
Heart-free I wandered on
  In the strength of the purple spring,
Forgetful of winter wan
  And the changes the seasons bring.

Till a bank my footsteps stayed
  With flowers and mosses o'ergrown,
Where sloping pines waylaid
  The songs from the ocean blown,
  The songs from the ocean blown,
That won through the fading mist,
  Like the laughter and tender moan
Of a goddess by mortal kissed.

And a cottage stood by the sea,
  In vines and roses dressed,
And a voice spake unto me,
  " I give thee food and rest."
A cottage stood by the sea,
  And I knew that dwelling bright,
By music fashioned to be
  The homestead of delight.

There many an idle day
  From toiling time I stole,
And of nature's passion-play
  Unravelled the mystic scroll ;
There many an idle day
  I summoned the wave and the wind,
Of half-built sonnet and lay
  The scattered rhymes, to bind.

And ever a stately Lady
  Before me in beauty moved,
And a glance in pride arrayed me,
  A glance and a voice beloved,
  A winsome voice beloved,
By music's fountain fed,
  That to sweet hopes unreproved
My timid fancy led.

'T is a merry morning in June,
  And the nodding daisies white,
And the waves and winds in tune
  Our wandering feet invite ;

'T is a merry morning in June,
  And far o'er the sands we stray,
And the morning and afternoon
  In beauty pass away.

Till a wreck our footsteps find,
  Like a drifting cage that lies
For the wing of the wandering wind
  And the restless ocean's sighs,
  For the restless ocean's sighs,
That change to a bridal song,
  As my Lady's soft replies
The sunset hour prolong.

On the gunwale her whiter hands
  Than the flitting sea-foam rest,
But, like steadfast nun, she stands,
  In sweet self-sorrow dressed ;
She stands like a steadfast nun,
  But, who looks upon my face,
May guess what hope has won
  My heart for its hiding-place.

What man is beauty's friend,
  For ever a longing sweet
And a subtle passion blend
  With that fair name incomplete ?
What man is beauty's friend,
  Or my Lady's face may see,
Nor fear what the bitter end
  Of treacherous joy shall be ?

Then I sighed : " Might a magic hand
   This windowed wreck remould,
And launch from the greedy sand
   New-heartened its timbers old,
And launch from its sandy grave
   Its sail on the swelling blast,
That warps the whitening wave
   And the strength of the gallant mast,

" Would Beauty across the foam
   With her faithful lover wend,
To music's classic home,
   Where summer forgets to end ;
In music's sacred home
   To watch the Tiber sweep
Past turret, arch, and dome
   From the clouds to the dark blue deep ?

" Where the lily sighs to the rose
   And the rose to the lily sighs :
' Again shall our petals close
   Unblessed of beauty's eyes ? '
   Where the rose to the lily sighs :
' Will the fairest never come
   From the frosts of alien skies
To the flowers of her Southern home ? ' "

At the words o'er my Lady's face,
   A tremulous love wave steals,
That with lips and lashes plays,
   And a hidden joy reveals,

And a hidden joy reveals,
That apparels the air in fire,
Till the heart of the ocean feels
The warmth of love's desire.

From the vessel she lightly stept,
And her cheek with blushes burned,
As, like novice in love adept,
Her face from my own she turned ;
Her face from my own she turned,
But my lips to her warm lips stole,
And my heart love's rubric learned,
And my soul was at one with her soul.

But she spoke with averted face,
And her voice was full of tears :
" Oh, love's short hour of grace !
Oh, sorrow's burden of years !
Oh, love's short hour of grace !
For thou knowest how dear thou art,
Thou knowest the love that sways
And for ever will sway my heart.

" Is thy love as strong to forgive,
As my own is to feel remorse,
You have asked me to love and live ;
I have poisoned your life at its source ;
I have poisoned your life at its source,
For my secret from thee has been hidden,
I am linked to a living corse,
And our love is a thing forbidden."

As my ears the poison drank,
    My life-breath turned to a moan,
My knees beneath me sank,
    And my heart grew cold as stone ;
My ears the poison drank,
    And, as one who listens and dies,
I fell on the rushes dank,
    And the mist drew over my eyes.

I lie on the beach alone,
    Crushed under the wheel of the night,
" Beloved ! thou art not gone,
    Speak ! speak ! thou voice of delight ;
Beloved ! thou art not gone,
    Come back, come back again !
Oh, lift me from my swoon,
    Oh, kiss away my pain ! "

The worms would not suffer me sleep,
    Though wrapt in lead I lay,
In a hollow grave and deep,
    That returned not the echoes of day;
The worms would not suffer me sleep,
    And I heard a whisper low : .
" Well, well may the lady weep,
    Who wrought this nameless woe.

" See how proudly in gallant trim
    Her vessel is bearing away ;
Does she think, I wonder, of him
    To the shifting sands a prey ? "

To the shifting sands a prey.
But I saw from my hollow grave
A lessening sail that lay
Cold, cold on the steely wave.

But again my heart-pulse beat,
And the fire in my bosom burned,
Again to my listless feet
The wandering paths returned ;
Again with my listless feet
I sought the unmeaning strife,
Where the headless herd compete
For the shadowy crowns of life.

Then I thought of a dream of fame,
That my yester-life had known,
Ere the cruel love-sorrow came,
And the joy to madness grown ;
The thought of a vision of fame,
Like a breath from the Northwind's lair,
Smote my languid bosom with flame,
And rebuked my youth's despair.

But Fame, can Fame's silvery tongue
Win open the gates of the past,
Reorder an ancient wrong
And the ways of the hours recast ?
Can proud Fame's silvery tongue,
Or the gods that live under its word,
Give life to a vanished song
In the lingering twilight heard ?

And yet no stranger I came
　　To misfortune, whose arrows knew
The chosen mark of my name,
　　Ere my years to manhood grew ;
No stranger to ill I came,
　　Nor to treacherous riches flown,
To my churlish kinsmen's blame,
　　And my friend to serpent grown.

But not winter's swift spur broken
　　In my naked side unfed,
Nor the slanders my friend had spoken,
　　As I drew him alive from the dead,
　　As I drew him alive from the dead,
To poison the light and the air,
　　Could match with one sweet moment fled,
Save as pleasures to heighten despair.

And I reach out my arms to the night,
　　To the night of the noontide sun :
"Speak ! speak ! thou voice of delight ;
　　Beloved, thou art not gone ;
　　Beloved, thou art not gone
Across the pitiless sea,
　　And thy lover weeping alone,
Weeping and dying for thee."

WAVE AND SHORE.

A bird sang over the crested wave,
    Proud lady, with glance so warm,
O follow, follow thy lover brave,
    Where none can follow or harm ;
Fly, fly to the golden Orient,
    Where seasons wax nor wane,
Where love, with gentle love content,
    The past forgets and pain.

A bird sang over the wave ;
    A bird sang on the shore ;
O follow thy lover brave,
O follow thy lover brave—
    Farewell for evermore.

A bird sang on th' unchanging shore,
    A wedded wife art thou,
And duty's voice persuades thee more
    Than lover's weal or woe ;
Forget, forget the tender song,
    That won thy thoughtless ear ;
Forget the feelings deep and strong,
    That drew your hearts so near.

A bird sang over the wave,
    A bird sang on the shore ;
O follow thy lover brave—
    Farewell for evermore ;
    Farewell for evermore.

THE STOKER.

What seek you, earth-born Lords, with one,
Who holds his patent from the Sun,
Who knows that life and death are naught,
But light and shadow of one thought,
One constant power, one linkéd wave,
Half seen and half within the grave?
Go, mouthing knaves, your thunder pour,
And make the world discordant roar,
And, when the earth's brief course is run,
I 'll toss the cinder on the Sun.

WANDERER.

Wild wanderer of the night,
What spurs thy careless flight ;
Dost thou not fear the net
By death and foemen set ?

" Of foeman naught I reck,
Nor death avoid nor seek ;
As friends, thick dangers lie
Round him undoomed to die."

Wild wanderer of the night,
What seeks your restless flight ;
Or wealth of hoarding gold,
Or glory's charm untold ?

" I seek what roses blow
Beneath the white plumed snow ;
I seek what flame lies hid
Beneath the billow's lid."

Wild wanderer of the night,
Stay, stay thine idle flight ;
Soft lips that sigh, " Return,"
For thee with kisses burn.

" Away, no homely joy
My spirit's hope shall cloy ;
Who wills, may fare with me
To forest-lair or sea."

DEL TEMPO FELICE.

My sorrow, like an ill-made dress,
  About me clings and dulls
All sights and sounds of loveliness,
  That nature's magic culls ;

In vain the birds of April sing,
  Or bloom the flowers in June,
No messages to me they bring,
  My heart is out of tune ;

I float on summer's dreamy tide,
  Or read the gorgeous rhyme,
That paints the forest's changing pride
  In autumn's golden prime ;

And think of pleasures long since fled,
 Of words unkindly spoken,
Of loving thoughts, alas ! unsaid,
 And ties too tender broken.

LEAP YEAR.

O turn aside and sit down here,
 And tell me, sweet Nineteen,
What sounds were those of frolic fear,
 That stole across the green ?

'T was sportive April's silvery tide,
 The frost-flowers round us snowed,
But like the flower of Summer's pride
 My prairie Beauty glowed.

In vain her fettered thoughts she spurred,
 The words all came up missing,
Like lissome Lamia, when she heard
 The fond familiar hissing.

At length new courage summoning,
 Her voice in music woke :
" We girls were playing bull-in-the-ring
 Around the school-house oak."

Now though the gossips may have their fling,
 And fog-horn censors croak,
What harm in playing bull-in-the-ring
 Around the school-house oak ?

But when I promised to be dumb,
  She whispered a word so sweet, '
Jove would have whipped Europa home,
  To catch but the shadow of it.

COMMON SENSE.

Banish idle poets,
  The world will love the light,
If their fancy's voice
  Woo not from the right :

Stolen rays from heaven
  Darken common life ;
Stolen dreams of peace
  Set our hearts at strife :

With life's honest toil
  Be our souls content ;
To the simple truth,
  Be our purpose lent.

THE GLOVE.

Prithee answer, dainty Glove,
His name, who asks is harmless Love,
Where thy tenant's footsteps rove.

Once within this citadel
Beauty's regent deigned to dwell,
A vestal in her sacred cell.

Warden thou of timid mind
Not with fetters swift to bind
The peerless prize that lures mankind,

That monarchs might with jewels strew
Thy threshold, or with kingdom sue
The sacred treasure once to view.

Nothing now so proud or vain,
But would deem its touch a stain,
Where such visitant has lain.

Yet my wing reluctantly
Craves with strange infirmity
To nestle in this nunnery,

And in every nook to slip
A lurking kiss, whose poisoned lip
Shall wound each truant finger-tip.

THE POET IDOL.

My gentle lady Palatine,
　　Tell me what sorrow has made thee grieve,
Or dimmed thy matchless glance divine,
　　Fed with the beauty the starbeams give.

A slave to comb thy silken hair,
　　Blackamoor proud af his tiny god,
A scribe to make each word his care,
　　Gardener to glean where thy steps have trod,

And what no other queen, thou hast,
  Poet that sings not for honor or gain
Thy praise in words that will outlast
  Palace of marble or hallowed fane.

The laureate bards for wine and gold
  Barter their birthright of sacred song,
But liefer I on vinegar old
  Nourished, than nature and beauty wrong.

Of living sov'reigns thou alone,
  Rulest the ocean, the wind, and the star,
By title the gods cannot disown,
  Won from the glory of nature's war,

THE RATTLESNAKE.

Thine only hope a memory sweet,
Why, foolish heart, so wildly beat?
Is it the midnight's mystic hour,
When buried thoughts renew their power,
That summons up a vision bright,
Lit by the torch of lost delight?
A winding stream of silvery sheen,
A jutting bank with hazels green;
Around, fair hills with waving crest,
In beauty's calm and music drest,
A place as fancy's pencil rare,
Of nature's choice the sov'reign fair;
Fashioned for the mellow time,
When day and night are set to rhyme,
And masking shadows wavering run
Between the balanced moon and sun;

A spot, where lovely maid would choose,
Unwise, her homeward path to lose ;
A spot, where prudent maid should pray
No gentle lover hidden lay.
But ah ! fond youth, untaught to guess
What danger lurks in loveliness,
Already in that wayward place
I see a peerless maiden's face !
Who, heedless of the closing flower,
That warns her of love's treacherous power,
The silence lends of heart and ear
A lover's idle tale to hear ;
How from the thirsty mountain side
A snake uncoiled its fatal pride,
And crept a living spring to taste,
That like an eye a cottage graced,
Where dwelt a maid, proud nature's child,
In freedom's beauty undefiled,
The only prop of aged sire,
His hand, foot, eye, his food and fire.
She, taught by sympathy's unseen law,
Dumb creatures to her love could draw ;
And one pet squirrel held more near,
Than aught except her father dear.
One morning, hastening to the spring,
A brimming pitcher back to bring,
Upon the sun-burnt board that spread
Its shield above the fountain's head,
She saw her pet with plaintive cry
Run to and fro reluctantly.
With eager step the maiden leaped
Where mossy stones round crystals slept,

And placed her naked foot upon—
But ere the foolish tale was done,
A thoughtless locust's arid note
The hearer's listening terror smote.
" The snake ! " she cried, and wildly flew
To arms that well their service knew,
And strove with many a fond caress
To lend cruel fears forgetfulness.

DIRGE.

Closer draw the winding sheet
Round my lovely Lady's feet !
Still, still, art thou, and marble cold,
Crystal form from beauty's mould !
Dumb th' enchantment of the tongue,
On which our deepest worship hung !
Mute the heart, that no dismay
Quelled, though flames walled up the way !
Dimmed the eye that looked upon
Unveiled the anger of the sun !
What slave so base that would not give
His life again to see thee live !
Yet all too sacred is thy bier
To know a mortal lover's tear ;
I, thy humble vassal true,
Render thee my homage due ;
I, who when the murderous pack
Fastened on my bleeding track,
Found within thy threshold rest,
Food, and charity more blest,

Death has found thee, and the grave
Claims thee, noble, true, and brave ;
Mine the task on it to lay
Glory's unforgetful ray.

THE BIRTHDAY.

Is this the day, the joyous day,
That knew maid Mary born,
Of beauty's light the purest ray,
The crystal of the morn ?

A glance no winter's frost will nip,
Her curls the sunbeam's care,
Red music trembling on her lip,
A neck the snow's despair.

Her winsome smile, her soft reply,
A foot by zephyrs framed,
Her breast, in whose calm harbor lie
All gentle thoughts unblamed.

Twice happy they, this joyous day,
Who hear her accents sweet,
And watch her hands in busy play
Their daily task repeat.

THE ICE FLOWER.

Maiden, whom I long have wooed,
Wooed with hope's unyielding prayer,
With the summer's changing mood
Colder grow thy glances rare.

Like poor Robin lingering,
  Lured by autumn's treacherous sky,
Trembling love delays his wing,
  On thy snowy breast to die.

But though thy heart all frozen lies
  In vestal glory beautiful,
Through the cruel forgetful ice
  Nature works its miracle.

Opening on my eager sight
  Starry blossoms peeping gleam,
Raying forth the fresh delight
  Of thy wakening maiden dream.

THE TRYSTING-TREE.

Prune with care this apple-tree,
  Wart and wrinkle smooth away,
Bald and barren though it be,
  Bind each bleeding branch and spray.

Once, when time and I were young,
  Beauty here her footstep stayed,
Once by sorrow's timid tongue
  Beauty's ear was here waylaid.

Blossoms round us fragrance shook,
  Quicker grew my charmer's breath,
And a sigh, a word, a look
  Made me captive unto death.

II

Still that tender look I see,
    And while love and life are dear,
Never shall this trysting-tree
    Hand unkind or careless fear.

AUTUMN INLAND.

In scarlet hose the school-girl goes
    To the school-house under the hill ;
Old women meet with shuffling feet,
    And wingéd voices shrill ;
And whip in hand the farmers stand
    Around the throbbing mill.

The river creeps, the meadow sleeps,
    Embossed with cart and plow ;
Huge hives of gold the harvests hold,
    The weeds forget to grow ;
Unfenced and strong, a tireless throng,
    The prairie breezes blow.

Well scenes like these the heart may please,
    But dearer far to me
The rocking shore, the billows' roar,
    The foam-flowers of the sea,
And furrowed plain, that yields no grain,
    But deathless melody.

THE MUD AGE.

I sit within our wooden house,
  I look on brick and stone ;
I see small eyes look down on us
  And noses, many a one,
Upturned, as they would hang us high
In warning to each passer-by.

I think how many years of life
  These purse-proud knaves have given,
To win that prize of human strife,
  A brick-and-mortar heaven,
And wonder not they hold in scorn
Poor artists in the mud age born.

SELECTION.

Am I not great ?   Have I not slept
  Beside the pismires' nest ;
And as the vermin o'er me crept,
  Their prudence seen and blessed ?

Bite on, bite on, brave insects all !
  Not purposeless you thrive ;
Beneath your venom weaklings fall
  That heroes may survive.

RECOMPENSE.

The clanging eagle's song
  Delights the wise and great ;
Their ears stretch wide and long
  To catch the swift debate.

But birds, whose merry lay,
  In homely plumage hid,
Allures the morning's ray
  Beneath the forest lid,

None heed, save bard unheard,
  Who wooes the simple strain,
And with it wings the word,
  That mocks a world's disdain.

Strange recompense, the wise
  Repeat the notes they love,
And songs their ears despise
  Alone immortal prove.

FRÄULEIN.

A leafy shadow, sunset-died,
  Half veils the bending Fräulein,
And under tresses loosely tied
  Dark eyes with hidden joy shine :
At length she turns and softly says
What few will hear and fewer praise.

Her words betray no tenderness,
  Alas ! that could not be,
And yet their simple spell no less
  Will long o'ermaster me,
When hearts, that beat too close to mine,
Forgetful hands to dust consign.

She says : '' How strange I did not know it !
  For when I spoke your name,
My cousin cried : ' What ! he, the poet !
  Have you not heard his fame ?' ''
A husband, Fräulein, seldom wears
Such jewels tinkling in his ears.

TWINS.

I have loved and hated well,
Which is wiser, who can tell ?
Love that sighs : '' No longer seek,''
Hate that nerves our purpose weak ;
Love that wraps us in delight,
Hate that clothes our souls in might ;
Love that makes the gods our slaves,
Hate that angry devils braves ;
Twin-born spirits, fierce and sweet,
Stay or guide my wandering feet.

FOUR SEASONS.

A pony, fishing-rod, and gun,
A smaller boy to share the fun ;
Some spicy cake, a stolen peach :
My prayers, kind Heaven, no further reach.

A glass of wine, a fresh cigar,
And merry maid in plumes of war :
If heaven but grant these wishes three,
The world may go to heaven for me.

A sober aim, and constant friends,
The respite social pleasure lends ;
A wife and child, a privy purse ;
Unwise, who wider fancies nurse.

Be mine a cottage by the sea,
Kind deeds that still remember me,
And hope to meet on heaven's shore
The faces love beholds no more.

THE GREAT WORLD.

AN EXILED RAY.

No beam from joyous Helicon,
No blossom of the morning sun,
Allured me towards the deathless choir,
Who weave delight with harp and lyre:

In dungeon dark an exiled ray,
By sunset left on earth astray,
Awoke my fettered frozen youth
To beauty, music, love, and truth.

THE TEACHER.

The flames, that laid my dwelling low,
   Illumined mountain peak and path,
And swift from treacherous friend and foe
   I fled to nurse my vengeful wrath.

But beating on the glorious height,
   The sunbeams and the starry sheen
Inspired my soul with peace and light,
. And filled my heart with love serene.

327

Thenceforth forsaken and alone
  I wander through a world of scorn ;
The beggar's dog disdains to own
  So vile a creature and forlorn.

My friends forget me and my foes,
  My kinsmen mock the forgéd tie,
The thief his golden cloak draws close
  About him, if I chance him nigh.

But healing each new deeper wrong
  With solace from the infinite,
Naked amid an arméd throng
  I battled for the higher right.

For wise and simple meet in this,
  That worse than penury's filing tooth,
Or shattered hope of heavenly bliss,
  They loathe the gentle face of truth.

Yet shall my footsteps vex no more
  The paths of men.   The wave and wind,
The mountain cave and desert shore,
  Betray not him, who loves the kind.

Unknown shall be my face and fate,
  My grave the wolf and eagle's maw,
My memory in fond debate
  Blind hate and envy's tooth shall gnaw :

But doubt ye not the truth, that burns
Within my soul's untroubled night,
Shall stir men's ashes in their urns
And call the dead to life and light.

ISIS.

I know thee, Lady, gaunt and grim,
I know thy colder touch than fate,
Thrice welcome, bitter dame, to him,
Whose pride like thine disdains the great.

The wiser sister thou of death,
Who hold'st him in thine idle mood
A jackal, whose unsavory breath
Disgusts Mephisto with his food.

Indifferent art thou to birth,
A Hapsburgh at thy careless sneer
Becomes a thing of little worth,
A scarecrow hanging from a spear.

The magnate, who devours our isle,
Is in thy truer glass revealed,
Beggar, whose worth could scarce beguile
A worm to leave the potter's field.

The priest, whose words of love fulfil
The simple heart with sacred awe,
Unmasked, becomes a wandering will-
O-the-wisp beneath thine iron law.

Our gods in terror of thine eye
  Forget their lofty speech and stride,
Like giants, when the dawn is nigh,
  In rags and shreds away they glide.

A friend I had, another life,
  A treasure dearer than the day,
Thy glance disclosed the hidden knife,
  That thirsty in its bosom lay.

But welcome mother, mistress, wife,
  I little heed what name thou art,
Though thou hast tortured me through life,
  Fear not, thou shalt divide my heart.

BETRAYED.

Thou hast the joy, and I the sorrow ;
Thou hast to-day, and I to-morrow ;
The honey on the lips thou hast,
Its sweetness I shall never taste ;
But in the cradle of my brain,
By sorrow sired and nameless pain,
A thought is growing more divine,
Than ere will spring from thee or thine ;
No rose-leaves will my pathway bar
To fountain-head of sun and star,
And from the crystal height I may
Forget the sorrow of to-day.
But thou, thou canst not all forget
The torture base, the bloody sweat,

Thy brother's trust, his prison made,
His toil with felon laws repaid,
And all the treason infinite,
That robbed his soul of hope and light,
And drove him bleeding from thy path,
Against thy house to nurse his wrath.

˙BEWARE.

Beware, proud World ! to leave oppressed
The humblest of thy creatures, lest
In melancholy's sunless mine
He chance upon a steel divine,
Whose edge shall cleave your torturing chain,
And break your sceptred gods' relentless reign.

THE BEGGAR'S PLEA.

Your gold for pleasure's sake you prize,
  It owns no other sweet,
Who would not else dull wealth despise
  And all the care of it !

But pleasure is a gentle thing,
  No heart ungentle may
Entice its swift and timid wing,
  Or long its flight delay.

Sweet pleasure is a gentle thing,
  In vain are pomp and state,
No joy can land and palace bring
  · With the lazar at your gate.

THE HEAVY CHANGE.

The voices of the sea are dumb,
  A chain is on the wind,
The clouds with broken pinion come,
  The lightning's eye is blind.

We hear no more of freedom's name,
  No more of equal right,
The words, that smote the world aflame,
  Are clothed in shame and night.

From freedom's loins a tyrant brood
  Have sprung to mock their sire,
And teach the toiling multitude
  With tireless thorn and brier.

But though the scorn of wise and great,
  Like Samson, blind they stand,
Upon the pillars of the state
  Is seen a giant hand.

MY COUNTRY.

My country ! would to God thou wert
  A country, not the lackey born
Of England, proud of honor's hurt,
  And basking in thy master's scorn ;

Save as thy parrot-scholars preach,
  Afraid to think, to feel, to live,
Ambitious but to steal and teach
  Thy children how to pray and thieve.

WAKE !

Sons of less degenerate sires
  A baser offspring now beget,
Round our country's altar fires,
  For greed and greed alone we sweat,
  And fame and nobler aims forget.

Word ! whose sounding wing a-wind
  Across the chainless ocean rode,
Voice and eye of dumb and blind,
  A spell to break the tyrant's goad,
  And lighten toil's unequal load,

Wake ! against a subtler foe,
  The drowsy charm of Capuan hand,
Arts that recreant heroes know,
  As bowed beneath the yoke they stand,
  And tremble at a slave's command ;

Wake ! whose wing from shore to peak
  The blinding spray of battle blew,
Whet the lightning of your beak,
  Your crimson music sound anew,
  And keep your chosen people true.

WHY, BROTHERS, WHY?

The vaulted heavens are high enough,
Why must we stoop beneath their roof ?
The earth is thick ; through its broad street
Why must we walk with fearful feet ?
With deep-scarred backs, for felon gods
Shall we still forge the fatal rods ?
In vain from shore to mountain peak
Shall nature's voice in music break ?
The earth is ours, and ours the sky,
Why, brothers, fear to live and die ?

WENDELL PHILLIPS.

A voice is silent ; such a voice,
  As in man's bitter need,
At times avenging Heaven employs
  To scourge the tyrant's greed.

A voice like that undying tongue,
  That stayed the setting sun,
When o'er the freeborn bema hung
  The cloud of Macedon.

Immortal Phillips ! can it be
  That thou art in the grave,
Whose words of strenuous liberty
  From death awoke the slave?

Whose wingéd wrath, unsatisfied,
   Against the baser foes,
That mine our free Republic, plied
   No blind or coward blows.

Thou dost not sleep, by heaven's high throne,
   Unvexed by wrong or night,
Thou hear'st thy mighty words march on
   And battle for the right.

THE UNKNOWN FRIEND.

Soul of my soul, whose tameless eye
   Has drunk my bleeding verse,
And feels the deeper misery
   My painted words rehearse,

Though known to me thy name nor face,
   Our love though oceans part,
I fold thee in a long embrace,
   I live within thy heart.

I know thy boyhood's laughter wild,
   Thy youth's enchanted pain,
I know thy manhood undefiled
   By lust or sordid gain.

Deep hast thou felt truth's battle pride,
   And deep the wise world's scorn,
And cursed the fetters vile, that tied
   A hand would wake the morn.

Repine not, tho' thy worth estrange
  Thy country, brother, friend ;
Thy nobler scope, thy wider range,
  Full recompense shall lend.

The exile, greater than his race,
  Beneath Fate's yoke unbowed,
Calls from his Alpine resting-place
  The world to burst its shroud.

SCIENCE.

Unsung, the song of Science
  In works of splendor hides,
And changing through the ages
  With changeless truth abides.

Of sleepless sage or toiler,
  Step-children of dull fame,
It spells the mystic passion,
  It breathes the sacred name.

From listening gods their sceptre
  Its wandering echo steals,
And through their desert dwelling
  The soul of night reveals.

ART.

What isles, that changing season
  Nor ancient night obey,
What temples these apparelled
  In larger light than day !

Of builder Art they witness
  The high creative rhyme,
That mocks at death's undoing,
  And parts the tide of time.

Here gods from heaven banished,
  Here lovers long unblessed,
Here exiled heroes wander,
  And they, who mourn, have rest.

FAME.

From darkness unto darkness
  A light of beauty creeps,
And Fame its fading shadows
  With careless sickle reaps.

From silence unto silence
  A voice of sorrow flits,
And Fame its frozen echoes
  With idle finger knits.

When thou, our mighty mother,
  Art gathered to the sun,
Will Fame record thy beauty
  And course in music run ?

THE SEARCH.

I bowed before the ancient word,
   I drank the sweet enchantment dire,
Each leaf by rustling poet stirred,   [lyre,
   Each thought that breathed from prophet's

I worshipped, till one nobler spoke :
   " Poor slave in motley livery " ;
The words my deeper spirit woke
   To seek the truth in liberty.

I whispered to a pearly shell,
   That held old ocean's fettered song :
"Sweet spirit, bid thine echoes tell
   The secret, thou has cherished long."

" I sang within my mossy cave."
   It answered : " Ere dull earth was born,
Such soul, as flitting mortals have,
   I gave them less in love than scorn."

Then plucking from the dust a leaf,
   " Sad minstrel, wilt thou not unbind,"
I whispered, "to a kindred grief
   The word that sways the pathless wind ?"

Then answered it with nature's pride :
   " From bud to fan my life was wooed
By zephyrs soft, till autumn-dyed,
   I fade a man of braver mood."

Through footless ways, 'mid gleaming stars,
  On bolder pinion swift I fly,
" Break, break !" I cry, " my prison bars,
  And bid my soul immortal be."

Ah ! faithless truth ! ah ! truthless faith !
  What horror blinds my glazing sight ?
Behind the stars Hope's fading wraith
  Glides silent into silent night.

The soul of soul within me dies,
  I fall as fall the stricken dead,
To rocks and clods my spirit flies,
  The mountains on my bosom tread.

Yet spoke no less the nobler voice :
  " The unrewarded are the great,
Though truth be death, in truth rejoice,
  Be godlike in despite of fate."

OM.

What art thou, Spectre of Despair,
Borne upon the wing of night,
Shaking from thy flaming hair
Seeds of madness and affright?
Whirlwinds on thy breast are fed ;
Earthquake waves beneath thy tread
Foam ; before thy glancing spear
Back the heavens shrink in fear ;
At the shadow of thy breath
Thronéd temples sink in death ;
And the gods in terror fly
The careless laughter of thine eye.
Now thy hand in idle scorn
Seems to beckon in the morn ;
Now beneath thy gathering frown
Doubly black the night has grown ;
Answer, though thy savage glare
From its roots my soul should tear,
Bravely have I lived and sought,
Through the charnel house of thought,
Truth, and dying, will die great,
Like a god, who wars with fate.

Then before me suddenly,
Like an eyeless corse, the sky
Sank, and, closing round my path,
Waves of fury broke in wrath.

" Good and evil is there none
But the live force forges on,"

Said the spirit. '' I am she
By fettered man named Destiny,
Soul of sov'reign motion,
Spirit of the viewless sun,
Ruler of the tireless force,
That spurs upon their fiery course
Linkéd worlds, and wakes to birth
The life, that paints the sullen earth,
That ideal, whose pregnant rage
Taught man to burst his brutish cage.''

'' Thou,'' echoed I, '' that spirit fair,
That made my youth's fond joys thy care,
Storing deep th' enchanted hours
With the laughter of the flowers,
Weaving a diviner ray
Round the beauty of the day,
Breathing on the dark blue night
A consecration of delight,
Or with footstep musical
Leading me through haunted hall,
Where the harp's sweet budded word,
By the minstrel's passion stirred,
Woke the gentle thoughts that lie
Restless at love's mystery ;
Far other than thy face half seen
Through trembling leaf that closed between,
When thy step outvied the fawn,
Startled at the touch of dawn,
And its whispering pinion fleet
Lured the soul with promise sweet ;
My backward eye still sees thee live,

Clothed with beauty fugitive,
Thy voice the oriole carolling,
Thine eye the day-star vanishing."

" Painted cloud dissolved in air,
Fair is foul, and foul is fair,"
Said the spirit ; " from the slime
To kiss the stars the cedars climb ;
The worm, whose breath pollutes the mire,
Lends the bird its minstrel fire ;
On sewer's filth the dying rose
Fed, to fresher beauty grows ;
With the courtesan's bitter shame
The vestal feeds her holy flame ;
The sable cook pours from his head
The sweat, that salts the princess' bread ;
The blush, that wins the lover's trust,
Wakes the murderer's brutal lust ;
The murderer's eloquent bones impart
A purer charm to plastic art ;
Through beauty's fading shadows wan
Breaks truth's iron skeleton."

" Art thou," then I, " that spirit proud,
Whose voice has long my manhood wooed,
In scorn of wealth or nobler fame,
Of love's delight or penury's shame,
To seek with undivided eye
The mystery of mystery ?
Or wandering by each haunted stream,
Where Grecian gods in beauty gleam ;

Or piercing through the populous haze,
Where spirits vast their shadows chase,
Unravelling the cords that bind
The Hindoo Trinity to the kind ;
Or worshipping in desert drear
Jehovah's awful voice of fear ;
Or spurring my soul's restless flight
Beyond the last star's glimmering light,
To Night's forgetful fountain spring,
Where tired Time sits with folded wing ;
Or searching for God's image hid
Beneath the heart's close shutting lid,
Ill search for him, who sees instead
The scorpion passions rear their head,
Avarice cloaked in pious dress
Wounding the friend, who comes to bless,
Friendship firing with the brand,
Whose bounty warmed its frozen hand,
The sleeping house of trusting host,
Taught too late true friendship's cost ;
Far other than the gracious mien
Of sacred truth's unveiling queen,
Vision fed with inward light,
Than morning's eye more joyous bright,
Raining from her golden hair
A quickening splendor everywhere,
Breathing word and glance of fire,
That make th' immortal gods aspire."

Then she : " The live force forges on,
Truth and falsehood is there none ;
Image of the masking world,

A lie in every word lies curled ;
Scholars burn their pious nights,
To glean the thoughts the drunkard writes ;
Trusting martyrs happy die
To gloss a doubting poet's lie ;
Education works its cheat,
That idlers labor's bread may eat ;
Tireless toil the patriot slave
To elaborate the social grave,
Where crime, reduced to fraud and law,
Holds the moral world in awe ;
Yet surging on through death and life
Sovereign force reigns lord of strife,
Who denies the live force must
Turn again to pregnant dust,
And with death's quick virtue feed
The wider growth's unpitying need ;
Witness, corner-stoned with fate,
The high imperial Roman state,
Whose rangéd law and living grave
My touch to freedom's eagles gave."

Then gazing on the Spectre's face,
I saw it lit with gentler rays,
And nature's spirit knew, that sways
With chainless law thought's hidden ways :
When suddenly within me stirred
The impulse of a sacred word ;
" I know," I cried, " a crystal name
Of power thy loveless force to tame,
A maiden in whose pure soul lies
A charm to move the unfeeling skies,

Though darkening in ether deep,
Sunbeams sink in endless sleep,
Though turning from the barren sky
Wasting leaves and grasses die,
Though circling earth, its heat half run,
A fagot drop into the sun,
Breathe but her name, and forth shall rise
A nobler world and clearer skies."

Then the spirit : " Wise art thou,
Of woman's heart the depths to know,
Though on thy lips her kiss be warm,
Doubt not she meditates thee harm."
Then I : " The gods, such lies who speak,
My hand shall into pieces break."
Laughing the Spectre turned and fled,
And left my soul to torture wed.

STAR-GAZER.

Diviner of the hidden stars,
   That hold if aught there be
Of truth, that parts our prison bars,
   And sets the reason free,
What solace for the human kind
Has heaven's envious veil confined ?

I hear the sacred prophet's word,
   As uninspired and vain,
As winds that pipe to branches stirred
   By barren autumn's rain ;
With thrifty tongue he wakes our fears,
And presses wine from sorrow's tears.

But thou, whose touch unlocked the chain,
    That bound us to the shore,
Whose rudder o'er the tideless main,
    Our hope and fortune bore,
Thou tamer of the bigot sky,
Thou wilt not bid us look and die.

THE NEW MOON.

My soul from lower worlds escaped
    Abides among the stars,
With forms by Fancy's finger shaped,
    Who reck not of the wars,
Dull mortals wage with appetite,
Disease, despair, and dateless night.

Reclined, I watch man-haunted earth
    Devour the circling way,
With glistening polls and golden girth,
    Tall peak and ocean gray,
And, ruler of the waters wan,
I see the Moon beside it run.

Diana, crystal-quivered queen,
    Of maidenhood the pride,
With sandals sheen and arrows keen
    To tame the leafy tide,
What hunter now with glazing eye
Invades thy beauty's mystery ?

Changed goddess ! whose unveiling smiles
    Endymion's slumber sealed,

Fond whisperer of wanton wiles,
  The sigh suppressed, the hope concealed,
Thou masker bold ! thy cold death's head
Another message might have sped ;

Another pupil thine, and thou
  Another teacher art ;
And well at sight of thy bent bow
  The troubled earth may start,
Who knows thee and thy weapon's fame,
And knows her naked heart thine aim.

Thy frozen fires, thy dusty seas,
  Unstirred by wing or wind,
Thy mountain-graven prophecies
  At war with living kind,
Strike home, as over ether's wave
Earth drags her slayer to one grave.

The lessening tide, the lengthening day,
  The seaport inland grown,
The heat that slowly dies away,
  The frost line creeping down ;
Forgetful bard and analyst,
By what strange gadfly are they kissed ?

That this wings words with music, that
  With plane and cross-cut saw
Plans high a house for reason's bat,
  In hope mankind to awe,
When Homer's name and Socrates'
Shall frozen lie in tropic seas.

THE AMBER GOD.

Swift Polar light, with beams less bright,
   Shake thy splendor o'er the sky,
From dim, sequestered seats invite
   Elves, that love thy veiling eye;
Hark ! the rocking plain and hill
Echo with their voices shrill.

Not thine the measured hour and road,
   Morning's struggling steeds obey,
The meteor's lamp, the lightning's goad
   Round a path a wayward play ;
Hark ! by rifted oak and pine,
Minstrels shrill in chorus join.

" No worshippers of whispering tree,
   Cavern-voice or sounding wave,
Our God as thought itself is free,
    Rending prison, chain, and grave,
From cloud to earth's deep cauldron spring
Ranging with imperial wing.

" Approach with touch that binds and frees
   Souls, whom beauty's magic sways ;
Approach and round thy votaries,
   Closer weave thy thrilling rays ;
And teach our tongues thy hidden charm,
Alien hearts to woo and warm.

" In rolling mist thy spirit hides
   Seeds of springtide's bounteous birth ;

By stalk and spray unchecked it glides
  Through the bolted door of earth,
And nerve by nerve the mighty corse
Wakes to bless its tireless force.

" Old ocean's bed with star-dust strewn
  Knows thy glances opaline ;
Its flowerless fields of sun and moon
  Vacant, own thy name divine ;
While radiant streams from line to pole
Thy unchartered reign extol.

" Thy guidance scoffing sailors seek,
  Tossed upon the blinding surge,
When whirlwinds, fanged with eagle's beak,
  Flight and instant peril urge ;
And shrieking from the flooded sky
Lesser gods in terror fly.

" For softer scenes and prayers less rude
  Leave awhile thy chosen home,
Forsake thy crystal solitude,
  Girt with icy tower and dome ;
And, Wizard, from thy sunless snow
Beauty's balmy blossoms blow.

" With music mild, with rapture wild,
  Languid love's fond fire intense,
With joys from toiling earth exiled,
  Grant thy minstrels recompense :
And lead o'er unpolluted ground
Song and step in mazy round.

" When stars are blind, and hope unkind,
  Youth and fading fancy gone,
Our lives in prison-house confined
  Suffer not to linger on ;
With thy swift flash, that sanctifies,
Close in death our leaden eyes."

THE EVIDENCE.

The sceptred honor of the gods of old,
  The rattling thunderbolts of frowning Jove,
  The purple empire of the queen of love,
The ghostly voice from Pluto's grisly hold,

The waves of fire from Hebrew prophets rolled
  Are spent ; in vain the sacred keys reprove
  The silent locks, that prayers nor curses move ;
Unpaid, brave Luther's hand works to remould

Divinity, or Calvin's skill to dress
  Law-gods with living terror ; to blind eyes
Dumb tongues are mumbling ; on the struck gods
    press
  Cruel reason's arrows, lords of the bare skies ;
Thou fool ! though words nor worlds the God con-
    fess,
  Undimmed in love's true soul His image lies.

THE IMMORTALS.

Immortal rise the gods, whom science slays,
  And nobler, breathing from the crystal sky
  A beauty born of silent majesty,
Whose sacred charm the victor's madness sways,

And our rebellious thoughts in music lays,
  As steals upon the soul's rewakening eye
  The meaning of life's hidden mystery,
Whose influence the unseen star obeys ;

Nor less his honor, who with chainless heart
  Piercing the subtle veil of hope and fear,
The poet's dream and the magician's art,
  That held in bondage childhood's painted year,
Beholds the cheating nebulous clouds depart,
  Yet wonders, what new suns their pride uprear.

PHIL. SHERIDAN.

At Winchester the Captain sleeps,
While Fame, in whose quick womb there leaps
A day of glory, vigil keeps ;
              Phil. Sheridan.

What sound borne on the morning gray
Has spurred him from his couch away,
As tho' a scorpion by him lay ?
              Phil. Sheridan.

Be not thy courser's proud feet slack,
That thunder on the smoking track ;
He bears our country on his back ;
Phil. Sheridan.

Now round the rider's path appear
The straggling soldiers winged with fear,
That fly and pause and wildly stare ;
Phil. Sheridan.

For while we lay in slumber's grave,
As o'er a bark the tidal wave,
Burst Early with his chosen brave ;
Phil. Sheridan. .

Crook's shattered troops disordered fly,
Brave Emory yields reluctantly,
And Sedgwick's veterans rooted die ;
Phil. Sheridan.

Speeding, more near the cannon roars,
His army's wreck about him pours ;
" By God," he cries, " the day is ours ! "
Phil. Sheridan.

" Halt ! comrades ; form and face about ; "
And high above the noise and rout
Arises hope-in-death's wild shout ;
Phil. Sheridan.

" Forward ! " Tho' death's gates open stand,
We plunge at our great chief's command,
As tho' dear life stretched forth her hand ;
Phil. Sheridan.

Like lion reluctant o'er its prey,
Or river meeting ocean's sway,
The rebel host their charge delay ;
Phil. Sheridan.

A moment, then, in terror fly,
As from our bayonets leaps a cry,
That folds the trembling earth and sky ;
Phil. Sheridan.

Whose naked hands the coward's brand wear,
From victors' grasp their weapons tear,
And with the vanguard onward bear ;
Phil. Sheridan.

They fly as deer, that wildly press,
With feet that pause nor toil confess,
To shun the hungry wolf's caress ;
Phil. Sheridan.

Ah ! ne'er before beneath the sun,
Since war its glorious reign begun,
From foul defeat was victory won ;
Phil. Sheridan.

Though sunk beneath the depths he be,
Careless he mounts the surging sea,
The lord of war and victory ;
Phil. Sheridan.

The wave, that tames the rocky shore,
The chainless tempest's sullen roar,
Shall sound thy name forevermore ;
Phil. Sheridan.

12

DETHRONED.

Supreme to river, gulf, and sea,
　That framed a golden land,
Two monarchs reigned, and bold were he,
　Disputed their command.

Bright ladies thronged their palace proud,
　And statesmen of renown,
Ambassadors before them bowed,
　And trembled at their frown.

Their fields were black with countless slaves,
　From dawn to closing day,
And white with sails the toiling waves
　Their harvest bore away.

No foeman's taunt, no son untrue,
　No word to curb their power,
Kings Cotton and Tobacco knew,
　In springtide's happy hour.

But now their fields with salt are sown,
　Their children's hearts with hate,
Their haughty flag is overblown,
　Their homestead desolate.

CHORIAMBICS.

THE RUSTLERS.

One day when my proud soul had soared
Above the stars, from bed and board
Divorced, by cruel hunger gored,
  A pagan fast,
I met a friend, whose kindred powers
Had spurred him high o'er heaven's towers,
A pace for this slow world of ours
  Too swift to last :

Our salutations duly done,
And interchange of hopes begun,
Since long the churlish winter sun
  Had sunk to rest,
" My friend," with prudent mind, I said,
"Could your wild fancy's flight be led
Toward that dull harbor called a bed
  In words undressed ?"

"It might : " Then he : "If first you led it
Sure footed, through the land of credit,
A treacherous spot, wher'er you tread it,
  Where things are mixed ;
But stay, I have a friend, who knew
Our better days, such friends are few,
If once that oysterman I view,
  We are well fixed."

He spoke, and soon our nostrils greet
A Bowery cellar's perfume sweet,
Where dwelt in happiness complete
        A German Lord,
Œstreich, whose hand of cunning knew
Of oyster fried the moment true,
And spices rare to make a stew
        By youth adored.

" How fat and saucy, like a king,
You sit, while scrubbing-brushes sing."
I mused, and wondered every thing
        So clean should be :
" A more particular man as I,"
Replied our host with dignity ;
" If you should find, it is no lie,
        Bei Gott, it 's me ! "

Then asking after Frau and Kind,
A wife and child are credit's mint,
My worthy chum began to squint
        At holy trust ;
A ship was out, a friend was in,
A favorite horse had failed to win,
An uncle rich was razor-thin,
        Mere pinch of dust ;

" Enough ! " cried Fritz, with generous
        pride ;
And leading us to room aside,
With steaming dishes soon replied --
        To thrifty praise ;

Till Jack, as proud as Turkish pacha,
My pipe with smoke, my glass with lager,
Peopling, trolled out a stirring saga
        Of worthier days.

THE VIKINGS.

Launch the black boat,
    Fly the wild raven,
Raise the war note,
    " Death to the craven ! "

Famine has fed us ;
    Wrinkled our maids are ;
Heroes that led us,
    Rusty their blades are.

Far on the lee
    Fadeth the dune,
Red from the sea
    Rises the moon.

Arrow of word,
    Plume of the night,
Shadow of bird,
    Swifter our flight.

Days twelve and three,
    North wind and wave
Sing merrily
    Hope to the brave !

Through the mist wake
  Steeple and tower,—
White the waves break,
  Trembles the hour.

Melody-haunted,
  Turret and dome,
Cadiz enchanted
  Smiles o'er the foam.

Bells' wild alarms
  Clang on the ear,
Shouting, " To arms !
  Norsemen are near."

Furiously
  Round us our foes,
Joy of the eye,
  Numberless close.

" Fang of the wolf,
  Beak of the raven,
Into hell's gulf,
  Death to the craven ! "

" Two-handed swords,
  Carve on your way !
Victory's lords,
  Wade through the fray ! "

Hand of the bold,
 Paid is thy toil ;
Captives and gold,
 Rich is thy spoil.

Fair Isabel,
 Fairest of all,
Tongue cannot tell,
 Love can recall.

Whisper unknown—
 Pleads the maid's part
Love's tender moan
 Deep in my heart.

" Pity her lot,
 Haco, my brother ;
Send without spot
 Child to her mother.

" Fair as her face,
 Over the mead.
Odin shall praise
 Love's gentle deed."

Stern his lip curled,
 Rose his hand up,
Swift on me hurled
 Red wine and cup.

Evil the blow
 Brother on brother ;
Never will know
 I such another.

Silent I stood,
 Silent I wept ;
Cold solitude
 Over me crept.

Laughed Haco loud,
 " Guard ye my brother,
Warriors proud,
 Home to his mother.

" Freya shall praise
 Thee nor thy wit ;
Perish the face,
 Kin would unknit !"

Whiter than snow
 Stands the fair maid ;
Under his blow
 Glistens my blade.

" Man with man fights,
 Viking defiled !
Coward only smites
 Woman and child."

Blood of my foes !
Red was my blade ;
Redder it grows—
Saved is the maid !

Blood my hand dyes—
Blood of my brother !
How shall my eyes
Look on our mother ?

FORT SUMTER.

The first gun, the first gun,
And the fort fired upon !
Have you not heard ?
Over mountain and hill
Up the stream and the rill
Flashes the word.

From the pine tree of Maine
To Nebraska's wide plain,
Silent men stand,
Till a low bitter sigh,
Till a hoarse angry cry
Sweeps over the land.

" You are speedy, our brother,
To inherit our mother,
Ere life is sped :
At the whim of your pleasure
Will you lay on her treasure
Strong hand and red ? "

Then a wan steely light,
Tipped with flame crimson bright,
　　Fills field and road,
And from mountain and lake
All the iron pathways shake
　　Under their load.

Forth from Sumter's low wall
Stalks a form grim and tall,
　　Royal of mien,
Such an one, since the tide
Broke the high Roman pride,
　　Eye hath not seen.

With a lash in his hand,
With a nod of command,
　　Lord of the fray,
" Up ! " he cries, " idle slave,
Set your scythe to the brave,
　　Blue coat and gray."

Little heed Glory takes,
Little choice Glory makes,
　　Hero and knave,
Rich and poor, 'squire and tramp,
Through the forest and swamp
　　Haste to one grave.

And the black faces wonder
At the hosts clad in thunder
　　Over them hurled :

And mankind stands at gaze,
As the thick battle haze
  Muffles a world.

THE " MUD MARCH."

" Brave comrade, why sit,
Like joy's counterfeit,
  Cheating the wine ?
The cup has no sorrow,
The cup has no morrow,
  Trust it with thine.

" While long-legged Jackson,
The black devil's black son,
  Chains down his sword,
And Burnside, annoyed
At friends undestroyed,
  Waits but a word ;

" Drink deep as the road,
Where yesternight stood
  Soldier and gun,
In snow, rain, and sleet,
Now heads up, now feet,
  Fearing the sun ;

" Drink deep as the stream,
That red to the brim
  Ran with our blood,
When down Marye's height
The death-laden light
  Rolled its red flood.

" Sink memory's pain,
Sink glory's disdain
 Deep in the glass ;
And if it lack leaven,
Add country and heaven,
 Let the toast pass.

" Count cups as the zeros,
That swell out our heroes,
 Blockhead and knave ;
Lame Porter the schemer,
And Halleck the dreamer,
 Hearse of the brave.

" Soon, soon for the fray
The trumpet will bray,
 Soon shall we hear
The message, that parts
True comrades and hearts,
 Knell in our ear.

" And up the long slope
Our chosen will grope,
 Stepsons of fame,
Till swift from the steep
A hand swoop to reap
 Glory from shame.

" Then, comrade, in haste
The warm Lethe taste,
 Truce to all sighs,

While discord's delay
Prolongs the brief day,
    Grudged to the wise."

STONEWALL JACKSON.

" Who can a bullet recall ?
Join me your hands, one and all,
    While my life spends ;
Think not I honor them less,
Though my own heart's blood I press,
    Comrades and friends.

" Soldiers, whom none may withstand,
Stay of our fair Southern land,
    Finders of fame,
Pledge me a warrior's word,
Never shall visit my sword
    Slumber or shame.

" Think how its wandering wrath
Baffled McClellan's proud path,
    Smote him and tamed ;
Think how its fury has left
Hooker of glory bereft,
    Bleeding and maimed.

" When on the swift battle-surge,
Shouting the Northerner's dirge,
    Foremost you ride,
Still let its point tip the wedge,
Still let its unconquered edge
    Armies divide.

" Others, when danger is sorest,
Earthwork may hide in or forest,
    You by this token,
When fence and battlement fall,
Naked shall stand forth a wall
    Firm and unbroken.

' When undishonored and free
Mountain shall look upon sea,
    Draw round my grave ;
Think not unheard shall be told,
How my true comrades of old
    Outbraved the brave."

Dumb by the red river-side,
Stonewall, in victory's pride
    Marked for death's prey,
Looked on the harvest of foes,
Looked on a glory that knows
    Time nor decay.

MOBILE BAY.

"Craven has sunk !" shrills through the fleet,
Farragut's oath stops our retreat ;
"*Hartford* ahead !" hark to the cry,
"Dare and we dare, die and we die !"

Hugging the fort, swiftly our ships
Enter the death-dealing eclipse :
Gun upon gun, flash upon flash,
Round us the bolts thunder and crash.

Lashed to the mast, soul of the brave,
On Farragut plows through the grave,
Black from the night into the bay
War-dog and ship wrestle their way.

Swift from the fort, vomiting wrath,
Bold *Tennessee* leaps on our path,
Fire against fire, mail against mail,
Slowly her guns falter and fail.

Haughty Mobile, dumb are her boasts,
Broken her hopes, captive her hosts ;
Mute lies the South, wrapt in despair,
Her such a hand smites in her lair ;

Her such a hand, master of fate,
Smites, and of Fame ends the debate,
Carving its deeds, reckless as wise
Deep on the key-stone of the skies.

THE FENCER.

Why do you blush like a rose ?
" 'T is but the wind from the street,
　Feel how it blows."

Why are your glances so warm ?
" 'T is but th' electrical heat
　After the storm."

Why do you tremble and sigh ?
" 'T is but a mouse brushed my feet,
　When you drew nigh."

RACHEL OF ROMNEY.

" Entrust without danger
Your name to a stranger,
 Lass not uncomely."
She stooped in her pride
And smiling replied :
 " Rachel of Romney."

"One short day and three,
With beauty and thee
 Shelter we beg,
Unfed this poor horse
Has borne sorrow's corse
 Many a league."

Through blossoms and grasses
A flame-image passes—
 Soon back again—
" Forbear further quest,
Remain mother's guest,
 Toss Pomp your rein."

With eyes full of grace
She looked on my face,
 Swift then as pard,
In melody sweet
Her fugitive feet
 Kissed the green sward.

" Hug, Sorrel, your stall,
Forget morning's call,
    Fear spur nor rein,
Your breath, trusty Rib,
Shall long round the crib
    Scatter the grain."

Strange, desolate house,
What strait hazardous
    Left it half haunted,
And hid in its gloom,
Like bird in a tomb,
    Maiden enchanted !

How dreamy the bed,
Whence danger has fled !
    Fondly reclined,
I watched one by one
The swift perils gone
    Move o'er my mind.

To Lynchburg, within
The dead-line I 've been,
    Reckless to see
My mother's dim eyes,
Grown young with surprise,
    Look love on me.

Too long my delay,
'T was "up and away,
    Make for the Ridge ! "

Through forest and swamp
One star was my lamp,   -
   Pathway and bridge.

Past mist-muffled crest,   ·
Through passes half-guessed,
   O'er the divide,
Like redskin, who.goes
Unseen through thick foes,
   .Darkling I glide.

At swift Shenandoah
'T is, "whoop and holloa!
   Halt! who goes there?"
As on through the brambles
My bleeding shade scrambles,
   Spurred by despair.

A young gelding, caught
At Lost River, brought
   Ease to my neck,
And softer the sound
Of hunter and hound
   Stole through the brake.

With swift foot and stanch
Potomac's South Branch
   Soon we have won,
And rock-armored hill,
Gray homestead and mill
   . : Fast by us run.

But truce to my dream,
Star yields to sunbeam,
   Morn summons me
Heart-vacant to wander,
Where lawns dimple under
   Vine, flower, and tree.

With checkered delight,
Dark colors and bright
   Wave round my feet,
And voices half seen,
Through crimson and green,
   Shower music sweet.

The loitering bees,
In gilt liveries,
   Sing, as they thieve,
And blossoms no wiser,
Though minstrel turn miser,
   Give and forgive.

But look ! who is coming ?
What live flower is blooming ?
   Rachel has risen,
As blithe as June-ray,
That edging the gray
   Breaks its cloud-prison.

The wayfaring wind
Would search far to find
   Shoulder so fair ;

But dark as the snake,
Half seen in the brake,
    Glistens her hair.

No stores of the town
Her vital charms own,
    Nature, her teacher,
In music who formed her,
With feeling who warmed her,
    Breathes from each feature.

At work and at board,
Her tenderest word
    Speaks to her mother ;
But glance, tone, and thought,
With magic inwrought,
    Mute hold another.

On flowery bank laid,
I watch the fair maid
    Order her house ;
Or, pinned to her pleasure,
Delightfully measure
    Paths perilous.

In coy loveliness,
Compliant recess
    Round us is glooming,
Or soothsaying trees
With low cadences
    Welcome our coming.

The Spring has come home,
And fruit trees in bloom
   Scent the soft air,
And runlet and thrush
Make meadow and bush
   Vocal as fair ;

But rays never born
Of sunset or morn
   Gem blade and spray,
And echoes, as sweet
As lure angels' feet,
   Round my path play ;

A dream in my arms
My soul subtly warms,
   Mocks it and blesses,
While love at her heart,
Who works so sweet smart,
   Timidly guesses.

Gold sinks overfast,
Bright hours are soon past,
   " Hostess, farewell !
In honor's increase,
May pleasure and peace
   Long with you dwell.

" But Thou, whose charms are
A mask for the fair,
   Turn not aside,

While hope strives to frame
A thought without blame
   Meet for your pride.

" Idolatry's lure,
No chain insecure
   Binds me to thee,
Oh, joy, if for aye
Love's proud jailer may
   Love's captive be ! "

The mother, who lay
Bedridden and gray,
   Lifted her head,
As mute to her will,
Her hand cold and still
   Sank on the bed.

Like jewel half hid,
By leaf's shrivelled lid,
   Glittered her eye ;
" My child's hand is given
To vengeance and heaven ;
   Stranger, good-by."

But who all alone,
Ere bridle is on,
   Steals from the door ?
" My sweet singing bird,
Is love's overword
   Cruel nevermore ? "

Then she : '' Why such haste ?
The clouds gather fast,
    Come under cover ;
When love bides at home,
Do wise wooers roam,
    Thou losel lover ?

'' While watchers are sleeping,
The harvest is reaping,
    Thy task is light,
When night strikes its noon,
Love proffers a boon,
    King would not slight.''

What statue of stone
That night had not known
    Love's mastery ?
Nor trembled with joy,
As wistfully coy
    Rachel drew nigh ?

In amorous gear
Of roseate fear,
    Fairer than praise,
With eager delay,
Like blossom of May,
    Glints forth her face.

Brave hand, shake for me
From night's dusky tree
    Apples of gold,

To blind Beauty's eyes,
Till love's witcheries
   Catch her and hold.

" Around your white throat
Your hair's silken coat
   Close let me furl,
That no glance come in
With sly hope to win
   Ruby or pearl.

" Divine lily set
In night's vase of jet,
   Ever as now
Your luminous face
The shadows shall chase
   Far from love's brow.

" When, Sweet, on the morrow
My joy turns to sorrow,
   Think once of him,
Whose life has but leave
In thine to inweave
   Gold, flower, and gem.

" From camp-fire to star
Bold climbers there are,
   Tamers of fate,
And soon glory's wing
Its master shall bring
   Safe to your gate.

" Soon, soon will you prove
Whom better you love,
  Stranger unknown,
Or war's chosen son,
Whom banner and gun
  Glorious own.

" From mountain to sea
Your hid charms shall be
  Known and adored,
And beauty and fame
Shall meet in the name
  Ralph Rutherford."

As bird, when, instead
Of young, a snake's head
  Greets its home wing,
With lips staring wide,
The maid from my side
  Drew shuddering.

" Why hasten to light
Your wax candles bright,
  Rachel of Romney ?
No lightning would dare
Blight blossom so fair,
  Rachel of Romney.

" Why whistle so loud,
Why whistle so shrill,
  Rachel of Romney,

To summon the cloud
Or dog from the hill,
   Rachel of Romney ? "

Look not upon death
With sword in your sheath,
   Out my brown blade.
" Come, night-prowling knave,
Why halt at the grave ?
   Be not afraid."

Through window and door
The gray shadows pour,
   Sword-blade and gun,
With cold wolfish eye
Unpitifully
   Round my path run.

With quick hand and wary
'T was cut, thrust, and parry,
   Never a word,
Till two giants grim,
May death harvest them,
   Mastered my sword.

I looked at the maid,
My life had betrayed,
   Silent she stood :
So lovely she seemed,
Methought I had dreamed,
   Vain dream and rude.

But hark to night's noon !
"Your word, Pretty one,
    Haste and fulfill,
To leave incomplete
A promise so sweet
    Suits honor ill."

With hand kind nor weak
She smote on my cheek ;
    Love answered her,
"Were I Beauty's steed,
Think not I should need
    Bridle or spur."

"Accurséd !" she cried,
"My three brothers died
    Facing the foe,
O'er father and lover
In prison-pens hover
    Vulture and crow.

"I swear by the rood
I 'd slay the whole brood,
    Ruffian and clown,
Each wide Northern mouth,
That hunts through the South,
    Eating her down.

"But thou, traitor-spy,
What death shalt thou die,
    Red Rutherford ?

Ere dawn, high on tree,
Your masters may see
  Treason's reward.

" Oh, had I but known—"
She turned and was gone ;
  Hopeless I stood,
And felt round my soul,
Like cold shadow, roll
  Death's solitude.

Then, sharp as a lance,
My mother's wild glance
  Pricked at my heart,
Oh, madness of pain !
The cord's tightening strain
  She may not part.

Now swift from the hill
The storm bugles shrill
  Led on the blast,
And fire, rain, and sleet
With furious feet
  Followed them fast.

Then trembled the house
With storm and carouse ;
  Freed from all fear,
In gorged merriment
The bushwhackers bent
  Over their cheer.

But far other sight
Made lurid my night,
    Yellow and red,
With lips large and mute,
The ripe battle-fruit
    Round me was spread.

Or worshipful priest
With gold-broidered vest
    Waved his white wand,
And tender-eyed nun
Undoubting walked on,
    Fagot in hand.

Or worms their blind head
Upraised from their bed,
    Balked of their prey,
That swayed by the wind,
With eyes staring blind,
    Troubled the day.

The hours travel fast,
When each hour 's the last ;
    Faster my brain,
To waste the brief time,
From fancy's black slime
    Sucks useless pain.

What vision is stealing,
What keen eye is feeling
    Hither its way ?

What madness and fire,
Slain brother and sire,
   Search for their prey ?

" Not vacant of grace,
Who once sees thy face,
   Rachel of Romney ;
Or spare me the shame,
That waits for my name,
   Rachel of Romney."

Her white finger tips
Press quivering lips,
   Flashes her knife,
On shrunk fetters laid
The generous blade
   Smites death to life.

" Fly, fly, you are free !
I ask not from thee
   Pardon or praise ;
If blood cry for blood,
Forgive me, my God,
   Dark are Thy ways."

One kiss like a sigh,
Too sacred to die,
   Soul pressed on soul,
Then, eager with care,
My swift step and bare
   Through my grave stole.

The clouds strained and parted,
And through the rifts darted
    Stars one by one,
And with wak'ning day
I saw our flag lay
    Cheek to the sun.

But long must I wait,
Ere hampering fate
    Lifts the red veil,
That hides from my prayer
A vision so fair,
    Love's praises fail.

REASSURANCE POLICY.

Wayward child of my heart,
Unforgiven thou art,
    Once to forget,
That the sun, stars, and moon
At thy bidding alone
    Rise, fade, and set.

When thy feet slyly peep
From the dusk wing of sleep,
    Think not in scorn
Of a lover would dare
Sword or adder to spare
    Thee but one thorn.

When thine eyes hide the light
From the desolate night,
 Dream once of him,
Who, with long, sleepless toil,
Fed thy name's wick with oil,
 Time cannot dim.

Where thou art is my home,
And thine absence my tomb,
 Quick with one prayer,
That these pale rhymes, that grow
Under shadow and snow,
 Beauty will wear.

GELIDA NOCTE.

From foam-cloud leaping
A bright star peeping
 In beauty's nest ;
Whispers Pearl-maiden,
With charms o'erladen,
 Soft be thy rest.

Sweet prayers surround thee,
Where slumber has found thee
 Lily of night ;
'Mid darkness lying,
Like germ undying
 Of heavenly light.

Love-doomed to wander
Thy window under,
 Hopeless I sigh ;

My heart fast beating,
One burden repeating,
    " Is she so nigh ? "

Wild wind, could my sorrow
Thy pinion borrow,
    Past were my care ;
Ere friends could aid her,
Or thought upbraid her,
    Her nest were bare.

PITY'S BEQUEST.

Child of beatitude,
Never may whisper rude
    Visit thy nest ;
I, who thy window woo,
Crave but one last adieu,
    Pity's bequest.

Harborless wanderer,
Ere fate my vessel spur
    Over the main,
Let one kind glance of thine
Comfort with dream divine
    Solitude's pain.

God, who thy beauty gave,
Made me thy beauty's slave,
    Chained me to thee ;
I but his mercy pray,
Shorten life's evil day,
    Since thou art free.

13

REPAID.

Reverencing love, hast thou come,
Mistress unblamed, unto my tomb?
Vex not with late guerdon of tears
Him, who thy white livery wears.

Youth and its strength freely were given,
Lady, to sing thee unto heaven ;
Lamp of my toil, soul of my thought,
Tireless for thy honor I wrought.

Flattering wiles, vanity's greed,
Pitiless hope's poisonous seed,
Lady, whose steps music waylaid,
Thou hast not left love unrepaid.

Drive not the warm snake from my breast,
Summon the mole back to its nest,
Over my grave let the thorns creep,
Trouble not thou, Lady, my sleep.

RAPHAEL'S SONG.

Know ye the song Raphael sung,
When the first sire into life sprung ?

Heavenly hosts, praise ye the Lord,
Worship the Power, bow to the Word.

Father of all, Ancient of Days,
Hark ! a new world echoes Thy praise.

Cloud-crested hill, crystalline sea,
Vocal with light, magnify Thee.

Beasts of the earth, fowls of the air,
Herds through the wave's furrows that fare,

Deep-buried tongues, rifting the sod,
Wonderfully praise Thee, O God.

What is Thy hand now fashioning,
Tree without root, bird without wing?

Into the mould, quickening run
Dust of the earth, ray of the sun,

Sigh of the wind, joy of the stream,
Shadow of night's tremulous dream,

Shuttle of frost, pulse of the wave,
Whispers that haunt forest and cave ;

Trembles the earth, rises the mist,
Nostril and lip, Lord, Thou hast kissed.

Image of Thee, splendor-arrayed,
Radiance-crowned, man Thou hast made.

Regent of earth, proudly his eye,
Winged with delight, measures the sky.

Angel and man, praise ye the Lord,
Worship the Power, bow to the Word.

JOSHUA.

Adonizedek,
　Proud Jebusite,
Comest thou out
　Harnessed for fight?

Slingers advance !
　Blow, trumpets, blow !
Israel's spears
　Forge through the foe !

Stay thy swift course,
　Wheel of the sun,
Till like a tomb
　Groan Ajalon.

On to Bethoron,
　Chase them and smite,
Jah crimson-handed
　Urges their flight.

Slake not your thirst,
　Spear point and sword,
Utterly slay ;
　Thus saith the Lord.

DEBORAH.

Victory-winged,
  Treading down wrong,
Rises exultant
  Deborah's song :

" Come from the byway,
  Thicket, and den ;
Israel's remnant,
  Quit ye like men.

" Barak arise,
  Utter the word,
Draw unto Tabor ;
  Thus saith the Lord,

" Pitched by the Kishon,
  Sisera's hordes,
Chariot-girdled,
  Burnish their swords.

" Search ye for Reuben,
  What do ye hear ?
Bleating of lamb,
  Lowing of steer.

" Search ye for Gilead,
  Asher and Dan ?
Galley and wall
  Bravely they man.

" Israel's glory,
    Who are to save ?
Naphtali's chosen,
    Zebulun's brave ?

" Hark, on Mount Tabor,
    Distant and low,
Nightfaring voices
    Steal to and fro.

" Faithful to death
    Under its crest
Israel's hosts
    Sullenly rest.

" Is it a lion
    Crouching to spring ?
Is it a wave
    Poised on the wing ?

" King-overthrowers,
    Swift from the steep
Leap Zebulun,
    Naphtali leap.

" Hail of the sling,
    Surge of the sword,
Wake in your wrath,
    Strike for the Lord.

" Planet and star
  Bend from your course,
Shatter and crush
  Footman and horse.

" Choked is the river,
  Crimson the plain ;
Who are the victors ?
  Who are the slain ?

" Sisera's mother
  Chides his delay ;
' Is it the spoil
  Lengthens the way ? '

" Out of the window
  Bending she cries,
' Why dost thou tarry,
  Joy of my eyes ?

" ' Guess ye, my ladies,
  What will he bring ?
Necklace and tire,
  Damsel and ring,

" ' Needle-work, cloth,
  Bright from the loom ?
Naked his sword
  Seeks not its home.'

"Look, woman, look,
 Footsore and wan,
Who through the dust
 Presses alone?

"Look, who is sleeping,
 Broken and spent,
Guarded by Jael,
 Safe in her tent?

"Hand to the hammer!
 Hand to the nail!
Helper and harmer,
 Thou wilt not fail!

"Hark to the shriek
 Stifled in pain!
Is it the nail
 Grides through his brain?

"Down he has fallen,
 Down he has bowed;
Vultures are weaving
 Sisera's shroud."

DAVID'S LAMENT.

Weep Israel, Israel weep,
Saul and his sons sleep their last sleep ;
Warriors mourn, children and wives,
Mourn for the joy fled from our lives.

Never may leaf, dewdrop, or rain
Gladden the hill, where they were slain ;
Bow to the dust, temple and tower,
Honor's increase dies in its flower.

Whom shall we now trust in or call on ?
Victory's lords, how are they fallen !
Jonathan lies pierced by the spear,
Desolate eyes, look on his bier !

What is the love woman has shown,
Generous friend, matched with thine own ?
Fountain of faith, harp of my heart,
Knit are our souls never to part.

Dearer than praise, dumb is my lyre,
Broken its strength, ashes its fire ;
Saul and his sons sleep their last sleep,
Weep Israel, Israel weep.

SOLOMON'S SONG.

He :

Daughter of kings, flower of the Nile,
Solomon's Song sues for your smile ;
Turn not away, whither to run ?
Where shall you hide, child of the sun ?

Whisper me, Love, whose was the care,
Carved without flaw shoulder so fair ?
Whose was the hand cunning to mould
Bosom and joint, pearl upon gold ?

Come, where the vine tangles the way ;
Come, where the rose lengthens the day ;
Come, where the breeze slumbers astir,
Heavy with musk, camphor, and myrrh ;

Come, where no false tongue will repeat,
Thick as the curls fall round your feet,
Praises, that spell nature's delight,
Echoes, that breathe love infinite.

Veil not your glance, winter is gone ;
Freeze not my heart, child of the sun ;
Solomon's Song sues for your smile,
Goal of desire, flower of the Nile.

She :

Whose are the prayers, trembling that creep
Into the quick dream of my sleep?
Sighing, " The dew runs from my hair ;
Cold is the night, colder despair."

Rise up my hand, dripping with myrrh ;
Soft be thy step, night-wanderer ;
Didst thou not hear, treacherous one?
Come back again ; thou art not gone.

Wilt thou my cry answer nor heed?
Desolate heart, sore is my need ;
Into the town, silent and fleet,
Red on his path follow my feet ;

Keeper and watch shout and draw near,
Helmet and shield flash back the spear ;
Pitilessly rent is my veil ;
Laughter and jeers follow my wail.

Sisters beloved, far though he fare,
Lead him again home to my care ;
Child of the sun, black though I be,
Solomon's eye turned not from me.

VASHTI.

Tyrant of Persia !
Vashti the Great
Careless surrenders
   Crown and estate.

Drunk with dishonor,
   Hoarder of shame,
Toothless thy wrath
   Strikes at my name.

First of all women,
   Strong to defy
Custom and law's
   Death-dealing lie,

Me, with his golden
   Sceptre, the Sun
Touches, and bids
   Ever reign on ;

Thou and thy lords,
   Back to the clay,
Nameless return,
   Worms of a day.

SHADRACH.

" Nebuchadnezzar,
Thou and thy crown
Wait on the Lord's
Pleasure or frown.

" Know, haughty king,
Israel's knee
Bends unto God,
Not unto thee."

Nebuchadnezzar
Rose in his wrath,
Courtier and prince
Shrank from his path :

" Worship the statue,
Torture and death
Wait on denial ;
Thus the king saith."

Dulcimer answers
Sackbut and flute,
Israel hears,
Hears and is mute.

BABYLON.

" Nations, awake,
  Gird on your wrath,
Compass with fire
  Babylon's path."

Heed not the word,
  Feast, Babylon !
Blinded, the sight
  Turns from the sun.

Hark ! to the cry,
  Wounding the air,
Is it the Mede's
  Wail of despair ?

Look at the river !
  Helmet and plume,
Banner and horse
  Leap from the tomb.

Messengers meet,
  Shouting in fear :
" This way the flames,
  That way the spear."

Waxes the king
  Pale as the priest ;
Sword-points unbidden
  Flock to his feast.

Lady of kingdoms !
　Throned in the dust,
Nergal or Bel,
　Whom wilt thou trust ?

Pierced with the lance,
　Mute in their gore,
Children and wives
　Please thee no more.

Whom the sword scorned,
　Over their grave
Toil without hope,
　Harlot and slave.

Wandering Arabs,
　Pitched by thy gate,
Whisper :　" Is this
　Dintir the Great ? "

H—l, at thy coming,
　Rises to meet thee,
Zion's oppressors
　Totter to greet thee.

Under the Lord's
　Curse evermore
Rot Babylon,
　Rot to the core !

JUDITH.

Victory's lord !
  Fenced with the spear,
Sleep, Holofernes,
  What is to fear

Speed with your dreams ;
  Sires to the dust,
Youths to the yoke,
  Maidens for lust.

Hark to the silence !
  Israel's pride,
Spirit of Jael,
  Stand by my side !

Generous sword,
  Death of our death,
Not for the guiltless,
  Steal from your sheath.

Slavewright and tyrant,
  Drunken with blood,
Wolf of the world,
  Ravening for food,

These are before me,
  These are to slay,
God of my fathers,
  Thee I obey.

THE KING.

Whose is the voice,
  Startles the night?
Captain and elder,
  This way the light.

Haste, Judith, tell us,
  What of the foe?
Glimmer of hope,
  Respite from woe?

" Men of Bethulia,
  Safe to her home
Not unattended
  Judith has come.

" Hark to the welcome
  Words of our friend,
Speak, Holofernes,
  Judah attend."

" Far from the battle,
  Pierced by no lance,
Music and laughter
  Wrought my mischance;

" Timbrel and dance,
  Anklet and tire,
Whisper and glance,
  Bound me with fire.

" Beauty's anointed,
   Clothed with delight,
Robbed me of reason,
   Ravished my sight ;

" False to dishonor,
   Fearless as true,
Judith unaided
   Smote me and slew.

" Water and earth
   Grudge not to bring ;
All will acknowledge
   · Death as their king."

GO, *LITTLE BOOK*.

Go, little book, on ocean's tide,
I launch thy pinion's stainless pride,
And bid thee seek thy wandering home
Amid the craggy billows' foam,
Careless the tempest's rage to brave,
And kiss the laughter of the wave.

Far other course thy keel will keep,
From ships the nation's wealth that reap ;
For thee no lamp with constant light
Betrays the treachery of the night ;
For thee no minster spires upbear
Above the mists their guiding prayer ;
For thee no harbor gates unlock,
For thee no anchor bites the rock ;
Thy flag, that stretches toward the shore,
Will greet the blue hills nevermore ;
The only light thy prow to speak,
Will be the lightning's fatal beak ;
The only nest, thy sail will know,
The furrow deep that whirlwinds sow.

Yet never blossomed on the earth,
Than thine a less ungentle birth,
For thou wert born of that rare time,
When lingers love with truth to rhyme,
And all thy beams in beauty laid,
When wanton zephyrs joyous played
On silvery harp, that stretched between
An April cloud and meadow green,

And earth and heaven laughed to see
The struggling sun imprisoned lie.

And all indifferent to me,
Whate'er thy changing fate may be,
For thou art child of one, whose soul
Hope's treacherous gifts no more control,
Who deems despair and bitter shame
Coequal with proud glory's name,
Who holds the giant atom's force
Of power to burst a planet's corse,
And each forgetful hour to be
Twin flower with immortality.

THE LYRE.

Touch not the sacred lyre,
    It stands by the highway,
Around its whispering wire
    The happy children play ;

But be he wise or dunce,
    Grey beard or rosy cheek,
Its strings, who touches once,
    Of life no more shall reck.

FIRST LOVED AND LAST.

O Love, my woodwild boyhood knew,
To whom my manhood's strength is true,
For whom I left the golden way,
Through friends and honors thick that lay,
Left half-tilled field with plow embossed,
The web and woof of life uncrossed ;

Thou, whom it charmed me more to hear
Remote, with gleaning heart and ear,
Than watch my lady's kindling eye
Or woo her unreluctant sigh ;
Thou, in whose praise the songs that strayed
From cave and brook my rhymes waylaid ;
For whom with tireless hand I sought
All gifts by Nature's spirit wrought ;
For whom I pressed with crimson feet
The grapes for mortal lips unmeet,
And in the folly of that wine
Half deemed myself like thee, divine,
O Muse, make not thy beauty strange
To him, whose love no lure could change,
The wealth of Pluto's palace dim,
Nor Circe's arms encircling him :
I am not now, as I have been,
With strength unsapped and vision keen ;
The vassal years have tyrants grown,
Misfortune's priest I toil alone,
Or hearing friends the largess blame
Of curses wasted on my name,
His viper tongue, my lover sworn,
Of Mammon's slaves the flatterer born,
Or her, who sighing on my lips
Her stealthy knife in poison dips ;
Be all forgiven, all forgot,
Like Brahmin's vermin censured not ;
Stepfather earth, relentless Heaven,
Be all forgot, be all forgiven,
If thou, my Love, wilt not forget,
Who on thy smile his soul has set.

THE DICERS.

My mistress, my friends, and my kin
   Looked on me with alien eyes,
Each breath, my lips sucked in,
   Was heavy with curses and lies ;
From mistress, from friends, and from kin,
   To the mountain and desert bare,
From the whirlwind my bread to win,
   I turned in my heart's despair.

As under the footing of fire,
   At my coming the grasses die,
But thick on my broken lyre
   The frozen ashes lie,
   The frozen ashes lie
Of a golden temple bright,
   That gemmed my morning sky
With a splendor infinite.

But now o'er the blackening waste
   What music is to hear,
Save bleeding feet that haste
   From the hungry were-wolf near,
   From the hungry were-wolf near,
And the lurking adder's bite,
   And the phantoms fashioned of fear,
That leap o'er the threshold of night?

And I looked at the eagle's wing,
   That rides on the restless wind,

Can Heaven no harboring
   For her homeless children find ?
I looked at the eagle's wing,
   It fretted the roof of the sky,
And I heard the mountains ring
   With a hoarse and angry cry.

And I looked at the mole, that sounds
   The depths of the hollow plain ;
Holds earth in its sacred bounds
   No respite for life's pain ?
Holds earth in its sacred bounds
   No rayless cavern deep,
Where grief's unhealing wounds
   In dreamless death may sleep ?

But near and nearer came
   The wolf and adder fell,
And behind me a wasting flame,
   That had burst from the portals of h—l,
Behind me a wasting flame,
   And before me a pathless woe,
And a sorrow, no thought can name,
   That pierced my bosom through.

So under the shadow of night,
   That knows not any sun,
I spurred my wounded flight,
   And my bleeding footsteps on,
I spurred my wounded flight,
   O hope ! before my feet
There glimmered a sudden light,
   And great was the joy of it.

At a gate by the riverside
  Our Lady of Sorrow stands,
Through a mist-hung valley wide
  My steps her glance commands,
  My steps her glance commands
To a hilltop high, where bend
  O'er an altar with tireless hands
Two Dicers reverend.

And one of the players is Death,
  Five dice before him lie,
But the other answereth
  Each cast with a single die,
And one of the players is Death,
  And I feel at every cast
Sweep by me the rustling breath
  Of a spirit that breathes its last.

But Fame, who shall picture her,
  That other with Death that plays,
The lip no passions stir,
  And the splendor of her gaze,
  The splendor of her gaze,
That illumines the starry dome,
  And the flight of the gods delays
From their desecrated home?

And once in a hundred years
  She takes her trumpet of gold,
And blows o'er the valley of tears
  A music of charm untold,
  A music of charm untold,
And the noble dead arise,

And a deathless name behold,
And the winner of the prize.

But now on my presence glare
 The eyes of a rabble rude,
And a nameless corse they bear
 For the wolf and raven's food,
A nameless corse they bear,
 And I look in its hungry face,
And the gentle features fair
 Of a long lost comrade trace.

But I looked in Fame's clear eyes,
 " I, too, will battle with fate,
My life on the table lies
 To help the chance of the great,
My life on the table lies,
 No other stake have I,
Cast, Death, your fatal dice,
 Cast, Fame, your single die."

EPITAPH.

Stranger, who shalt hither come,
Know, who lies within this tomb,
Never knew to turn his back,
Though round him closed hate's wolfish pack,
On his friend or on his foe :
Further nothing seek to know.

FINIS.